The Silver Conspiracy

The Untold Story of Christ's Betrayal

A NOVEL BY
PASTOR BLAINE MacNEIL

The Silver Conspiracy
The Untold Story of Christ's Betrayal
The Trilogy of the Cross Part One

Meet Me on Facebook

MacNeil Publishing

A Novel by
Pastor Blaine MacNeil
Copyright © 2018 Blaine MacNeil

Unless otherwise noted all Bible references are from the King James Version.

The Silver Conspiracy

Pastor MacNeil's Bio

Pastor Blaine MacNeil has specialized in small town and rural church ministry. He spent his career in parish ministry including seven years working as an interim pastor for churches throughout his home state of Minnesota. He has also worked as a hospice chaplain, helping others to prepare for their journey home to heaven.

Pastor MacNeil holds a Master's degree (2001) in Counseling Psychology from the Adler Graduate School in Richfield, Minnesota. He graduated from Luther Seminary in St. Paul, Minnesota with a Master's in Divinity degree (2004). He furthered his educational experiences by completing the chaplain residency program at the Veterans Administration Hospital in St. Cloud, Minnesota (2013-14).

He also served as a Major in the United States Air Force Auxiliary/Civil Air Patrol as the chaplain of squadrons in the Minnesota and Wisconsin wings. In his service to our nation he has earned two Commander's Commendation awards for his service. He has served in search and rescue missions as a ground team member, and as a flight crew member. He is a graduate of the North Central Region Chaplain's Corp College and was the Minnesota Wing and North Central Region Chaplain of the year in 2012.

He and his wife Melanie love spending time with their grandchildren.

Thanks

A great word of thanks is due to those three people who have helped along the way to make this book possible. Thanks to my proofreaders and editors, Orrine Hanson, Roxanne Jessie and my wife, Melanie MacNeil. Their technical expertise completed what my creative writing skills lacked. Their help and encouragement has gone a long way to help me in the completion of this three volume trilogy of novels.

Introduction

Note: This novel is the first in a trilogy covering Christ's betrayal, his passion and death, and his resurrection.

In writing this book I was challenged to present something that was uniquely new about one of the best know stories in the Bible. I have endeavored to write without contradicting the Scriptures. I have striven to faithfully take the Gospel accounts of Jesus' life and betrayal, and added true to their times fictional drama to it. My goal in this story is to fill your imagination with how the details surrounding this time in his life might have played out.

As you read this book, remember that from his earliest days in life our Savior, Jesus, had a pattern of overcoming death. It began in his earliest years, with his escape to Egypt with his parents. Early in his ministry he disappeared when Temple authorities wanted to stone him. Again, he vanished when they wanted to throw him off a cliff in Nazareth. Still again, he calmed the storm that would have drown him and his disciples in the sea. Additionally, when they brought the deathly ill to him, he healed them. He also raised the dead numerous times. In all of this we need to ask the question: *did Jesus ever feel the emotions of grief and loss, or actually fear for his own life?*

Alongside these miraculous powers that he demonstrated he also had another pattern in his life. That was the avoidance of death. He did not have to grieve or mourn when someone died, he simply restored them to life. He did not have to worry when someone was deathly sick, he healed them. He had full confidence in his power to escape murderous attempts on his life. And he, being the

Lord of Creation, had the power to control the winds and the waves. Now the question becomes: *What does this pattern mean for his future?*

This underlying pattern came to a head when his friend Lazarus took ill, deathly ill. Jesus did not go to him and heal him, instead he delayed, and it cost his friend his life. When Jesus did return, it became a turning point in his life and ministry. There he had to face the two angry sisters of the man and an entire town of people in mourning. At that point Jesus broke down and wept bitterly over his friend's death and over the grief he had brought to the man's family by his delay in coming to them. This time it was very personal to him. For our Savior, we also see by his weeping that the pangs of death were not lightened by him knowing that he would be raising the man back to life in a few minutes.

This situation sets the stage for his own impending death. Now he has had to face the death of someone close to him rather than prevent it. Soon he will have to face his own death and struggle in the garden with indecision. There he must decide whether, or not, to surrender and drink the cup poured for him. This novel takes the reader back to that time in his life when it was not a foredrawn conclusion about what he would choose to do. The question then becomes personal for us: *Can we journey with him at that time in his life, and take up our own cross and die to self as well?*

Pastor Blaine MacNeil

Chapter One
Who Do You Say that I Am?

A company of men were walking uphill on a gently winding road which led to Bethsaida, a city in the northern district of Caesarea Philippi. Their conversations could be heard but the sun shone so brightly on that day that the intensity of its great light made anything you gazed at difficult to see. As they neared they came into focus. First appearing at their center was a Jewish Rabbi who was called Jesus of Nazareth. He was instructing his students, but it was easier to hear him than to see him or any of his disciples. And if you were there on the road that day to see them coming, the first thing that you would have noticed was the sun's brilliance extending to everything. You could only make out what was to the side of you, and only then, with your peripheral vision. But before you, in the center of your vision, was the golden star that gave light to the earth by day. All you could see were its unending rays illuminating from it in every direction. As you quickly allowed your eyes to glimpse at this grand star, your mind captured a vision of circular waves radiating from it that told you of its intense power. From within the sun there appeared the faint silhouette of a magnificent dove with its sweeping wings hovering high in the center.

Now as the Rabbi and his disciples walked closer to you on the road you could see them starting to appear more clearly before you. First to come into focus was the one who was in the center and leading the rest forward. This was Jesus. As he drew closer to you, the blinding sunlight faded and at his sides and following behind him were his disciples. The Rabbi was teaching them and they listened. He questioned them, and they pondered aloud what the answers might be. When he was silent, the disciples brought their questions to him and he answered them truthfully, with knowledge and wisdom.

Before you, for some reason, their Rabbi slowed his pace and then stopped. His disciples, some of whom had been engaged in side conversations, quieted down as they too slowed and then stopped their walking. Then Jesus spoke, "So, who do the people you've talked with say that I am?" The Rabbi did not wait for an answer before he resumed his walking. Then his disciples followed after him.

The youngest in the group, John, spoke first, "Some have told me that they think you are John the Baptist, who Herod killed. They believe that you are raised from the dead and that is why there are miraculous powers at work in you."

Their Rabbi replied, "Yes, I can see that. There is a family resemblance between us isn't there?" The disciples understood that John the Baptist and Jesus were related.

Again the Rabbi put the question to them, "Who else do they say that I am?"

The disciple next to John spoke out; this was James, John's older brother. "Other people are certain that you are Elijah who has finally returned to us from heaven."

To this their Rabbi replied, "That makes sense doesn't it? Everyone is waiting for Elijah's return." Still again he put the question to them saying, "What else have you heard others say about who I am?"

A disciple who was dressed much finer than the rest spoke next. His robe was made of a finely woven linen while the others wore more roughly woven coats. This one was not the same as all the others who were from Galilee in the north. This one's accent told you that he was from the southern province of Judea. He was known as Judas the son of Iscariot and he said, "Some think you are the prophet Jeremiah, or at the very least one of the ancient prophets; perhaps Elisha or Isaiah, and that you have been raised from the dead and have come out from your tomb."

Rabbi Jesus did not respond to any of the answers his disciples offered him for the moment. Instead he slowed his pace and stopped walking as before. And as before, his disciples who had been discussing the question at hand in side conversations quieted down as they slowed and then stopped walking too. Now they were attentive to their Rabbi and anxious to hear what he would say. Jesus took a few steps forward and then turned to face his disciples directly but he said nothing. This was nearly unbearable for the disciples, to have their Rabbi, who they also considered a prophet, look at them so directly in silence as the question loomed among them. Jesus looked them over one by one as if he were weighing the nature of their character. Then he broke his silence asking, "But who do you say that *I am*?"

The tall disciple named Simon, who had been walking at Jesus' right side spoke out quickly and without a single forethought. "You are the one anointed by God, the Messiah, the only begotten Son of the Living God." As he spoke his face reflected his own astonishment at how the words had just flown out of his mouth. After he spoke, his face showed concern over what he had just said and he wondered, if he was right to have said it and make this claim about his Rabbi? He had spoken without thinking first. He had his own private hopes about who his Rabbi was. But now that it was out in the open he paired with it his worries as he wondered if he had just made a very presumptuous, and too lofty a claim. But regardless of his questioning, he did not retract anything that he had just said; instead he was determined in his heart to stand by it, right or wrong.

Nearly as quickly as Simon had spoken out, John's older brother James, James the Greater, also agreed, "Yes, that's right!"

All the others also joined in agreement heartily nodding as Simon now spoke again for them all, "Yes, that's what we all say."

Jesus smiled ever so brightly as he raised his right hand and placed it on Simon's shoulder, "How blessed you are Simon bar Jonah! By your own effort you did not come into this knowledge." Jesus shook his head first from side to side saying, 'no,' and then up and down to indicate he was saying 'yes' as he continued on, "But this was revealed to you by my Father in heaven!" Jesus then looked up to the sky above and spoke loud enough for everyone at a distance to hear him, "And from now on I will call you Peter, "the rock", because of your confession of faith in me. And this confession of who I am is the living rock and foundation that I will build my church on, and the gates of hell will not be able to prevail against it. To you I will be giving the keys of my Kingdom. By them whatever you bind on earth will be bound in heaven, and by them whatever you loose on earth will be loosed in heaven." Jesus paused and motioned with his hands for everyone to gather in closely, "Now all of you, I am commanding that you do not tell anyone that I am the Messiah. I also have to tell you something that you need to know, to prepare yourselves, for when that day comes upon me. This is difficult for you to hear, I know, but you must know what is to happen so that the Holy Scriptures may be fulfilled in me. I will return to Jerusalem soon and there I will be rejected by the leaders of our people. They will arrest me as if I am a criminal. I will be tortured without mercy at their hands. I will be charged and they will condemn me. They will raise me up and put me to death, and after three days I will rise from the dead."

Only a moment ago, the disciples had experienced the most noble and exalted point in their long and dusty journey to the north. Now that moment was suddenly over. They knew without a doubt that Jesus was the Messiah and their hope for a homeland that was free of foreign oppression was kindled anew. But their hope for a king who would rule over them in righteousness, which had suddenly grown as bright as the sun, now died like a shooting star that burns out as it crosses the night sky. Their emotions had fallen from what seemed like heaven's highest height to being suddenly dashed to pieces, as a great sense of deathful dread overcame them from what their Rabbi foretold to them; that he would not be accepted by their nation's leaders. Their hearts fell still further when he told them that he would be condemned and put to death in the end. They just stood there, paralyzed like frozen statues, motionless, dazed and speechless men.

This did not fit with their thinking. It was, in truth, impossible for them to even imagine it. Peter was the first to regain his composure from the shock of it. He moved like a parent with a stern look on his face when he takes his child aside to discipline him. Grabbing Jesus by the arm, he pulled him away from the rest and off the road they had been traveling on. He stopped and turned to Jesus, he gave him a stern look with his eyes and spoke ever so severely.

"Jesus, what are you talking about?" Peter's arms moved about to emphasize the intensity of what he felt, "Suffering and dying this way!? This must not and cannot happen to you! I have left everything to follow you because

I put all of my hope in you, that you would be our King. I make my vow right now before you and the rest, to fight and even give my own life unto death to keep you from this fate."

Peter blinked and there was a pause in what he was saying. He had a sudden vision of himself in the future but it was somewhat blurred to him and it was not entirely clear to him what it meant. He saw Jesus speaking in a banquet hall and telling him to bring swords. He shook his head and then felt a surge of strength from his vision that energized him all the more. He looked at the others and pointed them out to his Rabbi.

"Look, see, all of your disciples would do the same for you."

The disciples were watching and because Peter was nodding, so did they all likewise, but they had not actually heard what Peter said. They only nodded in agreement as a matter of politeness.

"All of your followers would pick up swords to fight and die for you."

Again he had a vision of himself at Jesus' side, drawing his sword to fight against armed guards in uniforms. Further empowered by this, he spoke with great boldness and a high level of confidence, "This will not be happening to you! You are the Messiah, and there will be no more talk about it!!!"

The Rabbi was momentarily surprised by Peter's great intensity and insistence, but as he placed his own thoughts into perspective he turned to look at all of his disciples before speaking out, with all harshness, against this disciple of his.

"Peter!!! You get behind me, Satan! You are not at all thinking about God's will for my life. You are thinking only about what you and other people want for themselves and setting God aside in the act." Jesus matched and surpassed the fortitude that Peter had just displayed; he even looked as though he was ready to knock Peter off the high horse of his pride, if he had to, as he spoke on. "Don't you realize that you and the rest of the world have no say in this matter; it is the Father who has asked me to lay down my life and for this reason I came to you. If you pick up arms to fight my enemies to the death, I will have to stop you and everyone who joins in with you. There is nothing you can do and there is nothing you can say to change or stop any of this! Nothing!! The words of the holy prophets must have their fulfillment in me. I know that you don't understand this right now, but after I rise you will. You have to trust me and accept what must happen. And as for yourself, don't be found resisting what the Father has ordained for me to do."

The man who had just looked like a stern parent bent on correcting a misbehaving child now appeared more like a weepy child who was being corrected by his parent. Tears swelled up in his eyes as he stepped down from the pride of his high headed position. As Peter spoke, his voice was broken as though he had been crying, "This – is - too – hard - to - believe. And I don't understand it, any of it, my Lord! But because you have asked me to, and insisted that I allow it, I will do as you say."

Given Peter's reaction, the Rabbi felt he needed to address the rest of his disciples about what he had said, so that they were all clear about what must happen and what was absolutely expected of them. He and Peter rejoined the rest and Jesus spoke these words to them all, "Listen to me all of you and mark my words." They listened carefully to him. "Remember what I tell you now. Very soon I will make my way to Jerusalem again and there my destiny will be fulfilled. They will take my life and on the third day I will be raised back to life." He paused now, out of necessity because he was shaken by what he had just shared about his coming passion of suffering and death. The disciples were now able to look him in the face and even into his eyes, and as they did they could see the sorrow and pain that lay ahead for their Rabbi. "Now that you know this, you need to ask yourselves this question; 'do you really want to keep following me?' If you do, then as my follower, every day of your life you must begin by denying yourself and dying to yourself by picking up your own cross. If you think you can save your life in any other way, like picking up a sword to fight, then you will lose your life by that same sword. But if you lose your life for my sake and for the sake of my Gospel you will find it, and save it for eternal life in heaven. Think it through, each of you. Think it through for yourself. What good would it do you if you could own the entire world but in the process of buying it you have lost yourself, and then you will also lose everything when you die? What value do you put on your life, on who you are and on who you will become? What will your life be like? What will you be like? You will become as nothing if you think owning the world is what makes for a good life. And if you are ashamed of me and what I have said just now, in this adulterous and sinful generation, then I will be ashamed of you when I come in my glory and in the glory of my Father. On that great and celebrated day I will return with legions upon legions of holy angels on my right and on my left and I will repay everyone for what has been done. But today, believe that standing among you right now are some who will not taste death before they see the day when I will come into my

Kingdom crowned in glory and clothed with immense power."

Jesus looked at them to see if any would question him or leave him, as some had in the past when they realized what was expected of them. This time his disciples all stayed. There was silence for the moment. What more could be said? There was nothing left to say. The Rabbi had made himself clear and the disciples accepted his terms for following him. So Jesus resumed walking to Bethsaida. The disciples, though they did not turn away, remained standing there for the while even though Jesus had resumed walking.

Chapter Two
Who Is the Greatest?

As Jesus walked on, he now rested in the idea that his twelve were willing to pay the cost and continue on as his disciples. He was more than fifty yards in front of them before they returned to walking. Their low mood after hearing that their Rabbi would be put to death was short lived and they reverted now to the high point they had just experienced when Jesus told them plainly that he is the promised Messiah. And why not go there, to that high point? They loved feeling that way and doesn't everyone? This they could accept with ease, that he is the Messiah. They readily heard those words from their Rabbi with willing and glad hearts. And though they had listened, they did not really hear Jesus when he said he would be rejected and put to death. They did not let those words linger in their thoughts for any longer then the short time they had lingered on that road. It was as if they had left those thoughts behind them at that place too. After all, it was hard to imagine, and even harder to accept, that this would happen and that he would be killed. But isn't this true regarding anyone's death? That kind of dreadful news takes time to set in, time to adjust to and time to come to terms with. For them, all they knew in their own high thoughts was that Jesus is alive, he is the long-expected Messiah, he is their newly rising King and they were excited about it, because they have the good fortune of being his chosen, to be his disciples.

But because of these lofty thoughts, a jealousy was now weaving its way into the minds and hearts of the eleven who felt snubbed by what Peter had blurted out so quickly. They all knew or at least had hopes, albeit subtly, that Jesus was the Messiah. The recognition that the tallest among them received from Jesus could have been theirs, if only competitive Peter hadn't said it first. But that man, many of them thought, took no consideration for the others and what they might have wanted to say. They resented that he took his liberty before first looking to the others to see if one of them had something to say. These fires of jealous contempt were now kindled and grew still hotter as the day grew warmer from the rising sun. They were preoccupied with thoughts of their own rise to bright futures as their heads sweltered from the heat of the day. The leaven of their own pride rose well in these conditions and it intermixed with the knowledge that they were not just followers of a true prophet, but of the Messiah himself. They took pride, and too much of it at that, as they relished in their own conceited thoughts; that they were his closest confidants.

Their pace was leisurely, that of princes out for a stroll, but not young John's. He could see that Jesus was some distance in front of him and so he hurried his pace to catch up with his Rabbi and be at his side. Then Peter took notice that John had moved and would soon be able to walk alongside Jesus before the others would. He determined that he was not to be outdone by that youngster, so he double quickened his strides. His jealous thoughts told him that if John got there first, Jesus might pass on some instruction to him that he is anxious to know too. Soon enough, though it took him some effort, Peter had arrived side by side with John before he could reach Jesus. He gave a little extra effort for himself and then he looked over his shoulder to see that he had just now passed John, and so he moved in front of him. He had been laboring so to get there, but now that he had achieved this forward position he slowed. John was not giving much attention to any of this and didn't consider it a race as Peter did.

Peter's sense of victory was marred though, when an unawares John stepped on his heel. "Hey, watch where you step!" he cried out.

To which John innocently said, "What are you doing? Why do you always have to be in front of me Peter?"

Peter solemnly denied it, "Me! I do no such thing!"

But John protested with the truth of his past observances, "Yes you do! You just did it! Again! You worked hard to pass me up, and then you looked over your shoulder to see if you were past me before moving right in front of me. Then you slowed your pace so I would have to slow down too, or run in to you. Old man, you shouldn't try to be in the front. It is too hard on your bones. Just because you think you're better than me doesn't mean that I should have to walk behind you, and at your age-ed pace."

Peter could not stand to be corrected, regardless of the truth, any more than he could stand to be wrong regardless of the facts. In his own defense he told John, "I'm not old and there is nothing wrong with me being in front of you or anyone else. And you walk too fast! The rest of us are just fine with walking together, at a more reasonable pace. Can't you simply join with us, and walk together with us, just this once? Huh?"

Now that the verbal sparring had begun, John came out punching in his own defense, "If you are fine with walking together with the rest of them then why did you bother to walk ahead of them and pass me up before taking a position directly in front of me on this wide road and presume to walk all by yourself?"

As the rest of the twelve caught up with these two disciples, Jesus was still about twenty-five yards ahead of them. Peter and John bickered on and the other ten didn't even take notice of it because they were bickering with themselves as well, which was common among them all on most days of the week.

Andrew and James the Greater were the first to catch up with Peter and John. They were carrying on in much the same fashion. Very defensively, Andrew stood up for himself and insisted, "I do too look the best, and I make the best first impressions of any of us."

But Andrew was blind to everything but his own mindset and didn't hear what he was being told by James, "Yes," he paused before thoughtfully going on, "you do Andrew, for the third time you do! Do you hear me? You're right, I agree. Don't you get that? You do! I concede, you do already!" shouted James.

Andrew finally heard what had been told to him, "Well, okay then. Finally. You're right to agree, after all it is true, I do look the best."

But what actually now happened is that he had been taken in, as James had set him up for an insult. "You do make the best first impressions. And then you open your mouth and never make another good impression again."

He was completely taken off guard by that low going twist in the conversation. He protested back, "What are you talking about?"

James had set the nail for the point he would now drive home, and by it establish his position securely. "Good looks don't make the preacher good at his job. I am a much better preacher than you, and here's why. I'm not always forgetting what to say and trying to fill the dead air that I've created with meaningless sounds like 'um' and 'ah' as I look stupid and hope my next words will somehow find their way into my mouth. When I preach, people like to hear me because my voice is deeper, it resonates, it carries better and I am never at a loss for words or what to say."

As the others approached them, Peter disengaged from his spit and spat squabble with John and looked back at them. He straightened up tall and shouted, "What are you two fighting over now?"

Andrew, a grown man by all outward appearances, now reverted to almost childlike immaturity as he expressed his hurt feelings and sounded off like a tattle tale. He lifted his one hand to his eyes to block the brightness of the sun and then pointed his finger at James, "He wants to believe he is better than me. But he is not comparing similarities among us. He's only fault finding, and the only thing he is proving is that he has the better imagination of the two of us when it comes to preaching."

Peter found that what they were fighting over was a great annoyance to him, "Preaching? Preaching!" He went on, "Well, if you want to know who the best among us is, it is me after all. I am the one who got the answer to the question Jesus asked us correct, that he is the Messiah. Add to that, I am one of the first to follow him. Clearly this makes me the greatest among us and today it has been proven. Don't take that badly though, you are all great." He hesitated and thought that he did not want to say anything too complementary to the rest, and so he added, "In your own ways I mean, you know. But, after all, think about it, Jesus called every one of us to be one of his twelve. But as for the greatest among us, I am the one who stands tallest above you all."

Andrew returned to his defensive posturing, "So what, that you are one of the first to follow him. I am the one who did follow him first, before you, Peter, and before any of the rest of you. I came and got you Peter, to see if you wanted to follow him too. And what if I hadn't? Think about that why don't you! So this clearly makes me first of all of us."

Peter stood still taller now as he stretched upward, "O yeah brother? Have you forgotten who put you to work as a fisherman, who taught you everything you know about it and paid you your wages? It was me, remember?"

The younger brother asserted himself as never before to his dominant sibling. "Yeah, I know. So what! Did you forget that it was our father who gave you those responsibilities in the first place? He taught you everything you know about it and you don't own any of the business, he does. And he was the one, not you, who paid me my wages."

Thaddeus, who was also known as Jude, stepped into the middle of the verbal thicket and raised his hands to speak, "Gentleman, gentleman, see here now." He used a softer tone hoping to calm the others as he spoke on, "Who is the greatest? I'll tell you who we can eliminate and you will find it easy to agree with my thinking. It is young John. He can only be, at best, as the youngest of us all, the last of all. And I have to add that I think he is too young to be counted among us in the first place." He looked straight at John and in a now condescending voice said, "You he pampers and the only reason your mother let you come along with us was because your brother James agreed to look after you."

John was not willing to surrender his position as being counted among them, let alone yield to being called the least regardless of his youth. He had just argued with Peter and successfully, by his own measure so he now made a sure and certain argument for himself to them all. "Well, I'm not the last one to reach the top of these dusty roads we have to climb. The way some of you huff and puff on them makes me worry that I might have to carry one or two of you on my back. In fact, I'll bet every one of you that I'm the fastest runner here and the most agile. I have the most endurance of anyone here; you all have seen that time and time again and don't try to deny it." He pointed his finger about and spoke on, "You old men, you are like the rear guard of an army that follows behind the rest because they aren't any good at fighting in the frontlines anymore. There are things I could tell all of you…" John's mouth remained open and in his thoughts he teetered back and forth with the idea of saying something brashly youthful or employing a mature discretion and saying nothing more. He settled for saying something in the middle, "But I know better."

James the Greater was not one to simply watch this battle by standing on the sidelines, "Now see here all of you! I am one of Jesus' closest confidants. I have been with him when no one else was with him." He confidently asserted himself and then looked eye to eye with the other James, James the Lessor, to assure that he would be heard by him, "And I clearly have greater standing than James the Lessor by reason of the simple fact that he is younger than me, that's why he is rightly called the Lessor."

The other James was no more willing than any of the other eleven to remain silent, so he came to his own defense, "Age is no measure as to who is the greatest among us. How could being older be better? Clearly I am more likely to outlive most of you. And so I will be able to carry out Jesus' mission well beyond your days upon the earth." He hoped to now fortify his words by calling on his brother Thaddeus to back him up, "What do you have to say about that brother?"

"Don't call on me thinking I am going to get tied up in all this mess. Listen to yourselves, all of you!" With an air of disgust he called out, "Age, youth, talent, responsibilities. Nothing, more nothing and nothing at all. I have already dedicated myself to *his* cause." Thaddeus had moved to discount what they all held so highly and then he went on to establish a new line of criteria for what should matter most among them. "I pay close attention. And I memorize his every word by heart and I bind them there. How many of you can say that about yourself?"

It was as though a flock of roosters had entered into a bragging contest on the road, with each one trying to outdo the other on their own terms.

Simon the Zealot, a man of few words but quick to take action, stepped up to speak. "Ha! I say allegiance and bravery are the greatest things! Allegiance to his cause and bravery in the face of opposition. These are the greatest qualities. When Jesus is crowned as my King in Jerusalem, at the Temple, I will serve him with unquestionable loyalty and unswerving devotion."

Simon Peter was quick to point out an error in what the other Simon had just said. "Simon the Zealot, they don't crown kings at the temple, they anoint priests there. They crown kings in what used to be Herod's Palace, which is now the Roman Praetorium, from where Pilate the Roman Pontiff rules Judea."

Simon didn't like being wrong and he didn't like being corrected either, even though the two go hand in hand. So now that he was worked up over being wrong, and then corrected, he waved his arms as he spoke again, and as if to enforce his point, he also clenched his fists. "We are going to Jerusalem and we may very well have to stand up for him against our opponents there." He looked around at everyone, "We may even have to face death. Now you need to know that I have taken it upon myself to most vigilantly look out for his personal safety; danger can come out of nowhere, and at any time. I am the one who's on guard to shield him with my own life if someone should try to strike out at him. None of you have thought about doing that one bit have you? How many of you are prepared to make that statement about yourselves? Huh? How many?"

No one had a response that directly stood against this new course in the flow of the arguing. Even still, that did not bring an end to their boisterous hen pecking and rooster strutting.

"Listen to me here." Judas' Judean accent stood out uniquely among them. "None of you manage the money that we need, the money that our benefactors give to me. And I remember the names of those who give the most. So having been put in charge of the ministry funds and because I hold the coin purse, I think it is already clear that I am in a high position of leadership, if not the highest among us all." As he ended his sentence he realized too late that it could be construed by his words that he might see himself as being higher than Jesus. So, though it was a feeble effort, he tried to make a quick attempt at patching on these words and still sound spontaneous, "Next to Jesus of course." And still his attempt to recover from the error that stemmed from his heart was made too late, as it cast an early shadow from the image of what was still to come.

The other disciples, all but one, had no immediate comeback for his words, well said as they were. Then Matthew spoke contemptuously down at him, "Don't presume that being in charge of the money is any great honor Judas Iscariot." Matthew was the one Jesus had called to serve him from his position as a tax collector. He did a good job of standing up and challenging Judas at his word. "I could easily do that job. Before I left everything to follow the Rabbi, I collected money from everyone for the tax. My fine home was well furnished, I wanted for nothing in this world and my purse was always full to overflowing. But I came to care nothing for all that I possessed. On the inside my life was very empty and I didn't know and could not find fulfillment. You count out the money, which is all you count for. Other than that you were the one he called last of all, which makes you last of all." His words were sharp and cutting, and almost enough to scare the rest into keeping silent. Almost enough.

Thomas, the most elderly among them spoke; his voice carried with it the sound of years of refinement and experience. He seemed at first to be taking the high road to bring the debate to its end. "Enough, enough of this boisterous talk, every one of you! Just listen for a minute to the voice of someone who is senior to you all. I believe that everyone needs to learn a little humility here. Now take just one of the countless examples from my life: I pray on my knees before God. That way I can pray most sincerely. And all of you prefer to pray sitting or standing up. But have you forgotten who it is that you are addressing? The Almighty, the LORD, and the God of all creation! You need to pray on your knees too, like me. You need to follow me in my example. That is how you too can best pray."

His words held the attention of the eleven for the moment because by then, at least in the beginning, he seemed to be appealing to them from higher ground and because he suggested that he wanted to bring their bickering to its end. But soon enough it became clear to the rest what he was doing. They felt tricked by his introduction, because he was asserting that his more holy and righteous than you practice of praying on his knees was better than their own ways. This battle of bickering birds was far from over as Bartholomew followed in Thomas' ploy by also using words that led the rest to think that the incessant fight was going to end because of how he invoked the words of their Rabbi. "I will say the final word on all of this and it comes from Jesus himself, so you better listen to me here and now. His word is the final authority among us and, as such, I have his endorsement on this matter. When I saw him, and mind you I was the first of all of us to see him, he declared of me, 'Here is truly an Israelite in whom there is no deceit!' Therefore, I have already been given the greatest endorsement he can give."

And still, as before, as they journeyed north, the terrible march of coveting to be the greatest pushed forward in ceaseless agony.

"That's nonsense!" Philip insisted. "I followed him before you. Besides that, I was the one who brought you to Jesus. Or did you conveniently forget that part? And you didn't see him first, he saw you first under the tree, remember? So, clearly, I rank before you."

And though the disciples were worked up over this unremitting matter, they agonized both for it to end and yet they were still were not willing to let it rest, not unless it ended with they them-self being recognized as the greatest one out of the twelve.

Their journey's end was now in sight as they were able to see the home of the benefactor where they would be staying. And, as such, Peter was truly right in his comments to the rest saying, "Okay, okay, that is enough, all of you! Just calm down everyone, and I mean right now. Clearly we are not going to solve this problem on the road while we are walking." Peter could not let it rest there though, not without setting the groundwork for a sequel continuation where he hoped he would see it come to an end, and only then if it was in his favor. He continued on, "Not today anyway. It will have to wait." With these words he could keep his egotistical hope alive regarding his self-assured claim to greatness, that is, that he is the greatest of all the twelve. "I will settle this all with you later when the time is right." And now he turned to do the right thing by instructing the rest in the practice of good manners. "I don't want this to go on any further. We are almost there. I don't want any of you bringing this into the home of our host. He doesn't deserve all of your arguing coming into his home today."

Chapter Three
The Greatest Least and Last

When the disciples arrived at Bethsaida they felt the full weariness of their travels. But more than that, they were down to the bone, deep tired from the volley of exchanges they made in their own defense of why they each felt they were the one who was the greatest. They were glad to reach the home of their host where they could sit down, rest and eat. And although they were twice wearied from the road and their arguing, they could not let go of their guardedness; they were still on edge, dulled only by their exhaustion. They were all ready to defend themselves if the embers of their heated exchange were for any reason stirred up again or given fuel.

Their host was having his servants prepare a large meal for supper, for Jesus, his disciples and the many guests who had come to learn from the Rabbi. The aroma of the meal stirred everyone's appetite as it roasted and sizzled on the open barbeque pit in the inner courtyard of the home. The twelve were hungry, and the pleasant fragrance of the food roused their appetites and reminded them of how starved they were. These elements: the weariness from the road, their maintaining the state of their extended defensive postures and the smell of the food that they could not yet eat all wore heavily upon them.

Since their arrival their Rabbi had been in a private conversation with their host, but now both of them came into the open-air courtyard, which was overcrowded with all the guests. Everyone wanted to hear what the Rabbi would soon teach them. Although every eye there was watching him, Jesus looked downward as he entered in silence and made his way toward the front of the crowd. He stopped on the way to his chair, faced his disciples, and spoke in a whisper to them, "What were all of you arguing about on the way here?"

There came an uncomfortable silence among them that was finally broken when Peter, as was his fashion, spoke first, "Oh... ah... nothing too concerning."

John followed, "Really, nothing at all."

James was a little more forthcoming, "Just a... ah... just a gentleman's dispute, nothing more."

The others kept their silence and guarded their eyes from meeting with their Rabbi's because they knew that he was on to something, and anything that they might say could not be better than the answers Peter, John and James had already offered to him. And even those answers did not really say enough to dissuade Jesus from his apparent suspicions.

As Jesus turned to go toward his chair, the disciples felt a momentary sense of relief. So, they let their guards finally came down because they believed that Jesus' question to them was now the final word on the topic for them, the one that had eluded them before. This was what Jesus purported to do; not to say the final word on it, but instead to get them to put their guards down and relax. And it worked. So now that they were disarmed, he turned back to face them, which conveyed to them that he didn't really believe that their arguing was nothing more than a gentleman's dispute. But the disciples were too tired to get worked up over it again. They merely wondered if he would chastise them now, in front of all those gathered, or later in private.

As Jesus took his seat and stretched out his legs he breathed a deep and long sigh of relief, and by it he set the mood for everyone, soothing and calming them all, especially his disciples. He looked about at everyone as if searching for someone or something. He saw a young mother who was seated almost directly in front of him. He asked her in a very gentle manner, "Woman, may I hold your dear child?"

The young mother reached up with her child in her hands and offered him to Jesus to hold and said, "My Lord." A look of delight was on her face because she knew that this was a special grace the Rabbi was extending to her and her son. The child saw on his mother's face a smiling assurance and a willing nod that this was okay with her. Seeing her approval, he gladly reached out his arms to Jesus as he was passed to him.

Jesus spoke kindly, "Child, come to me." The boy was very comfortable with this and in turn, he held onto Jesus. Everyone looked on and saw that the two were content to visit and share in each other's company, as if they had no other concerns in all the world.

Everyone waited patiently. What else could they do? The disciples recalled that, even though they had tried to put a stop to it, Jesus was glad to receive the children who parents brought to him for his blessing in the past. But this was not the same as that. No. Here and now Jesus went out of his way by asking to hold the child, and beyond that he was playing with him too. Which was a first. The child looked upward to the sky and pointed to show the Rabbi something up there. So Rabbi Jesus lifted this child up high, well above his own head and spoke quietly to him, "Can you see up there to the greatest heights? Your place is not up there among the birds of flight. No. Your place is here on earth among the rest of us."

The whole of those gathered strained to hear him, but only his disciples and those closest to him could. They were all very ready to cling to his every word, if ever he might speak to them.

Jesus then held the child in his lap and his eyes were still attending to him as he finally spoke to everyone, "Here is a question familiar to you."

He looked up at the crowd and then over to his disciples, "A question for your pondering. How do you become the greatest one among all of my disciples and followers?"

The twelve were too tired and too hungry to react defensively as they had to each other earlier. They were too drained to even react at all. Although Bartholomew did give a gentle elbow to Philip, even that was a friendly gesture as the two smiled and looked at each other.

The Rabbi continued on, "I am telling all of you this because from what I overheard from my twelve disciples who were arguing on the road that we took to get here, none of them has the slightest clue of how to become great in my Kingdom."

Jesus looked at his disciples for a moment and said, "They have no secrets that they can keep from me. They fought over who is to be the greatest and couldn't settle it among themselves." The Rabbi paused and gave thought to what he would say next, "You all need to know this. In my Kingdom fighting over who is the greatest isn't going to happen anymore. You see, you cannot settle important matters that way and still be my disciple. And the greatest among you is not going to be what you think either." The Rabbi paused so that what he would now say would stand out tall and clear to everyone. "In my Kingdom it all changes now." Again, he paused so that this message, that change was coming, would forever be in their memories. "Unless each and every one of you has deep changes in your heart and becomes like this young child, you will never share with me in my Kingdom. Ever. You must first become humble like this child to be considered great in my Kingdom. You may think of it this way, if I were to send this young child to you in my name, you must welcome him in my name and receive him as if he were me. So then if you were to welcome anyone, including this child, who I have sent in my name, you would be welcoming me. And when you welcome me you are welcoming the one who sent me, who is my Father in heaven. So begin to learn for yourselves that the one who is truly least and last among you is the greatest one of all, and let it be this way from now on among yourselves, all of you. And remember, I didn't come here for you to serve me; I came here to serve you."

Jesus looked down and gave his attention to the child again as he offered him his right hand and, in turn, the child placed his hand against the Rabbi's as they played together. Again, everyone waited patiently. It wasn't what they expected but it was good for them to be there. Even though it was a difficult lesson to comprehend, it was one everyone needed to hear and be reminded of.

Jesus then laid his hand on the child's head and looked with sincerity directly into his eyes, "Bless you dear child and may the God of Israel keep watch over you all the days of your life."

He lifted the child and reached out to his mother, "Thank you for your kindness in letting me hold your child." The young mother smiled and reached up to receive back her son as she joyously held him up to her face and spoke words of affection to him. The child reached to touch his mother's face as he was sharing with her the special blessing he had just received at Jesus' hand.

Chapter Four
Set to Go to Jerusalem

Jesus had been in Jerusalem several times before, but it was on the last visit that things became truly dangerous for him. It was there that his enemies were growing, both in number and in their fierce hatred of him. They had tried to stone him at the Temple and so, for his safety, he went north to Galilee. But, there too, he had faced opposition. Serious opposition. They did not pick up stones to hurl at him; instead they tried to throw him off a cliff to his death. Despite this, the Lord continued to teach and perform signs and wonders without number. There were many who now followed him and their numbers were continually growing; these were the ones who believed in him, and these all did so with the deepest sincerity. But those who stood against him, though much smaller in numbers, did so with even greater intensity and some of those did so with deadly intent. It was for the avoidance of them that Jesus had made his way so far north, north to Capernaum.

The time of his visit to Capernaum was all but done. It was in that peaceful time of evening when comes twilight, the time when the sky to the west grows rose pink and stars can first be seen in the eastern sky. The disciples were gathered outside around an open fire left burning from when it had roasted their evening meal. They talked and laughed about their day as they passed the evening away.

Their Rabbi was in their host's house but then he came out and approached them. "Listen to me, all of you." Though he had asked for their attention some of his disciples continued to talk on, but in softer tones and acting as if they were listening when they weren't. The Rabbi was irritated by their poor attempt at appearing to listen to him while they were still rambling on themselves. He spoke bluntly, "In the morning we are setting out for Jerusalem again."

Now their voices fell silent, dead silent, and their resistance to the idea continued on that way for a while until Thomas spoke out, "But Rabbi the last time you were there the authorities attempted to arrest you. They think they have a reason to put you to death. I don't think it is wise for you to go there again so soon, at least not publicly. Maybe you could go in disguise, if you even go there at all."

But he was a disciple, and not the Rabbi, he was a follower, and his Master had made his plans without consulting any of the twelve first. And why would he consult with them? He was the prophet. That was clear from Jesus' tone. When he did respond to Thomas it was with a short answer that was meant for them all to hear, "As I said."

Then he looked at their faces, each of them, to make sure they saw the look of unwavering determination on his face, and by its unyielding appearance, they understood what he meant. If it wasn't clear to them before, then it was clear to them now. "In the morning we'll get an early start and begin our journey there." This was what would be happening and Jesus left them with no doubts when he simply turned and went back into the house.

Jesus' last words to them were just as he intended them to be. Short, clear and simple. Jesus left them with the undeniable fact that his was the last word on it and, as such, the stunned disciples sat in silence until some time had passed.

James the Greater shook his head and spoke softly as if to ensure that he would not be overheard by anyone outside of their group. "I can't believe he wants to go there."

To which Thomas added, "I think it may lead to the end for all of us."

But John didn't see it that way as he questioned, "Is he going there to establish his Kingdom now?" What else could they think? Which was it to be when they would arrive in the Holy City, his death or his exaltation to power as their nation's King?

Bartholomew spoke with all lack of clarity, "It sounds like it, but I'm not sure." Everyone wondered, was he referring to the start of his Kingdom or to the end and his death?

Peter, who was certain as could be and as he always was, seemed to have every assurance of what would happen, because it was what he wanted to see happen, "But Jesus spoke about coming with glory and in the power of God in his coming Kingdom. Where else is he to rule from but in Jerusalem? And how can he go to Jerusalem and die when he is returning there to reign in power with legions of angels at his side? Don't start mourning his death when it isn't going to turn out that way. Why, with that kind of a force beside him who could possibly withstand his rule? We need to celebrate as we journey to Jerusalem with him."

And the truth be told, there really were indications of either outcome happening. But no one considered the possibility of both happening, no one but Jesus anyway. Not that he was going to rule as an earthly monarch as his disciples imagined. But he was going there to wage a war and conquer. And yes, angels would be at his side to assist him. As the evening gave way to the night the hot coals started to cool and the disciples continued in their ambiguous discussion of their views on what would happen. And though there was no end to their uncertainty of what the future held for them, there came an end to their discussion as they each, in turn, grew tired and went inside to sleep.

Chapter Five
Rejection in Samaria

When in Capernaum, Jesus set his face to go to Jerusalem once again. He also firmly determined the route that he would take. This was to be the shortest and the fastest way to the Holy City because it had an obliging terrain, the terrain of Samaria. Jesus had been there before and was well received by all because when he first went there he brought healing between His Father and all of their people. He was successful in his efforts and from then on, he enjoyed warm hospitality among the Samaritan people.

The Rabbi had spent the day before, and now the morning, in that tiny village. It was two hours past their noontime meal when he spoke to James and John, "Go on ahead of us to the next village and find a place where we can spend the night. We won't be staying on. Just arrange for dinner this evening and food for the journey in the morning before we head out at dawn." What he did was a common occurrence in their travels, to send two disciples ahead to prepare for their needs. But it was not customary for the Rabbi to stay only the night; he typically lodged for a day or two, sometimes longer, as he ministered to the people's needs.

James and John gathered their bags and staffs, and pushed on down the southbound road. They reached the next village; it was only a few miles ahead. It was a smaller village and the people in the streets seemed to be expecting them. The two were greeted by every stranger they came upon. There were not many buildings and so it was not hard for them to find the only inn there.

The two ventured inside to see a couple of people looking half asleep at a table and an Innkeeper who smiled gladly when he saw them come in his door. He stood up, brightened up and looked proud of his place. He was glad to have these two guests looking things over.

James was slow to speak and he did not initiate the customary greetings that must be exchanged so John spoke first and broke the silence that had become uncomfortable to him. But because of his youth it had not been his place to speak first and extend the greeting; it was always left to the eldest or the leader among them to speak first and initiate this. "We need overnight lodging."

He spoke with some nervous excitement before his older brother James should have spoken.

The innkeeper took note of his accent which was at first a heartwarming sound to his ears because he had hopes that these two might be disciples of Rabbi Jesus. He knew that he was in the region and now hoped his village might receive a visit from him. He was glad to ask, "You sound like you might be from Galilee?"

John was quick to admit to that, "We are." But in his stepping out so he could speak first, he had overstepped his customary place by assuming the younger could do just as well what his older brother had failed to do. John didn't catch on that his brother was offended with him by this. And neither of them realized that the sparring they would now carry out was taking them further out of step from the customary exchange of greetings they should have followed in.

They now began to indirectly challenge each other over who should do the speaking, which only lead them into their next terrible misstep. James pursued a course of jumping ahead of John in the conversation rather than starting over and starting out right. He went straight ahead to discussing the business at hand.

Though he was looking at the innkeeper, the expression of his face and the tone of his voice carried with it the sound of his irritation towards John as he spoke out, "There are thirteen of us. We are looking for supper tonight and at sunrise some food for our journey."

James quickly turned toward John and then back to the innkeeper again, "Nothing more" he concluded. He reasoned that John got the message he should say 'nothing more' by his quick turn in his direction. He also expected that the innkeeper would take it to mean that that was simply all they needed of him and that he would not pick up on the more subtle message included in his words which were meant only for his brother. How unfortunate it was for James that the message the innkeeper got was that James was telling him what he had intended only for John, that he wanted no further discussion of the details from him.

The innkeeper smiled and ignored his rudeness for the moment as he asked, "Are you part of the group that follows Rabbi Jesus?"

James nodded but said nothing as he stared intensely at John to quietly let him know he should remain silent.

The old man wanted to double check that he rightly understood what James and John wanted so he asked, "Dinner, rooms for the night, food for the journey, nothing more?" James coolly nodded again.

Offense was now doubly given by the brothers but the innkeeper had not taken issue over it, not for now anyway. "Yeah? Where are you headed in such a hurry?" queried the man.

John had understood the message that he should keep quiet but his youthful intemperate excitement about their destination overruled his self-control, "Jerusalem!" he blurted out.

James wished and then wished again that his brother had not said that. His posture dropped and his knees buckled under him a little as he caught himself preventing a fall to the floor. The innkeeper took silent note of this and though James saved himself from falling over, he could not prevent the fallout that was surely going to follow. He knew, though John did not, that the man would take offense that his village did not warrant so much as a half a day's visit by his Rabbi and that they wanted to leave right away for Jerusalem, a city that despised Samaritans.

James was right. The innkeeper didn't take kindly to the discourteous display the two fumbled into as they skipped over the proper social customs that should have first been extended by offering a proper greeting. But now the innkeeper who had been willing to overlook that infraction took real offense at the two just as James worried he would. The man managed to conceal his thoughts and feelings as he innocently replied, "Jerusalem is it?" The innkeeper didn't need to hear anything more from these two; he only knew he wanted to get them out of his inn and out of his village. *'If they are going to Jerusalem, let them be on their way to Jerusalem,'* he reasoned. Having thought it through he spoke again, "I wish I had something to offer you, I really do. But I am full up and short of help too."

James took the rejection out of stride and revealed his panic in his voice, "Then what about your village public house, can we stay the night there?"

There was a sort of public house they could have stayed in; it was actually a poor house on a community farm just outside the village. It was their local way of providing for their own needy. It was for anyone who was in need of housing and food, and if they would work the fields according to their abilities, they could stay in the house and share in the harvest it gave. But the innkeeper wasn't willing to send them there, not after the way they acted towards him.

Now the innkeeper set out to have some sarcastic fun with them, and he liked playing the actor and seeing other people's responses. He flung his arms into the air in a good display of overacting, "Public house? Public house! Does this tiny poor village look like it has a Public House?"

His ploy worked too, and now he could see a different side of the two demanding brothers. James was in a sweaty lather, "But the afternoon is almost over. Where will we stay?!"

And John added, "And what will we eat for our dinner?!" This was the reaction the innkeeper hoped to see in them and now it was time for him to drive home his point which he was glad to do as he added some sting to it. He shook his head 'yes' as he mocked them, "You said you are on your way to Jerusalem."

James and John nodded 'yes' along with him and their eyes looked hopeful.

Again the innkeeper's head shook in agreement with them, "So then be on your way to Jerusalem!" he shouted at them. He pointed both of his hands toward the door and it was clear in more ways than one that they needed to leave now.

John didn't pick up on the not so subtle undercurrent of the message. He was somewhat self-absorbed and still sulking. But James understood what danger they were facing and it made him fear for his safety, both his and his brother's. He quickly turned to John and made certain eye contact with him as if to warn his brother, 'We better be moving on. Now!' His eyes moved with intensity in a straight line to the door. His parting words were spoken and by their tone it was clear that his feelings were hurting, "Maybe the next village will have something for us." But he spoke this mostly for the sake of his brother to direct him on the need to quickly leave. James walked and shielded his brother from the danger he felt by stepping between him and the man as he reached out his hands and physically turned John toward the door and then securely marched him outside. John protested but James whispered to him, "Just keep walking, keep walking, we're walking out of here now!" John kept his silence, just barely, even though he was very nearly overcome with the temptation to stop and demand to know what was going on right then and there.

It was a short walk to the edge of the village where James felt it was safe enough to open his mouth again. There the brothers reflected on their encounter, but it was limited to their own conceited views and to what they wanted to make of it. James broke the silence, "You know, I'm not sure I believe this man. For being full up it was awful quiet in there. Just a couple of nobodies lazing about."

John added, "Yeah, and I don't think he was short of help, I think they were his help. What's going on here James?"

To which James also wondered, "You're right, what's going on here?"

John spoke with a critical tone as he questioned, "Did you notice how he quickly asked if we were from Galilee?"

James spoke on, "Then he wanted to know if we were Rabbi Jesus' disciples and where we were headed to. Then he lied to us! Twice, John, twice he lied to us!!" James' voice grew more angry as he spoke out. John, too, was getting worked up and as they spoke on, they reacted to each other and then overreacted off of each other.

James growled, "That makes me very angry. I don't care who that guy thinks he is. He is nobody to me. Who is he to lie to us and then refuse to give us lodging?"

John added a new view, "James, we failed here didn't we?"

James didn't give much thought to his brother's view point; he worried instead about what his Master's reaction would be, "What will Rabbi Jesus say? It's like these people are refusing to acknowledge him. All of Samaria gives homage to our Rabbi and this…, …this buzzard acted shamefully to us!"

John wasn't listening anymore because his anger had now turned inward on himself and it was giving him a bout of melancholy. He was getting down on himself and spoke in a strong and dreary manner, "We failed, didn't we James?"

James spoke sharply hoping to snap his brother out of his misery, "I don't think so! It was that innkeeper, he failed! And the village, they failed … they failed us and that means they failed the Lord!" James took all confidence in the equation he had just worked out and then concluded, "And now they should pay for it."

It never occurred to them that they were in the wrong and that they gave the first offense; it was not conceivable in their high mindedness that this was even possible. Now John's sense of failure turned from focusing on himself, and his brother with him, to focusing on the innkeeper. Unfortunately, his anger didn't stop there, because it was over flowing in abundance. So, great it was that it needed a larger target to hit than just the life of one innkeeper.

James, too, was fermenting his own anger and becoming intoxicated with it. Suddenly he burst out with a bright idea, "Fire!" he declared to himself and then as he turned and looked his brother in the eyes he asserted his idea again, "Fire!!"

John was quickly caught up in the mad frenzy that had now begun, "Fire, fire from heaven!" The two were thinking together in perfect step as they walked in one irreversible and regrettable direction.

They both looked to the heavens and James continued on, "Fire from heaven should come down and..."

James stopped and John instinctively completed the sentence, "... and take their lives."

The two brothers were enthralled with their plan; they turned slowly toward each other in great excitement as if they had done this before with some other fantastical plans of theirs.

John spoke gleefully, "Let them share Gomorra's fate..."

The sentence he started James completed, "... and let them be turned to ashes!" They acted happily as if they had just figured out how to cure all the world of its ills.

With all self-assurance James told John, "Here is what we will do. When the Lord arrives we will repay the village for how we were treated."

John, in fortitude agreed. "Then the whole village will be repaid for what they have done to us." Some time passed as the two muddled over their thoughts and plans.

When Jesus arrived he spoke with the two brothers, "Where are we staying? Over there?" as he looked toward the Inn.

James' voice carried with it a grave and stone cold tone, "Lord, you need to know that these people are unlike the others we have visited in Samaria."

John kicked in, "Word of you has reached all of their lands, and all of Samaria has received you with joy and offers of hospitality. But these villagers have been hardly willing to speak a word to us. They said that there is no lodging here for us, not even a public house to rest in. Then they said, "You are going to Jerusalem, so be on your way to Jerusalem.""

James' voice took on a righteous overtone, "Lord, for having treated you so rudely we will call down fire…"

Jesus, as a prophet, knew where this was going. "Stop!" he said without hesitating.

But it did no good. James and John were back on their compulsive roll again.

John spoke the next clause in their sentence, "from heaven…"

Jesus spoke more directly to them, "Don't say it!"

But the two brothers could not stop; they would not hear what Jesus was saying to them.

James carried on with the next clause "…and like Gomorra, let them be burned to ashes…"

And John with all enthusiasm rolled right in with the final phrase, "…for their failure to offer hospitality to you!"

The two brothers were so excited with their plan, they were sure Jesus would be all for it too. Unfortunately, for them they were entirely wrong. They had no idea how wrong they were which was why they would become forever known for this foul plan that they had dreamed up.

Jesus was now greatly angered over what they had conjured up in their minds; what should be the rightful end to the village for not extending hospitality. Jesus went face to face with these two in order to get their attention, "Stop it!" he shouted loudly at them both. Their Rabbi shook his head and with a look of scorn said, "What goes on in your two heads for thinking? How could you ever come up with a murderous plan like that! These people are not picking up stones to kill me or planning evil against me. And how could you not notice that they are insightful beyond your abilities."

James and John now turned to each other with the look of great fright.

Jesus continued on, "They know from what you told them that I am not going to stay with them other than for the night. They can see that I am hard set on going to Jerusalem and not staying to minister to their needs. And haven't you two figured out yet that I have come to seek and save the lost and give my life as a ransom for many? So how by your disastrous plan is God's love shown to them if they share in Gomorra's fate?"

The two brothers said nothing for the moment and the rest of the disciples stood by in silence not knowing what to do or say over such an overt plan to bring destruction on the people and their village.

James spoke first, but not to answer Jesus' question. He was still focused on his own concerns. "Then wherever will we stay for the night?"

John, too, was concerned only with his needs. "And what about our dinner, what will we eat?"

Jesus was irritated that they had ignored his question and so he ignored their questions. "Let me see, they don't have any place to offer us so we can spend the night. But, if you go ahead with your plans to turn them to ashes, then we certainly won't be staying here under those conditions! Either way, this is not a complicated problem you two! We will take ourselves to the next village where I am sure we will find our dinner and accommodations for the night."

Jesus turned away from the two and started walking to the next village by himself which was a sign that he was going to ignore them for a while so they could rethink their plans and come to a change of heart over the entire matter. As the Rabbi walked away he shouted his thoughts out loud for all to hear and he laughed, "Fire from heaven? These two have really got to learn to keep their anger in check." He mockingly laughed again. "Those two really are brothers aren't they?" All the disciples could hear the deep sound of disgust in his voice. "Brothers, two of a kind makes one pair and sons of thunder each they are ..., *sons of thunder* each." Now he took a deep breath in and sighed loudly as he said, "Come, let's be on our way."

Chapter Six
Almost Dinner

Jesus was well known and always a welcome guest in the village of Bethany. It was close to Jerusalem but also just far enough away for safety's sake. Many people passed through the crossroads there as they traveled to and from the Holy City. While the Rabbi was in residence there large crowds of those travelers stopped to hear him preach and teach. Beyond that, Jesus' friends lived there: Lazarus and his sisters Martha and Mary. For all these reasons Bethany was a favorite place for him to be.

Rabbis typically are seated when they teach and the crowds who gather to listen most often stand in the synagogues to hear them. When outdoors they would either sit or stand. This day the people were seated because there was much grass where they were. Peter, James and John also sat on the ground close to their Master who was seated in a chair that had been provided for him. The crowd was especially large, and though Jesus' voice carried well, it was not able to reach everyone who came to hear him. But there was an old world solution for this that Jesus often employed with the help of his disciples. He had some of his disciples standing in the crowds at intervals, where they were still close enough to him to hear what he said. After each sentence Jesus would pause and give the disciples time to repeat his words loudly to those further out. This way as they served as repeaters; with their voices echoing the Lord's words for everyone to hear.

As Jesus concluded his lessons that day, a man in the front of the crowd spoke out, "Rabbi, John taught his disciples how to pray. Could you teach us how to pray, too?"

Jesus paused and then nodded to the man to indicate he was agreeable to the request. Then he spoke,

> *"When you pray, say:*
> *Our Father, who art in heaven.*
> *Hallowed be thy name.*
> *Thy Kingdom come,*
> *thy will be done on earth as it is in heaven.*
> *Give us this day our daily bread,*
> *and forgive us our trespasses,*
> *as we forgive those who trespass against us.*
> *And lead us not into temptation, but deliver us from evil.*
> *For thine is the Kingdom, and the power,*
> *and the glory forever and ever. Amen"* [1]

Jesus had given them the words to say but now he wanted to instruct everyone further on prayer. "What would you do if your friend arrived at your door at midnight? What would you do for him? You would get out of bed, turn up your lamps and unlock the door as you invite him inside. Then you would put out some food for him to eat. But as you go to do this you see that you don't have anything left from your family's dinner to set before him and the markets are closed. So, what would you do? You would hurry over to your neighbor's house and knock on his door. When he answers you would say, 'My good friend has just arrived to visit me and I have no food left in my house to offer him. Please loan me three loaves of bread tonight and I will repay you in the morning.' But this neighbor refuses to open his door and says, 'Stop knocking on my door and let us sleep because we are all in bed. Now go home and leave us alone.' So then what would you do

---

[1] Matthew 6:9-13

for your weary friend at that hour? You would keep on banging away even louder on that neighbor's door. Then he would get out of bed and open his door to give you the bread you asked to borrow, just so that he can get rid of you and go back to sleep.

So remember what I have taught you about practicing prayer. Do not hesitate to speak up for yourselves and ask your heavenly Father for what you need and it will be given you. Don't sit around like a lame goat. Take action and search things out and you will find what you need. Knock without stopping, loudly if you need to, and the door will be opened for you. Because every one of you who dares to ask will receive what they need. Every one of you who searches will find what they need. And for everyone who knocks, the door will be opened for you. So, if you know how to provide for your children's needs, then how much more does our heavenly Father know how to provide for all your needs?"

Now, as the day was nearing its end the Rabbi concluded his teaching for the day. He rose to his feet, looked the people over and lifted his hands to impart his blessing on the people. He spoke out with a rich and deep voice, "And now receive the blessing of our God.

The LORD bless thee, and keep thee.
The LORD make his face shine upon thee,
and be gracious unto thee.
The LORD lift up his countenance upon thee,
and give thee peace. Amen"[2]

Jesus dismissed the crowd with those words and then intended to return to the home of his friends. But a Pharisee

---

[2] Numbers 6:24-26

55

with some of his friends approached him and said, "Rabbi, may I invite you to join me at my home for dinner? You and your disciples too?"

Jesus looked his way and nodded, "Yes, that would be nice, thank you."

Together they walked at a leisurely pace, the Pharisee led the conversation which was filled with little of anything meaningful. He simply chattered on with facts about the street they walked on, the homes and his opinions about the people who lived in them. Behind them a small but growing crowd followed and listened to everything that the two said.

When they arrived at the Pharisee's home Jesus was impressed with how well the man had done for himself to own such a large and well-kept residence which had a wide entrance with two doors that were both opened simultaneously by his servants, who bowed low as they arrived. Once inside, they sat as their feet were washed by his servants and the crowd that had followed them continued to watch and listen to everything, because the doors were left open. The Pharisee seemed to have a crooked and contradictory smile on his face as if he was enjoying having his feet washed but was not pleased about it at the same time. Jesus noticed that the man was holding his breath the whole time. His servants attended to his feet with what seemed like unusual attention to details and with much repetition. Both his feet were washed in the exact same manner and dried in the exact same way and to the final detail at that. The man was still smiling but clearly he was uncomfortable. Once the towels and water basins were taken away he breathed a big sigh of relief. Jesus wondered, *'is he holding his breath because he believes his feet had an unusually foul odor, beyond that of anyone's feet?'* But the Master didn't notice an unusual odor or anything else that was difficult to endure as his own feet were washed.

Jesus stood and looked down the hallway that led into the Pharisee's home; it had a large table in the middle of it, so large that you could only pass by it sideways. On the table there were several large basins filled with water and small towels in neat little stacks. The man now bounced to his feet and hurried himself with a merry excitement to one of the wash basins where he wiggled slightly as though this was a real thrill to him. Jesus watched on as the man had his servants empty a large water pitcher over his hands as he methodically interlaced his fingers and rubbed his hands, and fingers rigorously together. As he washed away he murmured and quietly hummed to himself. Then he attended to his nails and grimaced in discomfort as he scraped around his cuticles and under his nails with a manicure stick.

The Pharisee looked at Jesus and then turned his eyes to one of the wash basins and looked hopeful as if to say, 'go ahead and wash your hands, too', but Jesus did nothing other than look on. After that he rubbed the tips of his thumbs into the skin folds of his knuckles one by one as his servants again emptied another pitcher of water over his hands. It was quite an ordeal to watch. Never before had Jesus seen such devotion or meticulous care given to the washing of someone's own hands, let alone seeing someone take so much 'joy' over the experience.

The man stepped away from the table and Jesus moved to follow. But the Pharisee stopped; his posture suggested that he was blocking the way into the rest of his home. He gestured to the wash basin with his hand and said, "Don't you want to wash your hands too, before you eat?"

Jesus answered with an tone of unassuming ignorance to the question, "What is it?"

The Pharisee clarified himself, "You believe, of course, that cleanliness is essential in order for the godly man to lead a devout religious life, don't you?" The Pharisee presumed he needed to teach the Rabbi about his practice, "Of necessity, all precautions must be taken with everything that you eat and drink so that it won't contaminate or taint you, making you unclean."

Jesus continued in his position of assumed ignorance as he inquired of him, "Contaminate me?"

The Pharisee was glad to explain himself, "Yes. Contaminate you." He paused and gave the situation some thought before he added, "Before God, you know. Contaminate you before God. So, shouldn't you …" he paused hoping that what he said would be enough so that Jesus would follow in washing his hands.

But that did not happen. Instead Jesus replied, "Shouldn't I what?"

The Pharisee stepped back and looked Jesus over as if he couldn't believe the resistance he was facing from the Rabbi before he spoke again, with some anxiety appearing in his posture and his voice, "Wash your hands, of course…" He pointed with some insistence to the table and the tone of his voice now took on a distinctly demanding tone as he continued, "…wash your hands."

Jesus perceived that this man was guarding the way to the inner sanctum of his home because he could not endure the thought of anyone entering it without not only washing their hands, but apparently, he also had to find personal satisfaction in watching them do it. Jesus looked at him and spoke directly to the man's mistaken ways, "Is that how it works?" Then he rolled his head back as he billowed out in laughter over this amusement, "Is that how you think it works?"

The Pharisee stepped back as if he had been pushed, "But..." the Pharisee hesitated before speaking again because he was having difficulty understanding Rabbi Jesus' resistance, "...don't you want to wash before you eat? You must wash your hands, mustn't you?" The Pharisee was getting worked up over this impasse, and now his anxiety was rising. "Don't you care what might happen to you? Our forefathers learned the great importance of this long ago. So you must follow in their traditions very closely and I will have you know that it is for your own good."

Jesus' jovial attitude now took on a much more serious tone as it became clear to all those watching from within the house and from those on the street that the Pharisee was obsessed with a terrible compulsion. It was one that he had taken to a 'higher level', and made it a phony religious observance. Rabbi Jesus looked to the man with all seriousness and said, "Pharisee, listen to me carefully." Then he turned to the crowds who looked on and raised his voice for all to hear, "Everyone listen to me carefully and don't be misled by this man's so called religious observance here. Do not think that because you bathe in a fountain, have your feet washed for you, or wash your hands that you are in any way pure before God! You wash your food before you eat and your plates afterward which is good for everyone, but that is in no way a devotion to God. This Pharisee falsely believes that by his many precautions he can keep himself from being offensive to God as a sinner. This news that I share with you today may shock you, but all those practices don't have anything to do with pleasing God. Nothing at all. These so called 'religious observances' offend God because the Pharisee's focus is not about being faithful to the LORD but on trying to elevate himself above his own sinfulness. Does anyone here know that it is not about the dirt or the stink on the surface of your skin, but about what is inside of you from birth and what you do in life that soils your souls in sinfulness before God? In your hearts and in your thoughts, you are full of all kinds of sins: greed, wickedness, covetousness, lustfulness, murder, deceit and contempt for others. Don't be fooled any longer by this man's pretentious religious practices! Think for yourselves, and know the truth which is what Moses and the prophets wrote about it. God is the one who made the outside and the inside too. Practice mercy with others, make your confession of sin truthfully, practice repentance before God over the sinful things that are within you, and see that you will be cleansed of your sins by God through forgiveness from heaven."

The crowd of people watched with all seriousness and would not be distracted from hearing the truth. It was what they deeply longed to hear. The Pharisee was himself speechless as Jesus continued to teach the truth to everyone, "None of the Pharisees should be enjoying their *righteous* claims over what they do for themselves. What righteous deeds anyone does for them self produces nothing more than *self-righteousness*, which is a most terrible sin! If these men only knew God's truth about their lives they would have hearts so full of self-contempt, despair and anguish over their teachings; so much so, that it would consume their very souls. They carefully give a tenth of every last thing they have, even of meaningless, minute things like a dash of pepper, things that don't account for anything. What fools they are for doing this because when that is their focus, they neglect true righteousness, justice and loving God with all their life. They attempt to follow the Law of Moses but it is to a fault, and then they fail to see the reason for the Law in the first place. How sick and contaminated with filth are the souls of Pharisees like this! They are the ones who love to sit in prominent places at religious gatherings and have people address them by their titles everywhere they go; but beware they are more sinful than you can imagine. Self-righteous Pharisees, hear me out; your practices will only increase your misery and self-loathing, so much that you will be fearful to admit to it! You are infections hiding deep in the body that spread until death comes suddenly."

Another guest, a scribal lawyer who was an expert in the Law, was standing in the hallway beyond the water basin and he spoke out, "Rabbi, when you say these things about them you insult us too."

Jesus was just as direct with him as he had been with the Pharisee, "You lawyers, you too need to realize how miserable your souls really are! You believe that you can simply prescribe every possible religious observance to be followed so that sin can be avoided and eliminated from your lives. But by these you only make people fearful of doing anything at all and of going anywhere. And after you teach others to take all these precautions you don't even follow them yourselves. You are so very good at pointing out other people's faults but you fail to see your own. You accuse others of wrong doing but then, how strange it is that you never recognize their faithfulness, in essential things such as love and mercy. Somehow in all this, you grotesquely boast with sinful pride about your successes at producing righteousness. Don't you realize that any righteousness you produce by yourself is a terrible sin because it is the sin of self-righteousness? There is only One who is righteous and that is God, alone! The best you can hope for is to be forgiven sinners. But then, you too would have to confess that you have sinned in the first place. That would really be something to hear you admit to. You are fools for what you think, and believe and deceive yourselves with. How your souls have lied to your hearts and what twisted thoughts you have because of it. Do you think that you are doing a service to God by honoring the prophets he sent to you by giving them fine tombs? That will not erase the memory that it was your fathers who murdered them. You were born too late to share in their deeds but you have still found a way to join in their crimes by building those tombs. God has sent you prophets but most of them you rejected, persecuted and some you even killed. But now the time of judgment has come for all of those sins to be charged against you and this generation. All of the blood of the prophets that has been shed from the foundation of the world, beginning with righteous Abel, to the blood of Zechariah who was murdered as he stood in the Holy Temple between the altar and the sanctuary, you will be held to give an account for. All this will all be held in judgment against you and your generation. Don't you lawyers realize how terrible you really feel behind all of your deceitful games? May your heads be heaped full of condemnation until you turn to God for the help you need which only he can provide to you. Others come to you for help to find out how they can live faithful and godly lives. But then you give them the traditions and teachings of your prophet killing fathers and completely ignore what God has said about the faithful life in the Holy Scriptures. In this way you make void the Word of God so that you can uphold your traditions and fulfill your own self-centered interests. You do this over and over without regard for what God has said, and what learned men that you are. You don't even see how greatly mistaken you are. How is it that you don't see that you are invalidating God's word by what you teach and force others to do? You boast that you are experts in the Law of God, but in truth you know nothing about it. You criminals! You lock out everyone who seeks to be faithful and enter heaven by your mistaken ideas about what the Word of God says. You make certain that you have locked them out and then you don't even go in yourselves!"

Jesus stopped teaching and looked with disgust at the table with the water basins. With a single sweep of his arm he shoved everything on it to the floor. Water splashed onto his feet and so he shook it off in protest of the self-righteous practice of the Pharisee as he walked out the door and into the street with his disciples following him.

Outside Peter said to him, "Jesus, you came on very strongly against the leaders in there. Don't you realize that they are extremely upset with what you said so publicly against them? You didn't even stop what you were saying, so they could respond and explain themselves."

But the Lord was right to be deeply offended by the display the Pharisee put on, and over the way he tried to impose his misguided hand washing practice onto him. Everyone needed to learn the savage truth about it all.

The crowd that had observed all that happened continued to stand by hoping to learn more from Rabbi Jesus.

Then out from the house came a different scribe who addressed him, "Jesus of Nazareth, you were to be a guest for dinner at this man's house tonight. But you refused to follow the traditions and customs we observe. If you had not walked out he had every right to ask you to leave."

As soon as he ended his statement, a different Pharisee spoke out, "What do you have to say about this situation? Are you opposed to following any of the good traditions of our ancestors? Are you opposed to following Moses? Don't you care about becoming polluted?"

The crowd hung on every word that was being spoken and more people came running to see what the excitement was, speaking with each other, telling the newcomers of all that was said and done.

Though the scribes and the lawyers were expecting to speak with Jesus, to hear his answers and confront him over the incident, the Lord looked sharply at them and boldly exclaimed, "You will have to excuse me from discussing anything more about your practices, which, by the way, are not from Moses. My disciples and followers are pressing in to hear me teach and I don't want to neglect them."

The Lord was still feeling very offended over the demands the Pharisee tried to impose on him. But he felt the situation needed to be dealt with upfront rather than be compliant to it. The self- righteous religious leaders were admired for these practices by the people everywhere and the Lord needed to set things right, even if it meant taking a stand against them.

In the street in front of the Pharisee's house, he spoke out to the crowd of people, "Beware of the yeast of the Pharisees; their yeast is hypocrisy at its worse. Forget completely about them. You must know that any plant that my heavenly Father did not plant in his vineyard will be torn out by the roots, thrown by the wayside and left to die in the scorching heat of the sun. Forget about those hypocrites and the offence they took. They are no less than blind guides of the blind. Anyone they offer their guidance to will stumble along with them and both will fall into the same pit. If you believe in me and confess your faith to others, I will acknowledge you in the presence of God. But if you deny faith in me, how can I make your name known to the Father? But know this; if you speak a word against me, I will forgive you. However, if you blaspheme against the Holy Spirit of God, as these men have, there is no forgiveness for you. If you are brought before your synagogue leaders, before the Temple authorities or before a ruler there is no reason for you to worry about what you will say about your faith in me. Don't worry because you will have the help of the Holy Spirit to give you the words that you need to say at that time. These Pharisees, these scribes and lawyers are so worried about yeast in their bread and they warn everyone to avoid breaking the law on this matter. But the truth is that everyone needs to be warned about their yeast, the yeast of the Pharisees, which is what they falsely teach, and the hypocrisy of their lifestyle. Beware of the yeast of all of them, the Pharisees, the Sadducees, the scribes and the Herodians too. Nothing is covered up that will not be uncovered, and nothing is a secret that will not become well known among you. Therefore, whatever has been said in the dark will be heard in the light of day, and whatever has been whispered behind closed doors will be proclaimed from the housetops. I tell you, my friends, do not fear those who can kill the body, but after that can do nothing more. But I will warn you who to fear: fear him who, after you have died, has authority to cast you into hell. Yes, I tell you, fear him!"

Chapter Seven
Sabbath Cure

It was a bright sunshiny day that Sabbath morning and the village was quiet and peaceful. Rabbi Jesus had been invited to the local synagogue to read the scriptures and offer the day's lesson to the congregation. In the fashion of every Rabbi, he was seated in the front while most of the congregation sat on the floor or stood on the sides or in the back. The people's ears had grown tired of hearing the same old lessons, given by the same old people, over and over again. They lacked authority when they taught, they lacked the ability to share anything original. or even put a unique twist on anything by sharing their own experiences, from their own personal lives. For those reasons, the people loved to have Jesus visit. They loved to hear Rabbi Jesus because he did not simply repeat what others had taught him, as most of their religious leaders did, but Jesus taught as no one else taught. He understood everything in the scriptures, which he read with breathtaking mastery, and he could explain the depth of them well enough for a child to understand. Then he made his lesson practical, so that they could live what they gained from him, faithfully unto the LORD.

When the Rabbi began his lesson everyone's ears quickly grew attentive. "A man planted a fig tree in his fruitful vineyard. After enough years had passed and it had grown tall he came to visit it, expecting it to have matured enough to bear fruit. But when he looked at it there wasn't any. So, he called his gardener and said to him, 'Look at this tree! After these many years I expected there to be some fruit on it, but it is completely empty. I want you to cut it down and throw in the fire. Then you can replant this space with vines that will produce fruit for me.' But the gardener urged him not to do that saying, 'You should give it one more year. If you do, I'll till the ground and put down fertilizer around it. Hopefully, then it will produce fruit, but if it doesn't, I will cut it down and throw it into the fire.'"

In the middle of this lesson the people became unsettled. It was not because of what Jesus was teaching. It was because of the entrance of someone they rarely saw, a woman who they would rather not have seen, walk into their synagogue. It was her appearance that disturbed them. She was bent over at the waist, severely, and she had to use two canes to walk with. She needed to stretch her neck upward, and also turn her eyes sharply upward so that she could see what was in front of her. She walked, slowly, as she was in pain, severe pain, and she grimaced a little with every step. As she walked she put one foot forward with the greatest of effort and then, as she gently set her foot down, she took the greatest care to see if it was too painful for her to advance. By her expression she conveyed the message that she hoped everyone would understand her difficulty and that she was doing the best she could.

Some of the congregation that morning looked down as they saw her, shaking their heads in disgust. Others strained with their eyes to focus on the Rabbi, as if they did not notice her. Still others who were seated on the floor wiggled in discomfort and those standing became uneasy and their postures changed to project their impatience with her. Some, but only a few, stared at her and a couple of these made dirty looks at her.

It didn't take Jesus even the slightest moment to see that this woman was suffering. He was immediately moved with compassion for her and felt in his heart that he could not allow her to live like this any longer. Not one step longer. He stopped his lesson and while still sitting he looked at the woman with warmth and affection as he spoke softly to her, "Woman."

She was surprised that someone spoke so to her. She turned her head upward and, with a kindly smile to greet them, she looked around to see who it was that spoke to her. Typically, no one spoke to her, or if they did it was in a harsh tone with harsh words because the people there had no tolerance for her. When she saw that it was Rabbi Jesus who had spoken to her she smiled still brighter. But she looked as if she was uncertain why he would be addressing her so.

Jesus stood up tall, walked over to her and laid his hands ever so gently on her head and her back. His eyes closed, gently at first, then tightly and mightily, it was clear that he was concentrating very hard as he prayed in a whispered voice. He said his 'amen' and then opened his eyes and he looked as though he had been in another world and was now suddenly back. He refocused his eyes on the people around the room and then looked at the crippled woman as he spoke to her with overwhelming joy, "You are freed from your pain and your back is straightened."

Her face was in some kind of wonderful surprise as she suddenly let go of her canes, allowing them to fall to the floor before her. Then she flexed her back and stood upright as if it was no effort at all for her. As she stood up, loud snapping noises were heard coming from her back as it was made straight. She came off her feet with a bounce as she stood tall and whole again. The painful grimace of her face was gone; as was the weight of her long-endured affliction. This miracle had also erased her many deep and dark wrinkles away, making her look twenty years younger.

She looked about at the members of the congregation radiating a new and great sense of self-confidence as she broke out singing praises to God, raising her arms and looking to heaven. Then she looked at Rabbi Jesus and as their eyes met, her face grew still brighter and warmer. As she sang out she alternated looking heavenward, to the Rabbi, and to the congregation. She sang with such amazing beauty,

> *"O LORD my God, in patience I cried*
> *to you for help and you have healed me.*
> *You brought up my soul from*
> *despair and restored me to life.*
> *I will sing your praises and never*
> *cease to give thanks to your Holy Name.*
> *Look to him all you people and be made radiant;*
> *so your faces shall never be ashamed.*
> *He put a new song in my mouth,*
> *a song of praise to our God.*
> *I will forever tell of your wondrous*
> *deeds and your kindness toward me.*
> *Sing praises to God, sing praises,*
> *sing praises to our King, sing praises.*
> *O my strength, I will sing praises to you,*
> *O God my Redeemer who has*
> *shown me his steadfast love.*
> *Great triumphs he gives to his King,*
> *and shows steadfast love to his Anointed,*
> *to David and his descendants forever."* [3]

It was hard to make much sense of the congregation's reactions to the events of the morning. They were almost

---

[3] Based on Psalm 30.

giddy to hear Rabbi Jesus teach, but then they became very agitated when the woman who was crippled appeared. When Jesus went to her they were disturbed and they became outright angry when he healed her. It was as though they were more interested in having the lesson go on undisturbed than in seeing the woman healed. They were very put off by her appearance when she was crippled, but now that she was no longer crippled they were in an uproar.

Now the synagogue leader, Joash, believed he was speaking for everyone when he addressed Jesus, "No, no, no! Our congregation doesn't like this happening here in our synagogue on the Sabbath, this is wrong!" Then he turned to the congregation, "Listen to me!" He turned and faced the woman who was healed, and giving her a troubling look he said, "Everyone listen to me!" He looked across the room to ensure everyone was still listening as he spoke, "There are six days for working but work can never be done on the Sabbath day. Come on working days and be healed but don't come on the Sabbath for healing ever again..." He looked at Rabbi Jesus before continuing on, "...because it is a sin." He now stared with squinted eyes at Rabbi Jesus as he continued ranting on, "Healing is not allowed on this holy day and this, this event, should not have happened today! If you are coming to be healed of anything on this day of the week you will be involved in a sin because of it. And if you heal anyone on this day make no doubt about it you are breaking the Sabbath."

The congregation followed Joash's movements with their heads, nodding 'yes' as he nodded 'yes' and 'no' as he nodded 'no'. It was as if he was using some unnatural trickery to control their thoughts.

Jesus wondered, 'How can they be so blind so as to

think like this Joash and agree with him?'

Clearly God had worked this miracle on the Sabbath. And if God, who had commanded them to keep the Sabbath holy, had done this miracle on the holy day, how could it be a violation of keeping the Sabbath? Why couldn't the people make this simple logic work for themselves?

Rabbi Jesus became indignant with them and he cried out in disgust as he faced them down, "You hypocrites! Every one of you! How many of you have cared for his ox or donkey by bringing them to water on the Sabbath day? And haven't you read about how things were in the very beginning? Moses wrote that it was on the seventh day when God completed the work that he had done, then he rested for the remainder of the seventh day. So, all of creation was brought to completion on this day and you, you want to force her to wait to be made whole? How can you imagine that you can prohibit God from healing on this day? Shouldn't this woman, a daughter of Abraham and Sarah, who Satan held in crippling chains and bound her with pain for these many unbearable years, be set free from her torment on this Sabbath day? Yes, she has been rightly healed and made whole on this Sabbath."

The congregation listened to Jesus and at first they looked as if they might be smiling and nodding slightly in agreement. But then their expressions changed and it became apparent that they were disagreeing with him by shaking their heads in disapproval. Most of them, and most of all Joash, refused to speak to the Rabbi as they turned backs on him and the woman too, indicating their service was over. But there was a smaller part of the congregation that morning who joined the Rabbi and the woman as they left the synagogue, rejoicing in the wonderful thing God had done for this woman.

Chapter Eight
Twelve Missionaries

On the night before being sent out on their missionary journeys, Rabbi Jesus instructed his twelve disciples. He told them that up until that time their work as his disciples had been very limited but now that would all change. He reminded them of the most important lessons he had taught them in the past and said that these were exactly what they should preach and teach as they went out to serve. He said, "Tell all of the sheep of the lost house of Israel that the Kingdom of God has come to them and that they should repent and believe in me." He assured them that they were well trained and were now ready for this task and he called them his Apostles because they were being sent out by him with his message to do his work. Then he informed them about who they would be paired with as they were sent out: Simon who was also given the name of Peter, and his brother Andrew; James the Greater and with him his brother John; Philip and Bartholomew; Thomas with Matthew; James the Lessor together with his brother Thaddaeus; and finally, Simon who was called the Zealot and Judas Iscariot.

Now the morning came when they would go out with the full authority of their Rabbi and he gave them their final instructions before blessing each one of them. He said to them, "You are those who I have chosen because you have been faithfully with me all this time. You have seen my work and heard my message. Now it is time for you to go out to the towns and villages. I have laid hands on the sick and prayed for them to be cured and now I am empowering you to do the same. I am sending you in my name to preach and teach, to cure the sick, raise the dead, cleanse the lepers and cast out demons. But beware, because I am sending you out like lambs into the company of ravenous wolves. Therefore be as wise as serpents and as innocent as doves among them. You are to be welcomed by all and you must serve without accepting any offerings. Take nothing with you for your journey: not a staff, nor a bag, no food or money, not even a change of clothes. Whatever town or village you enter and its people welcome you, find out who in it is worthy and stay with them until it is time for you leave. Whatever house you enter offer them your greeting and if they are worthy let your peace rest on them saying, 'Peace be on this house.' If anyone receives you in peace, your peace will rest on them; but if they do not receive you, your peace will simply return back to you. Eat and drink what is set before you because as workers in the Kingdom of God you deserve the food they give you. Don't move about from house to house; just stay at the same home the entire time you are in their town. But beware of how they respond to you because not all will accept your message. Some will force you to answer for what you say and for the work you perform among them by compelling you to go in front of their village councils. Others will have your backs whipped because of me and the Gospel that you bring. When this happens don't worry about what you will say because, as you know, the words will be given to you at that moment from the Holy Spirit speaking through you. The message that you bring about the Kingdom of God will even turn family members against each other in hatred, but do not be surprised by this. You must know that I haven't come to bring only peace to the earth. My word not only brings division but also a sword with it to those who stand in opposition to the Kingdom of God. So, have no fear of them because nothing they do can be covered up so well that it won't become known to all, and there is nothing they can whisper about in secret that will not become widely known about them. When you enter a village or a town that refuses to hear the Gospel and they do not welcome you, leave that place and tell them you are shaking off the dust from your feet to protest them. Tell them that the Kingdom of God has come near to them but that by their words and actions they have refused to be included in it. Whenever they persecute you, you must flee to the next village. And know this, that whoever welcomes you welcomes me, and whoever welcomes me, welcomes the One who sent me. Everyone who opposes you, everyone who accepts you, these will each receive a just reward according to their actions. For those who receive the Gospel I will acknowledge every one of them before my Father in heaven. But whoever rejects you rejects me, and whoever rejects me, rejects the Father who sent me. And whoever gives even so much as a cup of cold water to you will receive a reward.

Now come forward to me so that I may lay my hands on you and bless you for this work." The Rabbi called his disciples to his side and laid his hands on them in pairs as he blessed each of them. Finally he lifted his hands and gave them this commission, "Go in my name and preach that all people should repent of their sins and live in faithfulness to God. Freely share the message of the Gospel and let them know that the Kingdom of God is here. I give you this authority: heal the sick, give sight to the blind and make the lame to walk. Preach my words and have all power over the enemy. Amen"

Chapter Nine
Herod's Court - Herod's Rules

Herod's court was, well it was Herod's. He was an undisciplined sort of person and to say that he was eccentric only begins to describe him. When he wasn't acting paranoid he was unpredictable, moody, conflicted, dangerous and deadly so. Because he lived in great wealth and in the luxury of his palace there weren't many things in his life that worried him. But if there was a rival to his throne, a threat to his power or an interruption in his pleasure he sat up and took notice. He was every bit his father's son and worse.

His father, Herod the Great, was the one who the Magi came to for help as they followed the star that told them of a newly born King in the land of Israel. Herod's scribes were able to tell him where the child was to be born by the prophecy in the Scriptures that foretold of the event. Herod told the Magi that he wanted to go and honor the new born King too. So, on the condition that they would send word to him on how to find the child himself, he told the Magi that they would find the child in Bethlehem of Judea. But the ruler secretly made ruthless plans to murder the child once he heard back from the Magi. The Magi were warned by God not to send word back to Herod and that they should quietly leave for their own countries. When Herod realized he was tricked by the Magi he went ahead with his murderous plan. Because he didn't know which child was born to be King, he took the life of every male child there who was of that same age.

This second Herod had been raised as a palace brat, in childhood and now as an adult he wasn't too much different. Just a little taller and a lot fatter. He had responsibilities, but he had his staff look after most of those details for him. Granted he was Jewish, but not faithfully, not even in the least, it was in name only. Like his father before him he was also a murderer. It was him who ordered the beheading of the prophet, John the Baptist, as well as many others who he considered to be enemies of the state.

When Herod was at court he did not like to sit in a chair. That took too much effort for him. So, being a lazy man, he preferred to recline on his couch. That way he did not have to constantly hold his head up or keep his back straight. And he limited how much official business he would attend to on any given day. He did not care if some matters were neglected until the next day because he alone came first. On this day, Herod was talking privately with two of his courtiers. They were keeping him entertained with humorous stories and offering him complements about his magnificence. It was Herod's court attendant Jared who oversaw, at Herod's bidding, who was allowed to enter or leave the room, and he controlled what official business was brought before him for consideration.

A palace servant appeared at the door to call on Herod, so Jared walked over there to speak with him. Herod glanced that way looking as if he was more irritated by the person than curious about why he was there. Jared looked at Herod for any reaction he might have and then he looked back to the servant as their conversation continued. Jared was also weighing in his mind whether to speak to Herod immediately about why the servant was there or to put him out and deal with it later. He knew that if he displeased Herod the rest of the day would not go well for him, or for anyone for that matter. He watched Herod with his peripheral vision, and as Herod looked over his shoulder in Jared's direction again their eyes met. Herod gave him a slight nod to indicate he was willing to hear whatever it was that was being discussed at his door. Jared felt a sense of relief, then he welcomed in two men who the servant had asked to wait just outside. Jared asked the servant to wait just inside the door and then whispered to the two men to stay with him. Then he approached Herod, bowed and waited for the ruler to speak. Herod ignored him for a time and then turned to look over his shoulder again as he spoke down to him in an irritated and pompous tone, "Well, what is it this time?"

Jared addressed his ruler, "Herod, my lord, there are two men here with a report of a new prophet in your land."

Herod strained to turn his head toward the door to look at the two men. It was clear by the look on his face that he saw them as an unwanted inconvenience. And while Herod himself was not overly intimidating, his palace guards who stood by the entrance with their swords and spears were. This was not a man anyone wanted to upset. He spoke and his voice was full up and overflowing with a distasteful attitude. He yelled at Jared, "Well, what are you waiting for? Bring them over here so I can better look at them."

Jared quickly turned to the two men and motioned for them to come to his side and then the three of them walked directly in front of Herod. There, Jared motioned to them that they needed to bow before Herod which they clumsily did.

Herod acted as if he was upset with the two men and yet he did want to talk with them. He now sat up so that he could attend to their report better. In his demanding way he billowed out impatiently a barrage of questions, "Tell me, what you have seen of this man that you call a prophet? What does he look like? What have you heard him saying? What is his name? Where does he come from and who travels with him?"

By the looks of them the two witnesses appeared to be overwhelmed by the onslaught of the demanding questions put them. It seemed as if they were more likely to run off in fright rather than speak out for fear of offending their ruler.

The taller one spoke first but his voice shook, "The crowds, they were so large. I couldn't get in very close."

Now that he had taken that brave step to talk, the other found the courage to speak too, "I saw him, them, with my own eyes. There were two of them."

Herod was not surprised but he acted as if he was. That kept the shadow of his intimidation as a fresh thought in everyone's mind, "What! Two of them?"

The shorter one spoke. He knew what Herod wanted to know; "They came into my village and preached to us. They called on everyone to bring their sick and injured, the crippled and those in distress to them."

Herod laughed as he threw his head back. He thought that it was idiocy to do such a thing, to ask to have those kinds of people brought out in public. "Why did they call for those hideous wretches to come?"

The tall one was now gaining confidence to speak out more, "The two men laid hands on them, each one, one by one. They laid hands on their heads and prayed for them to be made strong and healed. Each one was cured, not a one was left that was not cured."

Herod looked skeptical and he put on a sour face as though he was not so easily taken in and he looked the two over to size them up again.

But the witnesses were not put off by this. The short one spoke again making an even bolder but nearly unbelievable claim, "They even cleansed a disgusting looking leper."

Herod took a more serious look at the men, but so as to encourage them, not intimidate them. Then he spoke more kindly, "Who do you say that they are? Do you know their names?"

The tall one spoke first, "It was …"

Herod coached him onward, "Yes..."

"I'm not sure" he said.

Herod's face dropped in disappointment.

But the other witness was able to recall one name, "I think one was called John."

Herod suddenly stood up in a fright and looked paranoid as he shouted, "John!" He looked around to see who took notice of the fear that overtook him and he glanced around to ensure his palace guards where still awake and at their posts, next to the doors and all the windows. He muddled quietly to himself and seemed to be unaware of anyone else's presence, "This cannot be, I had him killed! I had John killed!" Then he ventured out a few steps from his couch and shouted at the witnesses with great offence, "John the baptizer I had beheaded! He's dead! Do you hear me? It can't be him, it can't, it just can't be him!" He looked down and his left hand went up to his chin as he thought about it. Then his hand rose to his forehead, which he tapped a few times and moved his fingers about as if he was picking at his thoughts to turn them over and draw some of them out. "His disciples, they came and took the body away! Who knows where they buried him? They will never tell me. Even if I could catch one of those conniving little bastards, they will never say. So there is no way to check to see if his grave is undisturbed. So then he is now raised from the dead? Is that why these powers are at work in him?" Herod was showing fatigue over where his thoughts had taken him. Clearly he was shaken and his face had grown pale as he staggered backward to his couch where he laid himself down again in near exhaustion.

Having been heard, and knowing that his report was received as true, the tall witness spoke again with ease, as if he had somehow become a trusted adviser to Herod, as he offered his opinion, "It was Elijah who was with him."

That report disturbed the monarch even more, "No, no, no! Not John the Baptist and Elijah too! I cannot handle another prophet like him right now!" Herod shook his head and rubbed his forehead as if it was injured by too much thinking.

The short one added, "We never saw John the Baptist before his death, but he had disciples. I'm not sure who these men were exactly, I only know what they did."

Herod looked up in distress. Clearly he didn't want to hear that last comment.

The witness wondered if he had overstepped his place with this man of great power, so he added a belated, "sir" to his last comment and looked down.

Herod took a minute for himself and gulped empty his gold wine chalice which was inlayed with jewels and then he called for more, as if it was going to cure him of this newly presenting problem. He looked at the other witness and asked him, "You, who do you say that they are?"

The man thought about it for a moment and then answered, "They are two of the prophets from of old, or at least they are like the prophets of old. Or maybe they are new ones who have been sent by God to serve in our land, by preaching and performing all these signs of great power."

From the back shadows of the hall a Pharisee, one named Kish, appeared before Herod. He bowed, and then he spoke, "I have heard recently of one Rabbi with twelve disciples and many followers my lord." He turned to the witnesses and asked them, "How many did you say were in this group?"

The witnesses answered in unison, "Two."

And the tall one added, "There were only two of them."

Herod was nearly beside himself in anxiety, "Is there anything else you have to say about him or them?"

The second witness spoke for them both, "No, my lord."

Herod raised his voice, "See these men out." Then he waved them off as if to wave off a fly. He sat up and put his feet on the floor as he spoke to Kish, in his demanding way, "Tell me more about this Rabbi."

Kish continued, "This new wandering Rabbi travels in a large group. He usually has twelve disciples with him and draws great crowds wherever he speaks. Reportedly he also heals the sick and raises the dead."

Herod shook his head indicating he had heard just about all he could take in for one day. His weariness was seen, in that his head didn't exactly go right to left but lower right to upper left in kind of an irregular oval movement. His arms had become flaccid, but he did firmly grip the arm of his couch for support and he muttered quietly to himself saying, "What shall I do?" over and over again.

Then Chuza, Herod's trusted financial steward of the treasury, stepped forward, "Sir, if I may." He waited for an indication from Herod that he had permission to speak before saying anything more.

Herod nodded to him and waved his hand with a drooping wrist to indicate he wanted to hear from him, 'after all', he thought, 'what worse news could come my way?

Chuza continued on, "Joanna, my wife, knows about this Rabbi. She told me that he is a prophet named Jesus who is from Nazareth. He has many devoted disciples and hundreds of followers."

Herod mustered up some energy and showed a renewed interest in the report he just heard. "I am puzzled about who this is, and I find this report intriguing. It could be that John has risen from the dead and is working with this man from Nazareth. It is said that when the dead are raised back to life, they have unnatural powers at work in them from the next world. That would explain these reports of signs and wonders."

"Sir," Chuza felt he needed to share more about what his wife had told him, "She said he recently sent out his disciples as missionaries and he called them apostles. He sent them to preach in his name and gave them his power to heal the sick."

Herod wearily nodded his head as he listened and then said, "They all trouble me. These reports, these religious men, they all trouble me." Then he reacted with an angry shout, "And they take a toll on my good nature!" But that little exertion nearly exhausted him and so he quietly muttered to himself again saying, "Bit by bit they wear me down, bit by bit they make me grow tired, tired and old."

Herod laid down again and took time to think to himself without dismissing anyone. A few minutes later he stood and spoke out assertively, "My experience, as was the experience of my father, is that these religious types don't last. They suffer the people to believe in what they say and to do as they ask. They lead many astray and upset the order of things. It is best, then, to have them run out of the land before they go too far and cause real problems. Whoever these men are, they are in my land stirring things up and I want them found and arrested so that I may question them. All of them. Especially this one who calls himself John. Then I will judge if this one is the baptizer or someone else. That John brought much trouble with him. I imagine this one, whether he is John or someone else will be the same or worse. I may have to have him and the other one put to death, this Jesus of Nazareth. And whoever they are, or he is, this time he will stay dead." Then he nodded to his court members and they knew that they needed to put things in motion as Herod had just ordered. The monarch now plopped down onto his couch, reclined and reached for his wine chalice.

Chapter Ten
Death Threat

It was a rare occasion when Rabbi Jesus wasn't working in his ministry. Even on the Sabbath he was *working*, which he was able to do without breaking the Sabbath Day of Rest. He once explained it this way, "My father is working still and therefore so am I." He took time to rest as he had need. The last time that happened was when his cousin John the Baptist was beheaded. He needed that time away to mourn the loss and come to terms with the death. Now with his newly appointed Apostles out on their missionary trips doing the work for him there wasn't really much left for him to do. He wouldn't allow himself to travel anywhere. He needed to wait for them to return and to hear them share the stories of what they had accomplished. So this became a time of rest for the Rabbi and he was enjoying with great anticipation the reports he would soon hear from his disciples when they returned.

He was sitting outside at a table in the courtyard of one of his patrons as the noon hour was approaching. In that time his disciples began to return to him from their travels and missionary work done in his name. Two by two they all came during that one hour and they were all filled with joy to be together again. The disciples exchanged stories of what they encountered and had done in the towns and villages they visited. Jesus sat quietly listening to the reports of their work and inwardly rejoicing in his heart. But before long he could no longer contain himself as he stood up and lifted his hands above his head and began to dance before the LORD as King David had danced before the Ark of the Covenant. And the disciples were as giddy as children for the joy they felt as they too joined in celebrating in the glory of the LORD. Jesus then led them all in singing the Psalm of David.[4]

> *"The LORD is my light and my salvation;*
> *whom shall I fear?*
> *The LORD is the strength of my life;*
> *of whom shall I be afraid?*
> *One thing have I desired of the LORD,*
> *that will I seek after;*
> *that I may dwell in the house of the*
> *LORD all the days of my life,*
> *to behold the beauty of the LORD,*
> *and to enquire in his temple.*
> *For in the time of trouble he*
> *shall hide me in his pavilion:*
> *in the secret of his tabernacle shall he hide me;*
> *he shall set me up upon a rock.*
> *And now shall mine head be lifted*
> *up above mine enemies round about me:*
> *therefore will I offer in his tabernacle sacrifices of joy;*
> *I will sing, yea, I will sing praises unto the LORD.*
> *When thou said, Seek ye my face;*
> *my heart said unto thee, Thy face, LORD, will I seek."*

When they were weary and tired from their celebrating they sat down to rest and Jesus spoke to them, "While you were away, I was sleeping in the night and I saw a vision of Satan's strongholds crumble like sandcastles being washed away by sea waves. I heard the chains of many who were held in bondage to him snap and break as they were set free. And I saw him hopelessly falling from heaven like a

[4] Taken from Psalm 27 KJV

flash of lightning as he tumbled down into the abyss of Hades."

Jesus grew euphoric and then looked at each of his disciples saying, "How blessed are you, all of you! Angels have longed over the eons of time to see what you have done in the Kingdom of God. I tell you today that in heaven many prophets and righteous men beginning with Adam and over the centuries have hungered and thirsted to see what you have begun. Blessed are your eyes because of what you have seen!"

He now looked heavenward to pray aloud, "O Father, what a joyous day in heaven and on earth this is! You have hidden the mysteries of your Kingdom from those who this world considers the wise and educated. But you have lifted the veil covering your secrets to those who are like infants and babes! This is your will in heaven and it has been fulfilled on earth according to your power, glory and might. Amen"

As the day continued, the disciples went about caring for their personal needs after returning from their journeys. Jesus himself relished in the day and all that his disciples return had held for him.

Then in the middle of the afternoon a man of the Pharisees, Kish, came to call on Jesus and speaking pastorally to him, as though he was an emissary of some kind. "Rabbi Jesus, Herod has heard about you and the work of your disciples on their missionary trips in his territory. Now he has issued orders to have you arrested. He is even threatening that he may take your life, as he did John the Baptist's. You should take him seriously and leave his territory immediately. His family dynasty has a long standing tradition of murdering anyone who upsets their powerful reign over the people they rule." The Pharisee did not himself wish to appear as a threat to the Rabbi. Instead he was working to help Jesus by sharing this difficult warning. Even still, the Lord's disciples gathered around him as if to shield him from the danger that was now threatened against him. And Kish's message brought about a strong response from the Lord but it was directed not at the Pharisee, but at Herod.

Jesus spoke boldly, "You can go..." but sitting and speaking these words was inconsistent with his intensity so as he continued he abruptly stood up, "...and tell that scheming fox that my time and my life are not in his hands and never will be! He can spew threats all he wants but he is just bellowing hot air. Go and tell him that I am casting out evil spirits from the people he rules over and I am curing the sick in his lands today, and I will do it all again tomorrow. I will complete my work here on the third day, then and only then, will I move on. You can tell Herod that he can try but there is nothing he can do to stop me. For this prophet must not be put to death unless it is in Jerusalem."

Kish received the message with the same calm nature he had spoken from, "I will bring him the message, just as you have said it. But you must know that it will only rouse his anger against you even more."

To this Jesus added, "Tell Herod he should know better than to try and hinder me. The good works that I do, healing the sick and making the lame to walk are done for his subjects, for their benefit."

To this Kish could only say, "Yes Rabbi, you are right. I will share this too." And with a kind nod of his head he walked away.

As Jesus and his disciples now stood about, the twelve were wondering what ever should they do now. Jesus calmly assured them, "Oh, do not worry about this Herod's threats. My destiny is not in his hands, but in my own and in Jerusalem." The disciples were then dismissed and they went back to caring for their own needs; all but the inner circle of Peter, James and John. These three and Jesus with them sat in silence.

Before long James knowingly looked at Peter and then at John before he spoke out, "Master, you are different on this journey to Jerusalem. Why?"

Jesus chuckled to himself and said, "Why do you say that?"

John spoke in a concerning voice, "You will not be deterred from going to Jerusalem where they will seek to kill you again. And even now, though Herod has just threatened to take your life, you plan to be in his territory for three more days. You were defiant in the message that you sent to that ruler but you used to leave the places where your life was threatened."

Peter then spoke, "We are worried about the safety of your life."

In unwavering confidence Jesus told them, "This is not the first time a member of that family has threatened my life."

John's concerning look now became one of surprise and James also looked with grave concern into his Rabbi's eyes.

But it was Peter who blurted out, "What! When did that happen?"

Jesus spoke matter of factly, "When I was a newborn child. The father of this Herod, Herod the Great, sought to take my life. He heard of my birth from visiting Magi who were searching for me and he felt very threatened by their report that I was born a King. That Herod was not willing to allow a rival to his throne live and so he ordered my death. But my parents were warned in a visitation from an angel to leave quickly. We fled to Egypt where we lived until he died, and then my parents came back to Nazareth to live." Their Rabbi paused as if a great burden was lifted from his shoulders by sharing about those early years of his life. Jesus continued, "Now that I take the time to reflect on it, it seems that from the beginning of my life I have been avoiding death in one way or another."

The three had meant to share their concerns with Jesus and to support him as his disciples. They had no idea the conversation would take this direction.

Peter reacted with great concern, "You've never mentioned this before. This Herod is evil, like his father before him. The father murdered countless people who were contenders for his throne, even his own children were among them."

James had an emerging thought, that there was some sort of pattern going on in all this, "So, beside threats from this Herod and his father," he paused in thought and then continued on, "the people in Jerusalem had already picked up stones to kill you when we were last there, but you escaped. Then we followed you to your home in Nazareth."

John now continued in the same vein of thought, "But they treated you even worse and wanted to throw you off the edge of that cliff and again you escaped. And now you want to return to Jerusalem where they will most likely try to take your life again."

Jesus looked at all three and then spoke, "It is true, I have had to avoid many attempts on my life from as early as my birth."

His disciples sat quietly, listening and not yet knowing what to think about all of this.

John reminded Jesus of what he thought was ahead of them if they were to continue on to Jerusalem, "I know the Temple authorities will try to arrest you if you teach there again. But they cannot put anyone to death. The Romans won't let them do that."

Jesus lightly laughed and said, "The Romans? The Romans were not there to stop them from picking up stones on that day when they first wanted to kill me. But I escaped from their hands because it was not my time to die then. And it is not my fate to die by stoning or by being thrown off a cliff either. I left those places because it is my Father's will that my work continue on."

Peter spoke out now, "Master, I am remembering when we were at sea. There was a terrible storm threatening to overcome us and we would have all died. But to the surprise of all of us you were able to calm the wind and the waves with only a word of your voice. You kept us all from death on that frightful night."

James also shared his thoughts, "Death has come near you so many times my Lord. And every time you have survived."

Jesus nodded, "I realize that there is more to it than that, now that I stop to think about it. I have avoided death in more ways than just those. In my ministry, whenever they brought those to me that were near death I was able to heal them and when they were dead I was able to restore their lives. I have been able to avoid death almost altogether; the death of others and even my own. But now, soon, the day is coming when I will no longer avoid death. Not the death of those I love nor my own.

The three listened carefully to every word he spoke and then Peter asked, "Is that why you have no fear of returning to Jerusalem?"

Jesus took his time to thoughtfully consider what his answer to Peter would be, "This time when I set out for Jerusalem I did so despite the reluctance that I have been hiding from all of you. Die, yes, that day is coming and soon. It is the Father's will and he has asked me to die for the sins of the world. And no one can take my life from me, the Father has commanded that. I have this struggle within myself, which is that I need to be willing to lay down my life so that I may take it up again. But I know that you and all my disciples will be tempted to take up the sword and wage war to keep me from my end. And there is already a war raging within my heart and it is carried to every inch of my being by the very blood that I will shed for the forgiveness of sin. Yes, there may come a time when we will take up the sword. But it will not be on that judgment day. I have taught you to pray to the Father, 'thy Kingdom come, thy will be done, on earth as it is in heaven.' Even so, in that coming hour I must pray this again, 'Father, thy will be done, thy will be done in my life on earth as it has always been done in my life in heaven.' The will of his Kingdom in heaven must be lived out in my life in his Kingdom on earth. If I lay down my life it is mine alone to surrender. If I do not lay down my life it is within me to say no and it cannot be taken from me by anyone. This is what is changing in me so that I may lay down my life. But until that time comes, when I will meet my death, I am already living in the dread of it."

Chapter Eleven
Wealth, War and Thy Kingdom Come

All the people of this village had collected themselves together for Rabbi Jesus to teach them. The synagogue was not nearly large enough for everyone, and so they sat on a grassy hillside, which served as a natural amphitheater. Jesus sat upon a chair that was brought out from the synagogue for him to use. He addressed the people, "Whoever comes to me, to be my follower, and does not love me more than their very own family members: father, mother, wife, husband or children, brothers and sisters, and even their own life itself, than they cannot become my disciple. Anyone who does not die to them-self daily, pick up and carry their own cross and follow me cannot be a disciple of mine. So, I am asking you to ask yourselves, each and every one of you, do you understand what it will take to be my disciple?

Think about it this way. If you are intending to build a high tower, what do you do first? First you sit down and estimate what it will cost you, to see whether or not you have enough money to complete it. Otherwise, if you skip that step, after you have laid the foundation and have begun to raise the tower, you realize too late that you will run out of money and cannot finish what you started. If you do it that way, then everyone around will see that you began something monumental but that you cannot finish it and you become a target of their ridicule.

Or, think about it in these terms: What if a king threatened to make war against a neighboring king without first calculating his odds of winning in battle over him? Then, after he has started skirmishes, he stops to ponder for himself whether or not he can, with only ten thousand troops, prevail victorious over a king who has at his command twenty thousand troops? Then he will have realized too late that he cannot possibly win and that he has humiliated himself before all the people. What will he ever do? In disgrace he will have to send a diplomatic mission to ask for terms of peace because the army of the other king has begun its march on his kingdom. So none of you can become my disciple if you do not first commit to dying to yourself and accept the cost of giving up loving all that you possess."

Now included in the mix of villagers who were listening to the Rabbi were two Pharisees, Abbas and Johiah, who stood nearby at the base of the hill, but apart from everyone else. They listened carefully, but their behavior suggested that they were not receptive to the Rabbi's lessons.

Abbas turned to speak quietly into the ear of the other, "This one makes me wonder if he is secretly calling for recruits to fight for his own army, and builders to construct a fortress somewhere for him."

Johiah pondered on that idea for a short time and then nodded, "I had not thought of it in that way, but you're right, it does sound like that doesn't it?"

"So, how in the world can we tell the difference if he is telling stories or calling his followers to action?" Abbas questioned.

"I don't think we can tell the difference if he is only speaking with examples or if he really is disguising his words to call for an army and the building of a fortress. Either way, he is implanting those ideas in the minds of everyone who hears his words" said Johiah.

Jesus continued in his lesson, undeterred by these two who stood out prominently and spoke while everyone else listened. "No slave can serve two masters because he will either hate the one and love the other, or be devoted to the one and despise the other. That is why you cannot serve both God and wealth. The Pharisees try to do both, but it cannot be done. They are the ones who justify themselves in the sight of others; but God knows their hearts all too well. The love of money that is so highly prized among men, that love is sinful and an abomination to God. So, beware of practicing your piety in front of others so that you can be seen by others as you do it. When you do that you have no reward from your Father in heaven. For the Pharisees love to give alms, but they don't do it to help the poor so much as they do it to gain recognition from others. Watch them and see what they do and how they act. They make a great show out of it on the village streets, in the Temple and in your synagogues. But it is all done, not for others, but for themselves because they love to be seen and praised by others for their good deeds. Their reward is not in knowing that the needs of the poor are met nor is it found in heaven. Being praised by others is the reward they want and it is the only reward they will be getting. They accumulate great wealth for themselves so they may live luxuriously even though it is done at the expense of others. Do not be like them because their master is not in heaven. Their master is found in their own purses and in the money it holds. These people think they can serve God and their wealth, but they cannot. No one can. They despise the Gentiles for their carnal ways but they are actually very much like them."

Both Pharisees took offence at Jesus' words, but it was Johiah who could no longer keep quiet about it. With a loud voice he shouted out to the people, "Oh, listen to this Rabbi talk about money. He lives off the support of the women who follow him."

Abbas joined him in like fashion, "What does he know about the cost of maintaining a respectable household? Nothing! He has no house, ha!"

The two took turns reviling Jesus as Johiah spoke next, "He thinks life is such a careless affair that you can just breeze right through it. If we lived like him we would be hungry, homeless and dressed in rags."

And to that Abbas add, "So, teacher what will you live on when you run out of things to say?"

The two took to admiring their own smart remarks and assumed that the crowd had received their words favorably.

But they assumed wrong as was proven by an anonymous and animated responder who called out, "Would the owner of these two stray jackasses collect his animals and lead them away please. Hee-haw, ee-aw." To which the crowd roared out with a short and hardy outburst of laughter. Needless to say, the two Pharisees withdrew some distance away from the gathering, but not so much that they could not hear what Jesus was saying.

Other than stopping his lesson for a short moment, Rabbi Jesus ignored them and then continued with his lesson, "Don't seek after worldly riches. As Solomon has said, 'The lover of wealth is not satisfied with gain.'[5] Instead, strive first for the Kingdom of God and his righteousness, and all that you need in this world will be given to you as well."

Seated in the front of those gathered there spoke yet another Pharisee named Ja'el. It was clear from his words that he differed from the last two, as he sincerely asked, "Rabbi, the Kingdom of God that you speak of, when will it be here and how will we know it when we see it?"

---

[5] Ecclesiastes 5:10

Rabbi Jesus was pleased to hear that question and he nodded pleasantly to the Pharisee before answering, "The Kingdom of God? God's Kingdom is not coming with things that you can simply see with your eyes. Someone might say to you, 'Look, it is here!' or 'Look, it is there!' Don't follow them, just ignore them. The truth is that the Kingdom of God is found within you and among you in your midst. Whenever God's will is done on earth like it is in heaven, there is his Kingdom's reign. So, live and do God's will so that his Kingdom may be found in you. The Law and the Prophets have ruled our faith until John came preaching and baptizing. Since then I have been preaching the good news that the Kingdom of God is at hand."

Jesus stood to his feet and looked at Johiah and Abbas saying, "But now everyone is trying to forcefully make their way into the Kingdom of God."

Then he turned again to the villagers as he pointed by nodding with the back of his head in the direction of those two Pharisees to indicate who he was talking about, "Some here are by their own efforts trying to push and shove their way in, even though they will never enter its gates by their own piety and their own righteousness. Those who will enter the Kingdom enter by God's righteousness alone and are living in vigilant repentance from sin, and sincere faithfulness to God. These are the ones who will enter heaven before the rest. Know this, all of you, that many will come and talk to me as if they are my friends saying, "My Lord, my Lord, remember all the things that we did in your name, preaching and doing signs?" But I will have to say to them, "Who are you calling me your Lord in this way as if we have been close friends? I cannot admit you into the Kingdom of God because I do not know who you are."

Rabbi Jesus had completed his public teaching for the day and, as was his practice, he stood to bless the people before he dismissed them. Then his disciples gathered with him as they withdrew to a more secluded setting so that he could teach them privately. "Soon the days will be here when you will long to see me again because I will be gone from among you. But know this, that just as the lightning flashes and the sky is lit up, so will I be when the day of my return comes again. But before that happens I must faithfully endure under great suffering and be rejected by all of our rulers.

After those days it will be like it was in the days when righteous Noah lived. Everyone was living without a care in the world; they were eating and drinking, and getting engaged and marrying. They lived out their daily lives as usual and ignored the prophet's call to repentance from sin by turning to God in a life of faith. They did not believe the prophet when he foretold to them that the flood would come to cleanse the earth of their evil and sinful ways, and still they refuse to turn so that they could be saved. Then, without another warning, the rain suddenly fell from the sky; the flood waters rose from within the earth and it was too late for them, because Noah and his family had already shut the door to the great ark. It will be like that again when the day of my return comes.

Remember Lot? Remember his wife? When Lot walked the earth, people lived out their lives as they wanted to, regardless of God's design. They ate and they drank, they went to the market, they built homes and planted their fields. But their hearts were far from God and their sinful lives were continually filled with only evil. Then came the day when Lot left the city of Sodom because the day of their judgment had come. Their lives were taken from them when heaven spewed down fire and sulfur because they refused to repent of their sins. Just like in those days, I will return from heaven and all the earth will see me. So, don't live like those who try to make their life secure by this world's riches, doing it independently from God's will. They are the ones who will lose all that they have in this world and then have nothing stored up for themselves in the next. But those who give up such pursuits and follow God's will over their own will are the ones who will keep their life in this world and receive eternal life in heaven in the world to come."

Chapter Twelve
To Sit on the Right and on the Left

Jericho was the perfect place for Rabbi Jesus to visit as he made his way to Jerusalem. He and his disciples needed to take a few days to rest and regather their strength after much serving and traveling. Jericho was surrounded by wastelands and desolation but the ancient city itself had an exquisite freshwater spring called Elisha's Fountain. Its waters were used to irrigate and make fertile its surrounding plains. It truly was an oasis in the middle of the dry and weary land that it was surrounded by. Jericho was a beautiful place that was also popularly known as the City of Palms and many wealthy people had made it their winter residence and lived in fine country homes nearby.

Rabbi Jesus and his disciples were guests at a private country villa owned by one of his patrons and they were very much enjoying an afternoon to themselves. The sun's warmth and the peace along with the quiet of county life so removed from the hustle and bustle of a large city soothed their weary souls.

Now as Jesus reclined in the sun and enjoyed the picturesque view of the countryside's landscape, Salome, the mother of James and John, came to him with her sons following behind her. She knelt to her knees and bowed low to the ground as a gesture of humility before the Lord. Her sons followed her example, each one kneeling and bowing low to the ground, with James to the right of her and John to the left, both just slightly behind her. Salome spoke directly to Rabbi Jesus addressing him with the greatest respect, "My Lord...," she thoughtfully paused before going on, "...as a mother I am asking you to do this for me." She paused again as before and then continued on,

"I wish you would do something for me, and for my sons." She paused again to glance and smile first to her right towards James and then to her left at John before continuing. Then she looked back at Rabbi Jesus, made a beautiful smile and with some excitement in her voice said, "Something special." Her many pauses suggested to the Rabbi that she was indicating that if he merely understood her and what she was saying so emphatically, he would be sure to grant her request.

Now, of the other ten disciples who were scattered about the area, Peter was the closest. He took notice of Salome and her sons approaching Jesus. He assumed at first that it was a private matter and paid them little attention. But he could not avoid overhearing some of what was said, for as close as he was to them.

Jesus attended respectfully to Salome's conversation with him as he asked her, "What is it you want me to do for you and for your sons?"

She no longer paused as she spoke, "When you arrive in Jerusalem to be our King…" her heart swelled up with a joyous pride as she tried to speak persuasively, "…appoint one of my sons to sit on your right side and the other one to sit on your left side so that they may help you rule in your Kingdom."

Peter's ear's picked up on the conversation, not because he intended to eavesdrop, but because he heard the words 'Jerusalem' and 'King'. Now he not only listened, but he caught Judas' attention who was nearby and called him over so that he too could listen.

Jesus spoke with a gentle voice of caring as he explained, "You do not know what you are asking me to do for your sons."

But Salome softly protested, "Yes my Lord, I do know. I want to see them seated at your right and left hand sides where they can rule the people with you in righteousness."

Jesus now spoke to Salome's sons directly, "James and John, are you able to drink the cup that I drink, or be baptized with the baptism that I am baptized with?"

They were both thrilled to be asked that question. It made them feel very hopeful and they took it as a sign that their mother's request would be granted. "We are able!" they both quickly said in unison.

Jesus nodded and spoke again to them, "The cup that I will drink you will drink; and the baptism which I will receive you will be baptized with."

Salome smiled with gladness as did James and John. Yet Jesus remained very somber because he understood what they did not. The baptism he referred to was a fiery trial of persecution and the cup was one of death.

The Rabbi spoke on, "But who will sit at my right or at my left side is not my decision to make. It is solely the decision of my Father in heaven. His and his alone."

Salome and her sons now felt a great letdown as they realized that they had asked Jesus something that he could not grant them. Their dreams of rising to these two exalted positions of greatness were now dashed to the ground and their hearts became heavy within them.

But this situation was not over, because there had already grown a strong resentment among the other disciples as word of their private attempt to persuade Jesus to grant to them such great positions spread to the other ten disciples.

Peter had called them to his side with an urgent waving of his arms and then Judas spoke to them. "You all need to know that James and John have their mother trying to persuade Jesus to name them the two chief disciples and to let them rule at his left and right hand side." Peter then said, "We need to confront them right now before it is too late and not just idly let this plan of theirs to go on." While Peter was still speaking he began walking over to Jesus as the rest followed and listened.

He ignored Rabbi Jesus as he interjected himself into the situation, speaking very assertively to James and John, "So you two think you can goat-butt your way into the two greatest positions of leadership beside our Lord without us knowing about it?"

Judas quickly jumped in and with a shaming and accusatory tone spoke down to them, "Who do you two think you are anyway? How long have you been secretly planning to do this? What exactly have you been scheming to do here? You two went behind our backs and tried to have your way by asking for positions that I don't think either of you are qualified for."

Then Peter spoke again, "I know what kind of rulers you would be too. Anything you don't like, anyone you don't care for would be consumed in fire from heaven by your orders."

Now the other disciples took turns raking them over the hot coals of their fuming anger. Andrew was next, "You should not have stooped to involve your mother in this. If you aren't able to make this request on your own, then clearly you aren't qualified to do the job in the first place."

Then it was Matthew who spoke out, "Yes and there are better qualified leaders among us for those positions than both of you. You two cannot simply work in secret to cut us out and then expect that there won't be a backlash upon you. We all have a say in who rules and who serves. So before you do something that foolish again, don't do it all!"

Jesus saw that there would be no end to this bickering and backbiting so he took the conversation back under his control, "Stop this! All of you! How presumptuous of every one of you to think of leadership positions in this way! You all know how the Gentiles live don't you? You are sounding more and more like them all time. Their rulers callously issue orders to their people for their own selfish benefit. They don't even given a second thought to how they treat the people they govern over and abuse to no ends. They are merciless and arrogant tyrants to their own people and the greater their power and position the worse they get. In my Kingdom, among those who serve with me, and for my disciples that I have trained, there is a different rule of law that we will live by; the rule of God's loving-kindness and mercy. I don't want you to act like ignorant Gentile rulers. If you want to become great, if you want to be a leader, then you must become a humble servant to everyone, and I do mean every last person, even to Samaritans and Gentiles. And if you want to be thought of as a ruler, then you have to become as a lowly slave to them all. Look to me and the example I bring to you. I didn't come here so that I could act like a Gentile ruler and be waited on hand and foot by others. I came here to serve you and to give my life as a ransom for the sins of the world."

The disciples stood there, some with open mouths wanting to say something but not knowing what, and others just dropped their heads in silence as Jesus turned away from them and walked away.

Chapter Thirteen
Deathly Sick

This day had been a particularly hot one, so much so that Lazarus quit work early and returned home. He was greeted by his sisters, but he merely gave them a nod and then rested quietly in the shade of the inner courtyard of his home, where he hoped a breeze might come and ease his discomfort. When the evening meal was served, his sister, Martha, called him to come to the table. But when he attempted to rise to his feet he found that his legs were considerably weak and his head light. He made his way inside moving slowly and cautiously on heavy limbs. Once inside, he breathed a sigh of relief, hoping a meal would refresh him. His face was very reddened and dry, but because of the low lighting that the lamps offered, neither of his sisters noticed this.

At the table Lazarus offered a blessing to the LORD for their meal. Then he took a bite of his bread, only to find that once he had swallowed it his stomach began to cramp down hard. "Oh-h-h, ahhh!" he groaned.

Mary, his younger sister, quickly asked him, "What is it Lazarus?"

Lazarus grimaced and grabbed at his stomach, bending forward in pain. "My stomach. I have sharp pains." Again he groaned, "It started this afternoon but it wasn't that bad, but now it is nearly intolerable. I have to go to bed, I can't stand this." He attempted to rise from his couch and was overcome with still worse pain. He became very lightheaded and was near to fainting as he collapsed back onto the couch. His sisters could see that he was dizzy as his head wobbled in a circular motion.

Martha instantly cried out, "Adonias come quickly!

Lazarus, you need help." She looked at her sister Mary and said, "Let's get him to his bed."

Try as they did, the two ladies were powerless to move their brother who was much larger than either of them. Adonias, one of their servants, was nearby and rushed into the dining room when Martha called him.

Mary said to him, "Lazarus is ill. Help us get him to his bed."

The servant took Lazarus' arm and put it over his shoulder, then took hold around Lazarus' waist. He lifted him to standing and helped him walk to his bed.

Martha carried an oil lamp into the room directly behind the two and stood at the foot of his bed as she looked at her brother in his distress. Mary followed her into the room and once Adonias had stepped away she knelt at the side of his bed and held her brother's hand hoping to comfort him.

Martha spoke to him, "Lazarus, I am going to send for the physician."

He broke from his silence and said, "Yes, thank you, send for him now."

Martha turned to their servant and instructed him, "Adonias go to the home of Benjamin the physician and ask him to come right away."

Mary cried out, "At this time of night? The sun set an hour ago! Where is Jesus? Shouldn't we ask him to come?"

But Martha, finding a certain calm within herself, told her sister, "Jesus has gone to Bethabara on the other side of the Jordan."

Mary's distress increased, "But that is more than two days from here. What will we do?"

Martha answered her, albeit indirectly saying, "Go quickly now Adonias." He nodded his head and hurried to put on his coat. Then he lit a lantern and went out the door and into the darkness of night.

Half of an hour passed before he returned with the physician. Adonias directed him into Lazarus' room. Benjamin carried a case with medicines and other items for his profession. He was a very tall man, tall among the tall, but he had a gentle presence and stood in silence for a moment before speaking, "Good evening, Martha." He paused to look at his patient and then asked, "What pains have overtaken your brother tonight that are so urgent?" Benjamin took off his head wrap and underneath it was a smaller skull cap, a sign of his devotion to the LORD.

Martha felt bad about having to call for him after dark, "Forgive us for calling on you at this late hour. My brother was overcome at dinner and now he has grown worse."

Benjamin nodded as he agreed, "Yes" and then he looked at Lazarus before sitting on the side of his bed. In his exam he first touched Lazarus' forehead and commented, "Warm, very warm to my touch." He motioned to have a lamp brought in closer and then he opened wide his patient's eyes and said, "Dull, dry, flat." Then he touched his ears, "Hot." He asked Lazarus to open his mouth and asked Mary to bring the lamp closer and hold it up so that it would shed more light on her brother. Benjamin looked inside and said, "Dry. Exhale for me." Then he sniffed at his breath, "The smell of fruit." There was a pause and then he asked Lazarus, "What did you do today?"

Lazarus was in distress as he weakly answered with a gravelly voice, "I worked in the fields and tended to the livestock."

The physician asked him to open his night shirt and then put his ear to his chest and listened, "The air moves and there is no crackling." He listened again for a while and then said, "Your heart is racing fast but is otherwise fine. Was the work hard today?"

Lazarus answered, "We got an early start and pushed hard."

Benjamin thoughtfully listened and then spoke to him, "Perhaps you overworked what the day was allowing you. It was very hot and its heat has taken its toll on you." Benjamin cautiously pushed down on his abdomen.

Lazarus reacted in pain and cried out, "Ahhh!"

The physician nodded knowingly, as if he expected this reaction.

As he released his hand's Lazarus again cried out even louder, "Ahhh!!"

Benjamin noted out loud his findings, "Hard to the touch and painful when pushed down, and when released."

Lazarus offered, "This afternoon I had a hard knot that began here in my upper stomach as a dull ache. But then when I got home it moved to the middle of my stomach. I don't think it is moving anymore. It is as if I ate rocks."

The physician asked, "Did you drink enough water?"

Lazarus told him, "When we were out in the fields one of our water skins burst and we ran out before the noon hour. When I got home I tried to drink some but it hurt worse when I did."

Benjamin turned to Martha, "Could you have a large pitcher of cool water, a drinking cup and some towels brought in please?"

Martha was so used to delegating that she simply looked to her sister and Mary rose to do what the physician had asked.

Then Benjamin asked his patient, "Did you eat much for supper tonight?"

"No" he said, "Just a bite. I just didn't feel hungry and it made me feel worse."

Benjamin had completed his examination and now explained his findings, "You gave too much of yourself to working today, and the heat of the day also took its portion from you. Your skin, eyes and mouth are dried out and inside you are parched from the heat of the day, and from overworking. I fear there is a slowing, perhaps even a stoppage of your organs because your strength was used up to the point of exhaustion. The food from your lunch has hardened, that's why you feel like you ate rocks. The heat of the day robbed the water right out of your body. Things are not moving along easily and so your organs are trying harder than ever to move the food through."

Mary returned from her errand with the water and towels and the physician spoke directly to Martha, "Here is what must be done. Keep him as cool as you can, open the window fully and let the night air in. Someone must wave a fan to keep cool air passing over him so that it will carry the heat away. This must be done until his forehead is no longer hot." He motioned to Adonias and then pointed to the fan. The servant lifted the large stiffly woven fan made from palm leaves and began to wave it slowly to get the air moving. "You must also cool him by getting him wet with cool water so that as it evaporates it will carry the heat away. He must drink as much water as he can. Even if it hurts, I don't care, he must drink it. No wine or anything else, just water all through night, in small sips and often. He must not eat anything tonight and nothing in the morning until this condition passes from him." Benjamin poured water on one of the towels to make it dripping wet and then whipped it gently over Lazarus' face, arms and chest to demonstrate what he wanted done for his patient.

Now he reached into his case and rummaged around until he found a small jar. He asked, "Martha, would you pour some water into that cup?"

She did as the physician asked and then handed it to him. He opened his jar of medicine and held it over the cup as he tapped at it gently to get some of the compound to fall into it. "Here Lazarus, let me help you up so you can drink this medicine. I know that your stomach is hurting, but you must pass it through and this will help you to do that."

With the help of the physician Lazarus leaned up on one elbow and gulped the medicine down as fast as he could. Then he fell back onto his bed and breathed a sigh of relief.

Benjamin turned to the sisters to ensure that he had their attention as he gave them the rest of his orders, "Lazarus, you must get up during the night and walk around a little every half hour and then again into the day. Have your servant Adonias help you in your weakness. That will help you move this along. I am afraid that the pains, even though they are sharp, will continue through the night. There is nothing I can do to ease that. And do not wear a belt or any binding clothing. I will return tomorrow in the afternoon to care for you again. Until then, drink as much water as you can, at least that entire pitcher before the daybreak if not more, and that much more again in the morning, before noon. Otherwise you must do nothing but rest until my return." He paused to think if there was anything else he could do or if there were any other instructions he could give, but there were none that he would say for now. He looked at his patient and said, "I will pray for you now Lazarus."

"We will call upon the LORD, who is worthy to be praised,

so shall you be saved from your distress.
In this infirmity we call upon the LORD;
to our God we will cry for help and
from his Holy Temple he will hear our voices.
Our cry to him will reach his ears
and may he save you from this illness. Amen"[6]

Then Mary, Martha, Adonias and Lazarus together said, "Amen"

Lazarus offered a grateful word to the physician, "Thank you for coming to help me at this late hour."

Benjamin nodded in his direction, and then Mary and Martha in unison added, "Yes, thank you for coming."

As they made their way to the door Martha spoke, "Adonias will see you safely to your home."

As they reached the door Benjamin turned back to look at the older sister and spoke with a concerned voice, "Martha, I have done what I can. But my cures may not be enough to..." he paused momentarily to share what he knew would be distressing for the sisters to hear, "...to bring him through this. It would be best if you sent for Rabbi Jesus. He loves your brother and I am sure he can do everything that is needed for him."

With that word Mary was sent reeling into a panic, "But he is more than two days away from here."

Martha knew her sister well; that she overreacts dramatically, and often at that.

Martha spoke calmly, hoping to soothe Mary, "At first light we'll send a runner who can bring him the message to come." Now she reached into her purse and pulled out a coin, "You must have this for your own needs."

The doctor received the coin and said, "Thank you for

---

[6] Based on Psalm 18

your kindness." Now, together with Adonias with oil lanterns in hand, they made their way out into the darkness of night.

Time seemed to stand still for the sisters during the passing of the long night. They remained awake and at their brother's side the whole time. Along with the help of their few servants they carried out the physician's orders, fanning Lazarus constantly, helping him drink the water and using wet towels to cool him.

Martha looked at her sister and now disclosed her fearful emotions, "Mary … we need to pray for our dear brother."

Mary silently nodded as tears appeared in her eyes.

Martha prayed, "God of heaven and earth, bring strength to our brother and restore him to health again." Then she began reciting a Psalm,

'"He that dwelleth in the secret place of the most High…'"

Mary joined her and together the two prayed,

"shall abide under the shadow of the Almighty.
I will say of the LORD,
He is my refuge and my fortress: my God;
in him will I trust.
Surely he shall deliver thee
from the snare of the fowler,
and from the terrible pestilence.
He shall cover thee with his feathers,
and under his wings shall thou trust:
his truth shall be thy shield and buckler.
Thou shall not be afraid of the terror by night;
nor of the arrow that flies by day;

Nor of the pestilence that walks in darkness;
nor of the destruction that wastes at noonday.
A thousand shall fall at thy side,
and ten thousand at thy right hand;
but it shall not come nigh thee.
By the mere glance of your eyes
the wicked are punished.
Because thou hast made the LORD,
which is my refuge, even the most High, thy habitation;
there shall no evil befall thee,
neither shall any plague come near to thy dwelling.
For he shall give his angels charge over thee,
to keep thee in all thy ways.
They shall bear thee up in their hands,
lest thou dash thy foot against a stone.
Thou shall tread upon the lion and adder:
the young lion and the serpent shall
thou trample under your foot.
Because he hath set his love upon me,
therefore will I deliver him: I will set him on high,
because he hath known my Name.
He shall call upon me, and I will answer him:
I will be with him in trouble; I will deliver him,
and honor him and with long life will I satisfy him,
and show him my salvation.' Amen" [7]

Lazarus was restless, but now as he heard the Psalm he, too was moved to prayer, "Oh, dear LORD! I am greatly troubled. Save me from this sickness and deliver me from its pain. Rabbi Jesus where are you? Why haven't you come?"

---

[7] Psalm 91

Chapter Fourteen
Mourning in Bethany

Jesus had long ago grown tired of the opposition he experienced from the religious authorities throughout the land. This was especially true about those in Jerusalem from when he was last there. It was in the Holy City that their power was the strongest and their resistance to him the greatest. So as he left Jericho he turned east where he found respite in a place near where John had been baptizing in the Jordan River. It was the village of Bethabara which was also known as "Bethany Beyond the Jordan."

Now it was at midday when there came a runner seeking Rabbi Jesus and carrying an urgent message for him. Upon reaching the city he did not stop to drink at the well or even to hear directions that he asked for. He listened to them as he ran. He came to the home where Jesus was lodging and, out of breath and parched, he was near to collapsing as he spoke, "Rabbi, forgive me, its urgent."

Jesus gave him his undivided attention, "You must be exhausted." He stood up to give him his chair, "Here, sit down; catch your breath and rest." The Rabbi looked to the servants of his host and said, "Please get some water so he may drink, and bring him something to eat too."

The runner shook his head 'no' and pleaded, "It's urgent, Mary and Martha sent me to bring you back to Bethany." A cup of water was offered to him and he drank it down quickly before he said anything else. "They said, 'Come quickly, now, Rabbi Jesus. You are desperately needed. Lazarus has fallen ill with a high fever. The physician came to help him, but even he said you were needed. Come and lay your hands on him before it is too late.' They are begging you to come."

Jesus listened with a heighten sense of concern and he began to worry because his friend was very ill, and his family was calling for him to come immediately. He inquired, "When did you leave from Bethany?"

The runner responded, "Only a day and a half ago. I have run most of the way, from first light until it was too dark to see the road."

He now intensified his plea, "Rabbi, you must leave now, they fear he will die without you. Come with me now, I will take you there."

Jesus poured him another cup of water and he gulped it down.

And the servant returned with a plate of bread saying, "This is freshly made and it is still warm. Eat it now before you pass out."

With the bread nearly in his mouth he said, "Thank you for your kindness."

The shock of this news had set in and Jesus thoughtfully bowed his head low and closed his eyes to pray and call on the LORD. Several minutes passed and then he opened his eyes and looked to the runner, "You want to take me there but you mustn't be going anywhere today. You need to eat and rest from your long journey. You will come with us when we leave, but that won't be today."

The messenger's commission from the sisters was still very compelling to him, "But Rabbi, Lazarus cannot wait, he is nearing death!"

Jesus sought to relieve his sense of urgency because his commission was to bring the message, not to compel the Rabbi against his will.

Jesus spoke with all calm, "Though it distresses me greatly to hear that my friend is so ill, I cannot rush to be with him. The Father has spoken to me and this illness will not lead to his death. I have seen that God has a purpose in it so that I may be glorified in it. By this many will come to believe in me when they see what the son can do. We will stay here for now and you will recover your strength before we will travel to Bethany."

The day finished out but not without the great concern over Lazarus preoccupying Jesus' thoughts. Sleep came easy to the Rabbi and he slipped away into his slumber. Now it was an ancient world belief that at the sun's setting the blue veil covering heaven was lifted away revealing the glory of the LORD. Therefore it was in those hours that the mysteries of God were best pondered. It was in those hours when these two places, heaven and the earth, were closest. As Jesus lay sleeping in those late night hours, the moonlight shone down on him through an open window. It was then that there appeared to him in a vision, a man wrapped in a white shroud, laying in his tomb. It was dark there and the blue-black vision of the tomb brightened a little to reveal that it was the body of his friend Lazarus. Jesus grew restless in his slumber and began to mournfully weep in near silence. He felt as if he was suffocating, unable to awaken himself to relieve his hunger for more air. Then came another vision; it was of Mary and Martha quietly weeping and sobbing at the opening to their brother's tomb. Jesus grew increasingly restless in his sleep and fought against his slumber to awaken himself, but he could not wake up. Now he wept aloud as he found himself still helpless, slumbering and struggling with the heavy weight of what was shown to him. Still now another vision came to him; it was of Lazarus laying in his tomb again, but then there appeared, superimposed over the corpse, the shadow of a Roman execution cross. He could see the outer edges of it, then slowly the rest was revealed. It was a vision of himself, beaten badly, a deep wound over his heart, his head lifelessly hanging down. And there were two people standing nearby; just like he had seen Mary and Martha weeping. But this was not the two sisters, it was faithful John, his disciple, holding his mother Mary as she wept with such sorrow that he could not bear it any longer. Jesus summoned his resources and forced himself to awaken. Suddenly he sat up in bed gasping for air as though he had been suffocating. He was overwhelmed by what he saw and he looked heavenward, only to be overcome with the feeling that he was not alone. Slowly he lowered his head and turned to look to the side of his bed. There before him was Lazarus, sitting on the edge of his bed right next to him. Jesus was astonished and fearful. He had not gone, intentionally not gone, to heal his friend, who died. Now his friend was sitting with him at his bedside. Jesus worried what Lazarus would now say, something like, 'Why didn't you come and heal me?'

But as Jesus looked at him, Lazarus reached out his hand and took hold of Jesus' hand in a firm grip. He looked Jesus in the eyes and with but one tear rolling down his face, he prayed to his Lord, "Jesus, come to Bethany and wake me from my slumber."

Jesus found himself still unable to speak, but as he nodded knowingly, his friend vanished into the dark of night. His eyes now showed his alarm and his bewilderment. His thoughts returned to the vision he just suffered. He threw off his covers, swung his feet over the side of the bed to touch the floor and prepared to get up. What he experienced was unsettling. He tested the strength of his legs before standing to insure it was not taken from him. He rose without falling, and then wrapped himself in a bed blanket as he went outside to sit and wait until first light. This night could not have passed fast enough for him, but he found the patience to wait and pray to his Father, asking why had his friend died when the answer to his earlier prayer was that this would not lead to Lazarus' death.

When first he noticed the lightening of the night sky, he went inside and anxiously spoke to his disciples, "Awake! Everyone, awake! We are leaving for Bethany this hour."

Peter sat up on his bed and cautioned his Rabbi, "If you go there the Temple leaders in Jerusalem will learn of it and then they will try to kill you again! And you say you are going near there again? The last time you were there they picked up stones to crush you with. If they see you, they will take your life, Jesus."

James, too, cautioned his Rabbi, "Why ever do you want to go there? Is it to die? They will be ready for you, and this time there may be no escaping from their hands."

Jesus spoke to them, "I am going to Bethany because my friend Lazarus has fallen asleep and I must go there to wake him."

But the disciples did not understand his meaning. Peter reasserted himself, "You will be found out and they will arrest you. They will bring charges against you! How can we keep you safe from them when you always go about so openly among them? Will you go in secret this time?"

Jesus nervously paced about between their beds and was unrelenting as he urged them to get moving, "Your time is anytime. My time is not here yet. The Father has shown me his will and what is going to happen. I know his plans and I will walk in his ways. Therefore, we have the light of day which will keep us from haphazardly stumbling. Those who don't know the Father's will have no guiding light to walk by. They will inevitably stumble and fall, just as though they were walking in the darkness of night."

This was one of the rare times when Jesus showed a sign of personal distress to his disciples. But it was not over the danger he might face by going so close to the Holy City. The disciples could not understand how he could at the same time be distressed, but not care about the threats on his life and still be so insistent about going closer to that danger.

Jesus, still pacing about with anxious worries in his every step, re-spoke his incessant reason, "We are leaving for Bethany. Jerusalem has to wait. My friend Lazarus has fallen asleep and I must go there to wake him!"

But to the disciples it just didn't make any sense. The disciples knew Lazarus had been very ill but they also knew that his illness had not alarmed Jesus when first he learned of it, so they concluded that it was nothing too serious.

James spoke to his Rabbi hoping to clear the confusion he had, "Lord, if he's fallen asleep, that's a good thing right? He needs his rest to get well again. What if we wait to see him later when he is fully recovered and has regained his strength?"

Jesus stopped and firmly planted his feet. He stared at each of his disciples to gain their full attention. Then he spoke with all insistence, "No! You don't understand me! Listen to me, all of you, and understand what I have been trying to tell you!"

Jesus tried to summon the words that he needed to say so he would be fully understood. But he was choked up by the difficulty of those words. He nearly wept as he spoke, his mouth and face quivering as he told them this bad news: "Lazarus has died from his illness." That having been said, he found new strength and the words he must say to his disciples. "For your sakes I am glad I was not there, so that you may believe in me. That is why we are leaving now. So that I can wake him from his sleep."

The disciples received the news in silence as waves of grief now spread over them. Lazarus and his sisters had done so much, more than any, to support Jesus and them in their ministry. They were all deeply indebted to them for the countless number of kindnesses they had shown in caring for their needs, both personal and for the ministry of the Gospel.

The disciples were in silence and frozen for a time, not knowing how to keep Jesus safe from capture and punishment, but knowing that they unconditionally must go to Mary and Martha in their mourning. They knew the sisters' grief would be too much for them to carry alone, and though death might await their Master, they knew they must leave in that very hour to be with them.

A tearful Thomas broke the silence that had come upon them, and solidifying the certainty of what they would now do, when he said to the rest, "Let's go with him so that we can die with him." And so they all rose in tearfulness to pack and prepare for the journey.

Chapter Fifteen
The Return

The village of Bethany was a somber place to be in the days immediately following the death of Lazarus. Mary and Martha had put their every hope in Jesus, fully believing that he would have come in time to save their brother's life when they sent word to him. But it was clear that when he did not arrive on the day expected of him that something was wrong. The sisters had worried themselves to exhaustion over their brother's worsening illness. When his death came they were close to collapsing. And added to that was their worry that something dreadful must have happened to the Rabbi. What else could explain his failure to come? It was not possible for them to entertain the notion that he had intentionally delayed coming when the life of their brother was in such dire need.

On that day, when their brother was taken from them in death, they both tore open their outer robes over their hearts as was the tradition. They sent word by their servant to the synagogue leader and their local Rabbi that their brother had died. The sisters then washed the body and made final finishing touches to his fine linen burial shroud, which was embroidered with gold and silver treads. They sprinkled a mixture of aromatic spices that they had prepared onto his lifeless body, and more of it in the shroud as they dressed him in it. It was sewn and tapered around him to fit like a contoured sleeping gown. His head was wrapped in a sheer linen covering with a cloth wrapped under his jaw and over the top of his head to keep his mouth closed.

In life, Lazarus had been a leading citizen of their village, and in his death everyone in Bethany mourned. But there were none that called on his sisters to offer consolation on those first three days. That, too, was one of their customs; that guests would wait to call. On the day following his death, in the morning, at about an hour past sunrise there came the pall bearers and a large number of mourners to the house. They were led by the Rabbi from their synagogue and joining with him were other men of stature from their local community. The sisters met them at the entrance to their home. There were no words exchanged between any of them only a slight nod by the Rabbi as he was silently welcomed inside, he and the pall bearers alone. The men surrounded the body and then in unison reached to lift the bed that he was laid upon. In one motion they lifted Lazarus up and then the Rabbi took his place in front of their processional. The body was next followed by Mary and Martha and the members of their household. As they walked out from the courtyard, those who had gathered to join in lined up behind them, as everyone made their way to the tomb where his body would be laid to rest. It was not acceptable that the men should cry aloud, but many of them did silently shed tears of mourning along the way. The women wept. It was expected that they should wail and mourn aloud. There was much wailing that day because the one who had died meant so much to so many who now somehow had to learn how to live without him in their lives.

The men carried his body into the tomb and gently placed it on a raised bed of stone. All of the pall bearers shed tears that freely poured out from their eyes, but not a one of them made a sound. Martha went in first, followed by her sister Mary. They held each other's hands and then hugged each other. Their weeping was loud as they made their final loving good-byes to their dearly loved brother. As they exited the tomb the large number of people who had gathered were anxiously waiting for them to come out, most in tears, everyone distraught with heartache. The Rabbi faced the people as he read a Psalm of David;

"The LORD is my shepherd; I shall not want.
He maketh me to lie down in green pastures:
He leadeth me beside the still waters.
He restoreth my soul.
He leadeth me in the paths of
righteousness for his name's sake.
Yea, though I walk through
the valley of the shadow of death,
I will fear no evil: for thou art with me;
thy rod and thy staff they comfort me.
Thou preparest a table before me
in the presence of mine enemies.
Thou anointest my head with oil;
my cup runneth over.
Surely goodness and mercy shall
follow me all the days of my life,
And I will dwell in the house
of the LORD forever. Amen" [8]

Then the Rabbi turned to face the tomb and silently gestured to the pall bearers that they should roll the stone over the entrance and seal the tomb shut. Once that was complete, he offered the Blessing of Aaron up for the dead man;

"And the LORD spoke unto Moses, saying,
'Speak unto Aaron and unto his sons, saying,
<u>*In this way you*</u> *shall bless the*

---

[8] Psalm 23

children of Israel and say unto them,
The LORD bless thee, and keep thee.
The LORD make his face shine upon thee,
and be gracious unto thee.
The LORD lift up his countenance upon thee,
and give thee peace.
And thus shall the Name of the LORD
be put upon the children of Israel
whereby I will bless them for evermore.'"[9]

Mary and Martha took several minutes for themselves, then they looked at each other and turned to face the Rabbi. Again he offered them a slight nod of his head, then he turned to lead the sisters back to their home. Their customs required that they stay in their home for the remainder of the day and also the following day too. The only exception to this was that they were expected to go to the synagogue in the evening for silent worship for at least seven days running. They were also to devote themselves to prayer at the seven appointed times for their three days of isolation. They were not allowed to work for an entire week, but that was not going to be a problem for them. So great was their grief, they truly needed this time to themselves without any distractions or demands made upon them. Many of the villagers came to their home during these first three days, not to call on the sisters, but to leave gifts of cooked lamb, warm bread and fresh produce for them to eat. In the evening hour of prayer Mary and Martha went to the synagogue. They wore their head covering high upon their faces and kept only to themselves as they were not to greet anyone along the way, nor was anyone to greet them either.

---

[9] Number 6:22-27

Four difficult days had passed since his death. A few guests had come to call after the three days passed. They did not stay long. The sisters suffered with melancholy and did not say much to anyone. They each silently harbored to themselves thoughts that they could hardly admit to, that Rabbi Jesus was to blame for their brother's death. No, not that he had caused the illness that took their brother's life. Yet he certainly could have tried to return and bring him healing which would have prevented his terrible loss in death that they now lived with. They each suffered times during the day when they broke down in uncontrollable weeping, living with thoughts of what might have been if Rabbi Jesus had only been there in the beginning, or if he had come back to them in time to prevent his death. But this did not bring them comfort. It brought them greater distress. They believed that even if the Lord did return to them, there was nothing he could do now that would help.

It was on that day, six days after they sent word for the Rabbi to come to them, that Jesus did return to the village. At the entrance was gathered some of the elders and other folk who would meet there daily to talk about their community's day to day activities. From a distance they could see Jesus coming to them. He and his twelve disciples formed a distinct silhouette on the road's horizon. Several of those gathered got up and carried word of his soon arrival to the home of the man who died.

Those who stayed greeted Jesus upon his arrival, "Rabbi Jesus, welcome." said one of the elders. "We had been hoping you would have come days ago. We sent a runner for you. But what is there to be done now? Lazarus …" he paused to regain himself, "… you need to know that poor Lazarus died four day ago."

The Rabbi nodded knowingly, but did not say anything about how Lazarus had visited him in the night of his death. Together, those who had gathered at the village gate and Jesus with his disciples walked to Lazarus' home to call on the sisters.

A village elder spoke to Jesus and expressed his sense of hopelessness, "We are all very grateful that you have finally come, but even now, what is there to be done?"

Jesus did not share in their grief at that time. Instead he was anxious to be with Mary and Martha again and to go to the tomb of his friend with them. He replied, "Why are you saying to me, 'What is there to be done?'"

But the elder did not understand what Jesus meant and he did not dwell on it either.

One of the villagers spoke, "We sent word to the sisters, that you are here. I am sure they will find some comfort in your presence even now."

Many more villagers joined them as they walked to the home. Though the two sisters were past their required time of confinement, they had not yet ventured out of their home, other than to worship at the synagogue in the evenings or to go to their brother's tomb to pray and be near him.

Now a guest arrived at their home with the news, "Martha, Rabbi Jesus has just arrived at the entrance of our village."

Martha stood with a start and exclaimed, "I must go and meet him." She grabbed a shawl to cover her head and ran out the door to meet him. As she was running, when she saw Rabbi Jesus ahead of her, her tears of sorrow returned as they had been on that day when her brother had died. She stumbled and fell at Jesus' feet, grasping them with her hands and crying out to him, "Jesus, my Lord, why didn't you come to us? Then you could have saved my brother from death." She wept uncontrollably and then paused to consider what she had just allowed her heart to share. She worried that by her words she may have offended the Rabbi in her directness. She withheld her tears for now and spoke again, "But...but..." She paused, not knowing what she could say to reduce her fear of bringing offense to the Rabbi. As she spoke, she did not yet know how her sentence would end. She went on, "But I know..." she knew she needed to say something but what ever could it be? She paused and restarted, "But I know that..." She stared at his feet intensely, "that ... even now God will give you whatever you ask of him."

Jesus bent down and reached out his hand to lay it on her head, then he touched her chin to move it up so that he could see her face. He took her by the hand and helped her stand. "Yes, you are right. Even still, believe in me and I tell you that your brother will rise from the dead."

Martha found the words and strength to face her Lord, "I can only keep on living by believing in the hope that he will rise again in the resurrection at the end of all the ages."

Jesus looked deeply into her eyes before saying, "I'm here for you now, and for Mary and for your brother Lazarus. I am the resurrection and the life. Everyone who believes in me, even though they have died, they will live again because of me, and everyone who lives and believes in me will never die. Do you believe this? Do you believe this about me? That I have come this day to waken your brother from the dead?"

To Martha, the words he shared were not believable; that her brother would live again that very day. In her world the people believed that in death the soul would remain for up to three days and linger near the body before journeying up to heaven. It was during those days that, if by a miracle from God, a soul might resume its earthly life by taking up its mortal body again. But now that the fourth day of death had come, that hope, however faint it might have been, was now fully passed.

The older sister replied to Jesus, but her voice suggested that she was not as believing as her words described, "Oh, yes Lord, of course. I believe that you are the Messiah, the Son of God who has been sent to us. But I must return home because my sister needs me near her side."

Martha bowed low and withdrew from Jesus' side as she hurried herself home again. Jesus followed, but at a more leisurely pace with the village folk and some of their elders as they continued in conversation along the way.

Back at the sisters' home when Martha returned she went to her sister saying, "Mary, he has finally come and he says he is here for you too."

Mary was curled up into a fetal position, holding her knees to her chest and her head was drooped down. Her eyes were red and swollen, and her face was long. It looked weary from much weeping. She heard those words but her face did not cheer up as she rose from her couch. "Where is he?" she asked in a saddened voice.

Martha spoke again, "Not far from here, on the road to our home."

Mary reached for her coat and threw it over her shoulders to wrap herself in and then covered her head as she pushed out the door. She rushed, walking and then quickening her pace to nearly a run as she hurried her way to the Rabbi. As she approached Jesus, her weeping returned. She simply could not hold back her tears and the sobs of greatest heartache. Like her sister, she too fell down at his feet and then reached out with her hands as if she were going to hold them. But she could not do it. She leaned forward to kiss his feet, but she could not bring herself to do that either. It was hardly noticeable to anyone else but she found that she was already making a fist with her hand. It was a telltale sign of the emotions she was only beginning to find inside of herself because the circumstances surrounding her brother's death. This frightened her and she backed away and rose up to her feet. She bowed and then looked at the Rabbi as her hands rose, one still clenched with a fist as she exclaimed, "Jesus, my Lord, my brother was ill and suffered terribly before he died." She wept as she went on, "We sent you word but you did not come to heal him and he died. You should have been at his side to pray and lay your hands on him. Then he would still be alive today. But instead of you, my sister and I were at his side when he died." She shook with embittered words, "But now that he is dead, what hope do I have now in seeing you again?"

She fell forward in exhaustion as she trembled with weeping. Jesus reached out to catch her and then lifted her up and held her in his arms. He looked around and saw that there were many others in the crowd who had bitter tears swelling up in their eyes too. Some cried again over Lazarus' death when they heard Mary share about that moment when he passed. But he knew that there were also tears among them being shed for Mary and the great loss she and her sister have suffered under. The villagers gathered around them and in silence they let their saddened expressions speak for them. They did not want Mary to suffer anything more, now that Jesus had finally returned to them. It was as if they had formed a shield; one that, if it was possible, was meant to guard her from anymore pains.

Jesus found that speaking to Martha about the resurrection of the dead did little to comfort her, and virtually nothing to bring her to the hope and faith that their brother would be returned to them alive on that day.

Jesus had planned to go to the sisters' home to visit with them there before going to the tomb. But now a new direction was urgently needed and he looked to the elder saying, "Take me to where have you laid him please."

The elder spoke tenderly, "Lord, come with us and we will take you there."

Now their conversation ended and a new somber hush lingered over everyone. Then two of the villagers walked off in the direction of sisters' home to meet Martha and bring her to the tomb too.

Coming to the village's cemetery, the procession of people that surrounded Jesus, which had grown still larger in size, thinned into a long and narrow procession following him. Jesus walked side by side with Mary and the elder. Then they were joined by their local Rabbi. As they approached the tomb, Jesus began to find that the journey was hard for him to complete. His steps became rough and his muscles had grown heavy and were tightening up and shaking. He found that his eyes had already filled with tears waiting to spill over and run down his face. He suddenly felt a very uncomfortable warmth flash across his body as sweat poured out of his pores. He could not take another step. He was unable to stand, and then he suddenly fell down onto his hands and knees. His tears fell nonstop and he wept hard, and without consolation. He gripped his coat over his heart and angrily torn it open with both his hands as he cried out in a weeping prayer of desperation, "Oh, dear Father, what has happened to my friend? I miss him so terribly much. Why did your glory have to come through this bitter heartbreak of death? I did not want my friend to suffer this way, or his sisters to bare this impossible burden of grief, or for anyone to be distressed. Why did he have to die, why must death come to anyone? Is there no other way? This is too much for me to bear, have mercy on me." His entire body retracted as if in pain as he knelt low to the ground.

The villagers had spread out from their narrow line and looked on at Rabbi Jesus as he wept so harshly. Many were heard whispering to each other and one woman spoke to the elder, "See how much Jesus loved Lazarus! But why did he delay in coming to him?"

Martha had arrived and she went to her sister and they looked on in silent awe as Jesus wept for their brother. They held each other in a loose hug as they wept one more time at their brother's grave.

Now a man spoke out in a louder whisper, "Remember, he healed that blind man. So shouldn't his powers have been great enough to heal Lazarus and save him from death?"

Jesus heard what this man said and groaned in his heart because he had been hard pressed between having to do his Father's bidding or to have acted against his will and rush to Lazarus' side when he still lived. He regained his composure and rose to his feet not paying any attention to those who had followed him to the tomb. He alone approached the entrance of the tomb and the sisters looked on. Jesus asked, "This is his tomb?"

The elder nodded to him, "Yes Lord, it is the tomb of the man Lazarus."

Jesus looked at it with restless eyes as he approached the stone that sealed the tomb shut and then he turned to those who had followed him there. He spoke out, pleading for help, "This stone must be rolled away."

Martha spoke with caution, "My Lord! It has been four days now since he died. His decay will overcome us if we open the tomb."

Jesus' eyes had become swollen from the tears that he wept and their streams had washed some of the dust from his face leaving trails beneath his eyes that ran down to the upper ridges of his beard. He spoke with an especially deep and firm voice, "Believe in me and what I am doing. Remove the stone. Then you will all see the glory of what God can do!"

Several men came forward, some of them had been the pall bearers; they looked to Mary and Martha, to the elder and their local Rabbi. No one spoke another word to object to the Rabbi's call to remove the stone so they did what he had asked. They stepped up to the round stone that was covering the entrance to the tomb and they laid their shoulders into it as they gripped its edges and rolled it away. Then they stepped back and looked to see what Jesus would do and wondered if he would enter the tomb to see the body of the dead man.

Jesus looked upward to heaven and prayed loudly for everyone to hear, "Father, thank you for hearing me as you always have. Hear me now and return my beloved brother Lazarus to me again, alive and well and show everyone the power of your glory." Now he turned and looked to the people who had gathered, and then he turned to Mary and Martha. His face grew joyous and his eyes bright as if they were twinkling with starlight. And looking again to the open tomb he spoke again with that same deeply rich voice, "Lazarus! Come out!"

Everyone was speechless; in their thoughts they had anticipated that Jesus was going to look upon the body as it lay at rest. But now they found themselves in a state of awe as never before, motionless in thought and unable to move even a limb. Before they could take their next breath then came out from the tomb the man, Lazarus, now alive and standing outside the entrance to the tomb where they had only a few days prior laid to rest his lifeless body.

He head was covered in a thin veil and through it everyone could see his eyes and they too sparkled as Jesus' had, with the brightness of a heavenly star twinkling with the glory of the LORD, the God of Israel. There also was, though seen only by Jesus, the sisters and Lazarus, the presence of angels who stood right next to Lazarus and there were more inside of the tomb and others scattered about outside of the entrance. Their images faded away as Jesus spoke again, "Free him from this garment of death and let him rejoin us in life again."

The men who had rolled the stone door away from the tomb came to Lazarus along with Mary and Martha and they helped the sisters to unwrap the cloth from around his head so everyone could see him. And they loosened the garment from around his limbs, so he could move about freely. Long and joyous hugs now followed, the three siblings together embracing and their voices were filled with the highest joyful laughter overflowing. The sisters let go of their brother and Lazarus turned to face Jesus and he bowed low to the ground. Then Jesus reached down to take his hands and lifted him up. Lazarus wiped away tears of gladness from his eyes and reached out his arms to offer a hug to his dearest friend. Together they rejoiced as if they had been lost to each other for a lifetime. Now it was time for all of Lazarus' friends to see him again, alive and returned to them from the tomb's cold and dark recesses. He and Jesus turned to the village folk and Lazarus went out among them to greet them all and show them that he was truly back from the dead. Now there was no more mourning or grief in Bethany and no more tears of sadness. Now was the time to rejoice as many of them joined together in circle dances of greatest joy and thanksgiving.

Chapter Sixteen
Witnesses Against the Resurrection

At the gate to High priest Joseph Caiaphas' palace, two simple men presented themselves. A very straight faced one stated to the attendant Noash, "We need to see the high priest."

Noash choked on a laugh as he looked them over from head to toe, and made a point of it. Those who typically came to the palace were chief priests or other leading religious professionals, the very rich or the very important in society. They were not typically two very simple folk from out of town. To Noash it was nothing less than humorous that anyone so plain looking as these two should presume to think that they could simply walk up, having neither appointment nor a letter of referral, and make such a request. He chuckled as he asked them, "Would you?"

There was an uncomfortable pause as he looked away, making it clear that he wasn't going to say more. It was up to the two to take the conversation further.

"We have information that he will want to know about" spoke out the straight faced one whose face looked as sober as a person could get.

Noash was not so easily convinced. "Information about what?" he asked.

The second man was less tight lipped "We are bringing word about what the Nazarene Jesus has been doing in Bethany. It is very alarming."

Still, Noash refused to open the gate for them. He had no real reason to do it, not yet anyway. And he knew full well that to let anyone in without having good cause could jeopardize his station in life as a worker in the palace. This was his livelihood and, as such, he not only guarded the gate, he was also guarding his job. He turned his head their way again and yawned. He didn't want to tell them to leave just yet. He wanted to show them that he was not alarmed just because they said what happened was alarming. He looked away and then back at them, looking them over again and told them, "I doubt that it takes very much to alarm you two. But whatever it is, it's not very alarming to me. But then what do I know? Nothing, other than that you two aren't coming in until you tell me what your little secret is. Then I will decide if you come in or if I tell you to leave."

The men of Bethany looked at each other and then stepped away. They reasoned that although they may not have the sophistication possessed by those who lived or worked at the palace they felt they could also play the cat and mouse game with Noash, according to their own rules. They turned away from the gate and motioned as if they would walk away without saying another word.

The one said to the other, "I am sure we won't have any trouble talking to a priest or even a chief priest at the Temple. Then they can help us see the high priest."

Noash knew that if their news was truly alarming and he turned them away, then when his actions were made known to the high priest, he could lose his position as the attendant at the gate. He called out to the two men, "No, wait. Let me tell you what I am willing to do for you."

The men returned to the gate and listened. "What can you tell me about the report you are bringing for the high priest to hear? Certainly, if it bears any merit at all, I can see that you speak with someone here, perhaps even the high priest himself."

The two came in close and spoke to him in hushed voices, and upon hearing their report Noash opened wide his eyes in alarm. He opened the gate and turned, he waved to a servant near the door to the palace to come over quickly. To the servant he said, "This is most urgent. On my word, bring these men to speak with the high priest. Ask for a meeting with him and do not delay. The high priest will want to meet with these two men as soon as possible, I assure you."

The servant bowed to Noash and left with the two men. He led them down a walkway through an outdoor courtyard and then into a grand double door entrance. This brought them into the wing of the palace that contained the offices and meeting rooms that were used for the running of the nation's religious and local governmental affairs. The servant led them down a hallway and into another room with another set of double doors. He asked the two men from Bethany to wait just inside the entrance and he crossed the room to meet with those on the other side.

There were several great floor lamps with broad bowls where open flames of burning olive oil could be lit to give light to the room. But only two of them were lit on this day, so the room was dim and full of shadows. As they stood at the door they could see directly through one of the lamps. Blended in with its flames they were able to view the faces of several men, including the high priest. They all were engaged in a discussion of some kind. The two noted how strange these men appeared. The appearance of those they would meet with shortly was not a kind one. It was in fact a little worrisome to the men from Bethany because as they saw the other men through the tongues of the flames, the poor lighting enhanced their wrinkles and the shadows under their eyes, giving them very aged and cruel appearances.

The servant spoke to the high priest who bent his neck to listen to him. Caiaphas looked at the witnesses and pointed to the men saying, "Bring them to me." To those with him he said, "You will need to listen to this too."

The servant returned to the doors and spoke to the men, "He will hear you right away." They all ventured forward and when they were close enough to the high priest they knew enough to stop and bow.

Caiaphas looked at the men and said, "So, you say you know something about this Nazarene, do you?"

The first man brightened up and spoke immediately, "Yes, we were in Bethany."

The second quickly stepped in, "We live there. A man from our town, Lazarus, became very ill. His sisters sent a runner with a message to Jesus asking him to come quickly and heal their bother. But Jesus didn't come and the man died."

Then the first one added, "Some said that Jesus was afraid to travel that close to Jerusalem again."

Caiaphas grew impatient with the details that he considered an unnecessary nuisance. He wanted to hear the essence of the story and nothing more, so he said, "Is there a point to this story?"

The first one spoke up again, "Yes. Jesus came but the man had already been dead four days."

And not wanting to be to be left out, the second shared, "Then he ordered the tomb to be opened."

One of the chief priests there named Zerubash reacted to that, "What!?"

The man nodded and then went on, "He insisted that he would be able to raise him from the dead."

Now chief priest Elam objected to that possibility. "What in the world…? Not after four days dead he's not!"

But the man from Bethany went on undeterred, "Jesus called out the man's name."

And the other reenacted how it sounded speaking in a deep voice, "Lazarus!"

Still another chief priest, Akiv spoke out with concern, "That poor man's family! How they must have suffered. How could they endure it? After all they had already been through and now this travesty."

The man from Bethany continued to share, "That's just it. He was very ill and died."

He looked to his friend who then went on, "We are both witnesses to that. We saw it with our own eyes. Then they sealed him in his tomb."

The two continued to take turns telling the story as the other spoke, "When Jesus called out the man's name he rose from the dead and walked out of his tomb. Alive!"

There was an uncomfortable silence. But that was not the end of the report. The first one added, "Now most of the village believes that Jesus is a truly great prophet. 'Among the greatest of all' they are saying. Some are even calling him the Messiah. And the people of our village are telling everyone who passes through Bethany what happened. Many stop to see Lazarus and talk with him. And they are becoming believers in Jesus."

Chief priest Elam took to anger as he looked at Caiaphas, "How is this fool able to create such illusions?"

Chief priest Akiv reacted in his own way, "He may have actually raised the dead man back to life."

But Caiaphas wanted to discuss the story privately. He gestured with his head and eyes to the witnesses and looked at the chief priests, suggesting that they should talk privately without them present. He turned to the two men of Bethany, "Thank you for coming. You were right to come to me and make this report." Then he spoke to the servant, "Bring these men by the kitchen for a meal and give them something for their purses for their trouble in coming here."

Both of the men responded with gratefulness as they bowed, "Thank you for your kindness." And with that the attendant walked them out.

Caiaphas looked at those with him and simply said, "I think we need to assemble the Sanhedrin, and alert them to this report and find out more about this Jesus of Nazareth. Hopefully we will get enough of our members here to deal with this. We will regather at three." With that said, Caiaphas withdrew from the meeting and the others went their way.

Chapter Seventeen
Conspiracy Meeting

Caiaphas, the ruling high priest, summoned his leadership to an urgent meeting which was held behind the closed doors of their assembly room in the Temple complex known as the Hall of Hewn Stones, or in Hebrew as the Beth Din. It was the Council Chamber of the Sanhedrin which was their Supreme Court and governing body. The Sanhedrin was the government of the people of Judea and they answered to their Roman rulers who oversaw everything. They had seventy-one members, all men, beginning with the high priest and any former high priests. The rest came from the ranks of the chief priests, scribes and ancients. The priests were mainly Sadducees. The scribes were legal professionals made up of mostly Pharisees. The ancients were elders. They were laymen made up of tribal leaders and heads of prominent family lines. These were primarily Sadducees. Because of the short notice that was given, there were only about twenty-five members attending. Their operating rules specified they must have a quorum of twenty-three to make any judgments, save one. All seventy-one members must be present for them to render judgment over someone accused of being a false prophet.

The chamber was filled with the low roar of conversations among its members who waited for the high priests to enter. As Caiaphas came into the room, the conversations came to a quick end. The room went quiet as they all turned in his direction, as if at attention. He climbed up the three steps of a raised platform where he took his seat. The former high priest Annas, the son of

141

Seth, followed directly behind him and he also took his seat.

Caiaphas addressed the members who had gathered, "So this *prophet*, this Jesus of Nazareth, what do we know about him? Is he a troublemaker? What does he want?" Bar'Gidon, a leading Pharisee spoke up in a start and with a laugh, "Troublemaker? Yes!" Everyone in the room reacted to that, affirming what he said in a low roar of comments. Hebrek, a Sadducean chief priest spoke next, "We have been watching him for some time and we know what he is teaching our people. We have sent many from among our ranks to examine him. Even the Herodians have gone to talk with him. Everywhere he goes he publicly challenges the authority of our members and other devote men of prominence, including synagogue leaders. He says things that are disrespectful and very damaging to the traditions of our forefathers and religious practices. He tactfully converses with us and then tricks our members with his cunning, which turns the people away from us. So far, no one has been able to overcome his crafty words. He is very shrewd and twice as devious towards us."

Caiaphas was not happy with what he heard, but nothing had been said that was incriminating against him, and so he asked, "Can anyone tell me if he has broken any of our Laws?" The room was silent; no one there had anything they could say that would show that the Rabbi was guilty of sin.

After that Neriah, a Pharisaic scribe, spoke about his experience, "All I can say is that he turns our questions into an opportunity to discredit us and turn the peoples' hearts against us. And it's taking its toll on us. Now, when we go out among the people and into their synagogues, we are frequently not given the honor our office is due us.

Abihuel, a scribal lawyer from among the Pharisees spoke, "And now, because of his words, we are being treated with outright disrespect by the people because of how he has spoken to us in public and because of what he tells the people about us. And he does it in our very presence."

Annas, the elderly high priest found it difficult to sit still and hear these reports. He stood up and ripped open his coat as a sign that he was infuriated. Then he lifted his hand up quickly as if he was throwing ashes over his head. "This is outrageous! This man is performing so many signs that he sways all the people away from us. And then he grips them so tightly that they think he is already a prophet." The voices in the room rose to a low roar of concerned voices.

Caiaphas stood to his feet and urged Annas to sit back down with a sweep of his hand in the direction of the old man's chair. Caiaphas was calm as he responded to the old man's show of disgust. Then he addressed the members again, "I have just received a credible report that many people believe that this Nazarene has raised back to life the man Lazarus of Bethany who had supposedly been dead four days. Now the people of Bethany are telling everyone who travels through their village about it so that word of this is also spreading through Jerusalem." The orderly meeting took a new direction as it now became highly charged with emotions.

The roar of the room had risen to its highest, and a Sadducean ancient known as Dothan the Counselor, came to the front, raising both his arms and making a panicked address shouting out, "So many of our people have gone after him. He gathers followers everywhere he goes and they are found everywhere we go, even in Samaria."

Whatever Caiaphas' calm was, was now shattered at the mention of Samaria. That alone was enough for him. He stood tall and with a deeply authoritive voice called out, "Filth! Worthless filth those Samaritans! No true prophet would go out among them!" His face grew red with anger.

Bacchus, another one of the scribes, came forward and shouted out, "This Rabbi Jesus has even gone into Tyre and Sidon."

Caiaphas was turning a deeper shade of red as he reacted in revulsion, "He has even gone to the Gentile pigs?"

The meeting was turning into a free for all shouting match as its members yelled out their accusations against Jesus of Nazareth.

Chief priest Zerubash saw that the high priests had lost their grip on the leadership of the meeting, and so he went to the front to calm the room and return it to some level of order. After he had shouted for a few minutes calling for quiet, the room settled down on its own accord. Then everyone noticed that he was waiting to speak to them. Zerubash used a calm voice as he spoke out, "Yes, I have heard many reports of where he has been and what he has been teaching. I have even heard that he has been to Idumea and also to the east beyond the Jordan. Who knows where else he has visited? He travels almost constantly. And worse, this week the Gentile pilgrims arriving for the Passover have come to the Temple asking us to see him, as if we have some control over him."

A Sadducee called Lael added, "We know that among his followers are disciples from John the Baptist and at least one of his disciples is a national Zealot."

The noisy roar of protesting voices rose slightly as Zerubash nodded in agreement with him and asked the members for silence again as he turned to Caiaphas, returning the leadership of the meeting back to him.

Caiaphas now rose to speak, showing a much more composed front because of the influence of the chief priest's work to return calm to the meeting. He paused to think to himself. "Are there no limits to his pursuits?" Then went on, "So, many people believe in him and are becoming his followers? Does anyone have an estimate of what their numbers have grown to?"

Saulus one of the Pharisees spoke, "It has become sizeable."

But that vague reference would not suffice for Caiaphas as he inquired further, "They must number in the..." he paused as his mind struggled for a number that was not too threatening for him to image, "...in the what? How many are we talking about here, a few hundred?"

The Pharisee did not want to respond. He acted as if he was no longer part of that conversation by looking down at his feet and preoccupying himself with gazing around the room.

Caiaphas wanted to know his answer and then carried the conversation forward asking with a higher number, "What? Thousands?" He looked directly at the Saulus who seemed to have an idea about the numbers, but still he did not answer. Caiaphas spoke on, "More!? Well, then how many, damn it all!? I order you to tell me now!" Caiaphas' voice shattered any remaining calm, making it clear that he needed an answer to his question and would have an answer no matter what.

Saulus shrunk back and cowered from saying anything more to the face of the man who had so much power and influence in the affairs of their nation.

A Sadducee next to Saulus stepped forward and spoke up with a clear but reluctant voice, "Tens of thousands,

Caiaphas, tens of thousands." Caiaphas' face dropped. His mouth dropped. His voice fell silent.

Now that the truth about the numbers was being told a Pharisee known as Jael found the courage to speak out, "It could be even more than one hundred thousand when you combine those in Jerusalem with those pilgrims coming into the city from Galilee and from abroad for the festival." After he spoke he withdrew to the back of the room taking on a low profile. He didn't like having to share that news and didn't want to be drawn into further controversy.

The room was still and quiet as everyone took stock of what they just heard, because it was very shocking to them all.

Then a reluctant Caiaphas took the conversation in a new direction as he asked in a quieter almost exhausted voice, "You have informants don't you? What have they said that we can charge him with?"

Bar'Gidon answered, "We haven't been able to place an informant into the inner circle of his disciples."

Caiaphas wanted more specifics on the Nazarene as he appealed to his council for something that would be useful to them, "A man who leads such a public life like his cannot have secrets. We need to find out everything we can about him, especially what he has said. How many witnesses do you have that can testify against him, if he is charged before the Sanhedrin?"

A nervous Zerubash added a point of Law, "We must have at least two credible witnesses who agree fully in what they say. Their report must be about something that shows the man has broken the Law of Moses. More witnesses would be better, but whatever they say against him it is essential that it is a serious offense if we hope to have him put away for it."

Saulus sounded like he was trying to sound hopeful for their cause but he really didn't have any assurance in his tone when he answered the high priest, "The reports we get are many, but only one or two of those giving us this information are willing to appear and testify, if it comes to that."

Hebrek added, "All his disciples are from Galilee, like him, and they are a very tight group. All of our informants have Judean accents which doesn't help them make inroads into their group."

Now a bolder Pharisee named Jacob spoke up with a voice of hope for their deceitful plans, "There is one among them who is Judean, his voice gives him away."

The low roar of the room returned again as those present murmured their doubts and worries with each other. Then a scribe called Bacchus, who was considered to be one of the finest legal experts in the city, came to the front of the room, stood in front of Caiaphas and turned to those gathered. He raised his hands for the room to quiet down, then said, "Don't worry. We are able to produce witnesses, I assure you of that." Then relief was seen spreading over everyone's faces.

Caiaphas gave his advice to help those who were working on catching the Rabbi in his words: "You have to send in spies who aren't dressed in expensive robes. Have them dress as the people do in Galilee. Find out what his ambitions are. If you can't get a spy into his inner circle, then try bribing someone who is already there. Get to it, and get it done right away. I order it."

Caiaphas thinking about what else might need to be considered spoke to his council, "So is this the worst of it?"

Dathan the Counselor told him, "No. We have been getting sporadic reports for months that are not good."

Caiaphas, feeling the drain of all that he has had to hear and consider, summoned his reserves and motioned for him to go on.

"We have been hearing reports that people have been wondering if he is the Messiah. That is what first brought him to our attention. Then there came a report that he said he would bring destruction on us by calling down fire from heaven. Two of his disciples, referring to the destruction of Sodom by fire, were ready to call on heaven to do the same thing to a village they had passed through."

Following him, Bar'Gidon spoke up, "Recently he was heard saying that he is 'not here to unify our nation.' Instead he said he is 'going to bring division and disrupt the peace among us by the sword.' He spoke about 'an army surrounding Jerusalem and tearing down the Temple.' He states that 'the Kingdom of God is coming soon and that everyone entering it must use force.'"

Caiaphas, looking straight at these two men, strained to concentrate on what they said, which led him to ask, "Has he raised an army? Does he have armed followers?"

Bar'Gidon answered, "We don't know."

Caiaphas had grown weary, but Annas was not feeling drained so he rose to say, "If we let him go on like this ..." his emotions grew strong and he stuttered, trying to find a way to say, "...ev, ev, everyone ... will b, b, be believing in hi, hi, him!" This he incompetently sputtered out with a growing rage in his voice which grew stronger as he went on, "And if we lose our influence with the people and he gains their loyalty," the old man thought as he drew his conclusion, "how will we be able to appease the Romans? This man does not submit to us and he certainly will not submit to the Romans. If he will not work with us and them, then all will be lost." He spoke scornfully with a noble touch.

Saulus, feeling a bit of panic, reacted to the thought of being squeezed between the people revolting against the Temple authorities and the Romans drawing their swords to secure their hold over their nation. He spoke with great concern, "Anything we do against him could lead the people to riot against us, or even cause an uprising."

Bacchus spoke out as if he couldn't help but say, "Many among us fear that he, … ah … he …"

Caiaphas was not in a mood to allow him to bring up something of importance only to see him become reluctant to finish his sentence, "What else!? Just say it!?"

Neriah swallowed hard trying to moisten his dry throat so he could speak what Bacchus couldn't bring himself to say, "…that he may declare himself to be the Messiah and that his followers would be glad to put him on the Throne of David."

The room suddenly erupted in a high roar of shouting protests. The members, in their alarm, swung their arms and hands in a great show of outrage.

Caiaphas felt that calmer ways needed to prevail among them. After all, this was not the first pretender to come along and hold some sway with their people. He let the court members blow off their steam for a minute and then rose to his feet, raised his hands and motioned downward while calling out, "Quiet down! Everyone! Know this; his secretive Kingdom is full of tricks and false reports that lead the people astray, nothing more. The people, they are weak minded and easily fooled."

Abihuel objected to this, "But it was that Baptizer John who preached that the Kingdom of God was at hand: and

149

now this Nazarene is preaching that the Kingdom of God is here."

Bar'Gidon followed his comment quickly, "And the people will follow him to their own ruin."

Annas was not likeminded with Caiaphas as he spoke out in support of this Pharisee, "Yes, and in the process they will bring destruction upon us and our homes. They will provoke them to come and destroy our Temple, our livelihoods and our nation! And with all the pilgrims now coming into the city for the Passover, what can we do?"

The room erupted again with fast running voices of panic.

Caiaphas once more raised his hands and motioned for the room to find its calm again, "Listen! Listen to me now! I agree that he must be arrested and held so we can keep him from swaying the people any further. It is unfortunate that this is happening when the festival is so near, but it is nothing more than that. Simply unfortunate."

Annas spoke out with advice and orders, "Arrest him, yes. As soon as possible. But not during the festival or in public view. We don't want to spark an uprising when this, this … this…" his mind searched for a contemptuous name to call him but none came to him, so instead he let the rancid tone of his voice show his feelings, "…*this prophet* is taken."

Again the room reacted with a fast running of rumbling chatter, but this time there was a sense of confidence and assurance in their tenor, as if they felt good and that they were doing the right thing.

Caiaphas felt a sense of relief by this too; a feeling he welcomed, because his reserve was nearly to the point of being overdrawn. He spoke loudly to the room, "Calm down everyone. Calm down." His voice carried with it a soothing manner that settled the hearts of those who had been roused to alarming levels. His voice had a warming reassurance to it, "I will have him quietly arrested as soon as the opportunity presents itself. Thank you all for coming on such short notice. This is all we need to do for now. Thank you. That is all for now. Thank you."

The room turned to quiet conservations amongst small groups. Caiaphas turned to Annas and together they walked out discussing the plans they had laid.

Chapter Eighteen
The Dinner Party

Earlier in the week Jesus had been invited to a dinner party to be held in his honor, for having raised Lazarus from the dead. It was going to be held, of course, at Lazarus' home. That morning Jesus served as the Rabbi at a synagogue in the city of Jerusalem where he read and then taught on the Holy Scriptures. Following that he remained in the city and visited with some of the members of that congregation in their homes. As the afternoon reached its midpoint, he began his journey to Bethany, to the home of his good friend Lazarus.

The sun would set in only a few hours as Rabbi Jesus and his disciples drew near to the home of Lazarus. There were two barbeque pits that had been dug outside just for this occasion. In each one there were several lambs being roasted. Their rich aroma filled the air. Mary and Martha had asked many of their friends to help in the preparations for the dinner because there would be an especially large number there. Guests were arriving, and though some had entered the house, most were outside in the courtyard, gathered around Lazarus as he waited to greet his beloved friend.

Jesus and his disciples came into the village and some children ran ahead to announce his soon arrival. As the Rabbi came down the lane, everyone waiting grew quiet and turned to attend to the arriving prophet and miracle worker.

Lazarus went forward to greet Jesus with a warm hug and placed a kiss upon his cheek. "Welcome to my home Rabbi Jesus" he said.

Jesus, of course, hugged his friend in return and in his

own special way said to him, "It is good to see you again. Very good."

And with that said, the two walked together into the courtyard of the home. The guests were well prepared for his arrival, and as is typical of their celebrations, musicians played a moving melody that lead to jubilant dancing by all. Jesus too, with Lazarus at his side, could not help but join in the wonderful festivities and he danced as well.

Soon the call to dinner was made by Martha and the guests took their places. No room in the house was large enough to hold such a crowd, so the traditional dining table and its couches were moved outside to the courtyard which was surrounded by the home.

Lazarus invited Jesus to join him at the head of the table and he spoke out for everyone to hear, "Welcome! Welcome everyone! Welcome to my home and to this dinner party. Our guest of honor is here, Jesus, my dearest friend." Lazarus paused to put his arm around Jesus' shoulder and tug him in tightly. "Tonight we give him the great honor he is due for the miracle that he worked in my life. Though I was dead he brought me back to life. He is truly a great prophet of the God of Israel." And then he turned to Jesus directly and said for all to hear, "Jesus, tonight I offer you my seat at the head of my table for there is no one greater than you who should be so honored."

Jesus nodded to Lazarus in a kindly way and then he took his place on the couch at the head of the table, the place that on any other night would have been Lazarus' to recline on. Lazarus went on, as is the custom at such formal meals, to direct everyone to where they would be placed for the meal. Lazarus, of course, would be on the right of Jesus; then Peter was placed on Jesus' left side, followed by James and John. On the right after Lazarus, Judas was invited to recline. Lazarus then placed a few leading people from Bethany, intermixed with the rest of the disciples at the table. There was not nearly enough room for all the guests to be placed at the table, so the many remaining guests stood for the meal and were served their food in a buffet line.

Finally, the food for the meal was brought out on many great platters loaded down with roast lamb. Other dishes of fresh vegetables and bread came out, along with many pitchers of wine. Once the table was set, everyone's voices fell silent and they all looked to Jesus at the head of the table to lead them in the blessing. Meal time prayers in those days were not said to actually give thanks for the food so much as they were said to worship and bless the LORD who was worthy of their praises. The Rabbi looked around at everyone seated at the table and turned his eyes heavenward. He sang in a deeply rich voice,

"Blessed are you Holy One, the God of Is'rael.
For you provide us with all that we need in life
from the bounteous riches of your creation.
To you we give our praises, our thanks
and our lives in faithful service. Amen"

The room now broke out in joyous conversations as the food was served onto their plates and the dinner was underway. Those serving the meal walked about inside the U-shaped dining table and kept everyone's wine glass and plate full. It was one of the finest of meals a person could enjoy and it was in honor of the one who had done one of the greatest things a person could experience, that is raising someone, Lazarus, to back life again after having died.

Martha had naturally taken the role of being the chief

steward, overseeing every detail; a job she was well suited for. She was accustomed to taking on the role of serving others and getting things done. She had already spent many days planning and preparing for it, and now she was thriving in her element as she labored, both to supervise the meal and laboring to serve along with the others.

Mary also worked diligently as a servant so that the meal would be a great blessing to the Rabbi to whom she had once said, 'If you had been here my brother would not have died.' Now her heart was healed from those deep wounds of having felt abandoned by Jesus who had not come in time to save her brother's life from the grave. Her heart was healed of the loss of her brother in death. Her mourning had given way to joy and her once broken heart now felt that it could endure anything, because she had seen the glory of what God could do when hope was no more.

For days now she had been secretly treasuring in her heart a gift that she wanted to bestow upon her Lord. And what could be a more fitting time than to do this at the dinner given to honor him. She had no thought or doubt of whether to do it or not. She had every assurance that she should do this, as if it was an appointment from God, that she must give to her Lord. Gladness filled her heart to overflowing and yet she was able to keep the secret of it to herself in the days preceding the dinner. But now as the meal was winding down the time had come.

Mary had been inside the table area serving with the others, but now she stepped outside the table and walked around to the head of the table where Jesus was reclining. No one had taken notice of her there, as of yet. Then she knelt down at Jesus' feet and took out an alabaster jar filled with perfumed ointment which had been wrapped inside of her sash. She broke it open and its fragrance quickly filled the air, complementing the rich aroma of all the fine foods that had been served. She poured some of it onto Jesus' feet and began to rub the rich ointment in. Slowly the guests, one by one, who had been consumed with eating the meal and engaged in conversation, stopped what they were doing. Its most delicate scent had taken captive their attention and they looked to see where it was coming from. Mary continued to pour more onto his feet until the jar was completely emptied.

The atmosphere was near serene and it was a very beautiful sight to all those who looked on. Now the people of her village saw what healing had been worked into her heart and privately they all were swept into awe as Mary showed what great love she held for the Rabbi. Those who supported Mary as she had endured in grief at her brother's death now found healing for their own hearts and all that they had suffered. The dinner guests breathed in deeply, over and over, to take in its wonderful aroma.

It was unthinkable that anything or anyone should disrupt such as wondrous sight. Even still, that very thing happened. Judas, who was put out of sorts by this action, rudely all but destroyed the evening. He stood and pointed with the length of his arm to the tip of his finger as he accusingly shouted, "What is going on here! What's this you are doing you foolish woman?!"

The guests became highly alarmed over his reaction, and he completely disrupted the relaxed and serine atmosphere that had prevailed only a second ago. Everyone took offense at him and many spoke under their breath comments of disregard for his behavior. Even those reclining next to him moved over to the other end of their couches or stood and stepped away.

Judas was incensed and very much calloused to those about him and their reactions to his offensiveness. Still he spoke on in a shaming voice, "What are you doing! Don't you have any idea what the value of this ointment was? If you wanted to do something for our Lord I would have told you what he needed. But this perfume was probably worth over 300 days wages. It should have been sold and the money donated to the needs of the poor who have nothing to live on! Now you have wasted its entire contents by putting it on Jesus' feet of all things! ..." Judas meant to go on but he had already said much too much.

Jesus who was still reclining on his couch now rose up high on his arm and stated loudly in forceful and in no uncertain terms, "Leave her alone Judas!!"

Judas mouth fell silent and hung open as he came to realize he had misspoken himself in a most grievous way.

Jesus spoke on, "Don't worry yourself so; there will always be many poor folk who are in need, so you can be generous with them anytime." Now the Master rose to his feet and addressed everyone there, "But me, I will not be with you forever. And all of us, you included, will honor her for what she has done to me. She has, in advance of that day, anointed me tonight to prepare me for my burial. She is the guardian of this requirement and she will hold this good work in her heart as a trust until that day comes. And now as a fitting memorial to her, wherever the story of my life is told, she will be remembered for the kindness she has shown to me this evening." Jesus now turned to Mary and offered her his hand to hold as he said, "Thank you, Mary of Bethany, in the presence of these guests I give you my blessing."

Even though Judas had so terribly disrupted the peaceful celebration, Jesus' words and the blessing given to

Mary restored the atmosphere to what it had been. Everyone's hearts were restored to the special atmosphere and feelings they had been enjoying so well. But for Judas this was not true. He quietly removed himself from the gathering, withdrawing to a quiet place away from the home to be alone.

Chapter Nineteen
Son Crest Over the Mount of Olives

Even though it had been a late night at the dinner party, Jesus was the first in the household to awaken in the early morning. As he rose, he noticed the savory aroma of roasted lamb lingering everywhere. He looked outside to see vapors of smoke still hovering over the aromatic barbeque pits. He breathed in deep the fresh morning air, and took joy in the fragrant scent of perfume that he had been anointed with the night before.

It was very early, at first light, when the Rabbi stirred his disciples, James and John, and put them to task saying, "Go ahead to Bethphage. When you get there, you'll see a donkey tied to a post and at its side will be a colt that has never been ridden. Untie the colt and bring it to me. If anyone asks, 'What are you doing?' just say 'The Lord needs the colt for now, but he will return it to you later today.'"

Along with Jesus, there were also many in the village and as far away as Jerusalem who rose early that morning. The word had been spreading widely for many days about the resurrection of Lazarus, and thousands of pilgrims passing through the village of Bethany had heard it. They were on their way to the Holy City to celebrate the Feast of Unleavened Bread and the Passover, and word of this great miracle circulated among them. These people carried the word to Jerusalem, where it spread quickly to nearly everyone. This is what gave rise to the large crowds that came out to the village so early on this Sunday morning, to see the great prophet.

As James and John made their way to Bethphage they were being passed by many people who were on their way to Bethany to see Jesus. The people asked if one of them might be the Rabbi they were told about. James said to them, "You are seeking Rabbi Jesus, the prophet from Galilee. If you go into Bethany and ask, you will find him." Then the two brothers continued on to Bethphage and once there they found the colt as Jesus said they would.

James began to untie it and again, just as Jesus had said, one of the bystanders asked him very directly, "You there, what are you doing? That's not your animal."

James handed the lead cord to John who was acting a little nervous about taking someone's beast. James whispered to him, "Be calm brother." Then he turned to the man who spoke to him, "Yes, but Jesus our Rabbi needs the use of your colt. We will return it to you later in the day."

The man smiled as if somehow he was already prepared for the answer, "Rabbi Jesus? I see. Go ahead, he can use it."

James and John hurried back to Bethany with the colt and entered the house to tell their Rabbi that they had returned. When Jesus stepped out of the house with the rest of his disciples, he was overwhelmed to see that there was waiting for him a multitude of people beyond number who had been patiently waiting in silence. As he looked around it was clear to see that there were more people in the village than ever before. They wanted to see the prophet who worked with such great power from God. Those who knew of him pointed him out from among his disciples to the others. They wondered, 'If this man can raise the dead, what else can he do?' Though it was a rare event for someone to be miraculously returned from the dead, it did happen occasionally. Every Jewish person was taught in childhood about the time when Elisha raised back to life the son of the Shunammite woman. There seemed to be rumors of the dead being raised back to life that would circulate among the people in every generation. And, earlier in the Rabbi's ministry, rumors were widely heard about the daughter of a synagogue leader who he raised back to life from the dead, and also one about a widow's son. In each of those instances Jesus had laid his hands on them and they lived. But what made Lazarus' resurrection so spectacular was that he came back to life after having been dead four days. And Jesus did not lay his hands on him, but simply called out his name and commanded him to come out of the tomb. And the man came out alive!

James and John first placed their coats on the animal's back before helping Jesus to sit upon it. He began his journey to Jerusalem with his disciples following at his sides and behind. Even though the day was just getting underway, more people were coming in a steady stream on the road from Jerusalem and making their way to Bethany to see the prophet. As people saw Jesus coming they reverently took off their coats, and laid them on the road like a carpet. It was for them as if a great king was coming toward them. Still other young men climbed up onto the palm trees along the way and pulled down branches and dropped them to those below who used them also to carpet the road.

Even though the narrow road was filled with swarms of people, as Jesus drew near they moved quickly out of the way until he passed. Then they returned to the road to follow behind him. All along the way the people rejoiced by dancing and singing loudly beyond measure because there was a new prophet in their land. They rejoiced, and greatly so, because there had been no prophet, other than John the Baptist, among them for over four hundred years. Now not only was there a new prophet but this one was mightily attested to by his great signs and wonders. And added to this were the sweet memories that were kindled among all the people because it was time to remember again the renowned days of their ancestors. The days when Moses led them in the first Passover and out of Egypt. When they gained their freedom from Pharaoh, and left their bitter lives of slavery that they had been subject to. It warmed their hearts deeply to know that God had not forgotten them, or simply abandoned them to the Roman occupation, but now, at last sent this prophet to them.

The people endlessly called out their greetings to their new prophet, singing praises as he came near to them, "Hosanna to the Lord, save us now!" and "Blessed is he who comes in the name of the Lord; he is the King of Israel!" Others proclaimed the great miracles that he had done, "By the power of God he raised Lazarus of Bethany, four days dead, back to life." Still others shouted, "Son of David! Hosanna to the Son of David! Blessed is the coming Kingdom of our ancestor David!"

Jerusalem itself was still in the shadows of the early morning light because the sun had not yet risen above the Mount of Olives. And now on this day as it rose up in the blue sky, so also Jesus was ascending the mount, riding on the colt, just above its rising bright and golden rays. When he arrived at the summit the sun was also, just then, rising above it. It cast a brilliant light over the entire city of Jerusalem, including the Temple. Its bright beams powerfully shone over everything the eye could see. Many in the Holy City who took that moment to look at the sun's rising also saw Jesus there, mounted upon a colt. He appeared inside the circumference of the sun, which looked like a very large halo round about him. There Jesus stopped for a moment and circled with the colt three times before going on.

Just as Jesus was arriving at the summit, Elamadad, a chief priest, had arrived at the home of Rabsaris, another chief priest. The rising sun caught his attention and he looked to the east to see Jesus arriving at the mount's summit. Rabsaris was just then coming out of his house and he, too, looked to the rising sun.

Elamadad asked him, "What does that look like to you?"

Rabsaris responded by saying "What is going on here?" and then in a very angry and demanding tone said, "Who is that?" His voice grew even more gruff with every word, "It better not be that Nazarene." He shook his fist at the Rabbi and then told his friend, "Quickly, we have to get to the city's gate to see what all is going on." They raced on foot through the streets as fast as they could to get there before Jesus arrived and they watched everything that happened.

Jesus now began the journey down the western slope. As he descended, the shadows of the early morning hours in the city were chased away by the ascent of the sun that brought with it the light of day. As he made his way still closer to the city, even more people went out to join him. Many more were waiting at the Golden Gate to greet him with shouts of great praise as they had done along the entire journey. Many bowed in homage to him. Others waved to him and some lifted up their hands in praise to God.

Before entering the Kidron Valley, Jesus passed by the cemetery of Gethsemane, and as he did he began to weep. The crowds rejoiced so loudly that the words Jesus now uttered were only heard by himself. "Jerusalem, my beloved Jerusalem! How is it that you became the city that killed my Father's prophets and stoned to death those who he had sent to you in love? So many times I have wanted to gather your children in my arms as a hen gathers her young under her wings! But you were not willing to come to me so that you could have life. If you could only know what I must suffer so that the world may be forgiven their sins. If you could only know what must happen so that peace with God can be made for everyone! Are you able to see that for what you will do to me with your own hands, your Holy House will be abandoned by God? But now your eyes have lost their sight and these things are hidden from you. Now your days are numbered and your destruction certain. All because you did not understand the prophecies that must be fulfilled during the time of your visitation."

As Jesus approached the Golden Gate there were inside and out a great number of people to greet him, and some of the people began to dance to the rhythmic sounds of drums which loudly announced his arrival. The crowds that had awaited him cheered and shouted out his praises again and again without ceasing. They pressed in on each other to see the prophet. Parents lifted high their young children so they too could see him.

Waiting at the gate were the two chief priests who had become very disgruntled by the large public display that had been going on. Rabsaris and Elamadad shouted loudly to hear each other over the roar of the people.

Rabsaris was outraged, "It is him, Jesus! This is not good. Not at all."

Elamadad half-heartedly agreed, "I suppose not. But why, what are you thinking?

"Do you remember the days when our people were conquered by Alexander the Great?

"Of course."

"They ruled over us until the uprising of the Maccabees."

"Yes, I remember."

Rabsaris explained, "Remember King Jehu? Remember the Maccabees?"

Elamadad chuckled, "Of course I do, why are you asking?"

Rabsaris went on, "When the people rose up against the Greeks and won their freedom Jehu was anointed king. Then the people laid their coats on the steps for him to walk on and they shouted, 'Jehu is king.' When Simon Maccabeus entered Jerusalem after destroying that great enemy, the people shouted thanksgiving and spread palm branches for him to walk on. This stunt this Galilean has just pulled off has too close of a resemblance to those two events to be ignored."

Elamadad didn't think much of the history lesson, "I see what you are saying, but so what? Do you think these people know about those days?"

Rabsaris went on, "I am sure enough of them do. And not only that, I am sure that the Romans have already taken notice of what is going on here. I'm sure there is an historian among them and, at the very least, he will recognize the connections and alert his commander to it."

As Jesus came through the gate and into the city, those surrounding the two chief priests continued to sing Jesus' praises and to tell the story about Lazarus' resurrection. One person who had just then arrived at the gate from inside the city turned to the priests and assumed that, as religious authorities, they knew what was going on and so he asked them, "Who is this?"

Rabsaris gave him a dirty look and told him, "It is no one, just a fool riding a donkey. There is nothing to see, just go home and forget about it."

But before the man had moved on, a jubilant woman stood in front of them and proclaimed, "This is the prophet Jesus who brought Lazarus back to life after four days dead." The man nodded with excitement and left the priests to join in the celebration.

Rabsaris was now angrier than ever before and spoke with hardened determination, "I'm going to put an end to this spectacle!" He shoved the people forcefully out of his way, not caring who he might hurt, and approached Jesus yelling, "Jesus of Nazareth! Jesus of Nazareth! Listen to me! You must listen to me!!!" The Lord turned his head and looked to the man who continued ranting, "You must order your disciples to stop this ... this charade immediately!"

Upon hearing Rabsaris, Jesus looked around at the crowds and listened to them calling out his praises which filled him with a new sense of overwhelming joy. The Rabbi looked at the priest, grinned widely and leaned lower to speak to him, "Priest, listen to me! Even if these people could be made silent, the very stones around us would shout out, even louder than the people are."

Elamadad was standing nearby and went to his friend to say, "You see, you can do nothing. He doesn't respect us. And look, the whole world has gone after him; there are even Gentiles among them! There is nothing anyone can do."

Rabsaris' eyes grew wild and he grunted his words out as he looked his friend in the face and said, "I'll see about that. I am going to report this to Caiaphas immediately.

You keep following him and see where he goes, what he does, and who he talks to."

Jesus continued to slowly make his way through the crowds at the gate and into the city. He turned left on the street that led to the Temple. Once there, he dismounted the donkey and asked James and John to return it to the owner.

Elamadad followed behind at a short distance, though it was not easy for him as so many were pressing in on all sides to see the prophet. The Rabbi walked through the Temple and entered all of the rooms that were not restricted to him. He saw the sacrifices that were underway and the rites of blessing for baby boys just eight days old coming for circumcision. He also saw that there were people leaving with the lambs that they had raised and brought to the Temple for sacrifice. He was distressed that the priests had rejected their animals, on the grounds that they were not perfect enough. All the while he spoke to no one. Lastly, he came into the Court of the Gentiles and saw the money exchange and the lambs they were selling at more than ten times their normal value. This made him stoop over. It brought tears to his eyes that welled up until they ran from his cheeks and down onto the floor. With his hands he gripped his clothes over his chest as if he were holding a broken heart, trying to bring it comfort. His disciples had been following him throughout all this but were silent the entire time, carefully observing his every movement. Minutes passed and now Jesus let go of his clothes and lifted his hand to wipe away sorrowful tears from his face. He stood up straight and looked about to see where the entrance was and then made his way out of the Temple, not having said a single word. He walked in silence, surrounded by his disciples who provided a shield of anonymity for him all the way back to the home of

Lazarus where he rested quietly, alone and as if in mourning.

Chapter Twenty
Temple Leadership

About the time Jesus was leaving the city of Jerusalem, Caiaphas, who was at his palace, learned about the grand entrance he had made. Pharisee Elamadad went to his palace to alert him of it and he was soon joined by Rabsaris who had followed Jesus from when he entered the city until he left it and returned to Bethany. Caiaphas was enraged as he heard their report. As he listened he shook not only his head, but also his fist in the air as well. This kind of an upset, just days before Passover, was a great offense to him. So he ordered an urgent meeting of his Sanhedrin for that afternoon.

Not all the members were able to be found on such short notice, but those who were found came to the Temple immediately. As they assembled in the Judgment Hall of Hewn Stone they were in an uproar, talking loudly in small groups. They only had the brief report that was given to them when they were called to the meeting, yet it was enough to enrage them. When their High priest came into the room everyone grew silent as they turned to face him. He took his seat and waited for the aged Annas, his father-in-law, to come in and take his seat. Then he spoke, "We will begin by hearing the eyewitness report of the Nazarene's entrance into the city this morning.

Rabsaris came to the front and addressed the members, "This morning as I was leaving my home I was joined by Elamadad and we saw this Rabbi Jesus descending the Mount of Olives on a donkey. There were crowds beyond number with him. Then we rushed over to the city gate and with our own ears heard the people shouting to him saying, 'Hosanna to the son of David. Blessed is the coming

Kingdom of our ancestor David. Blessed is he who comes in the name of the Lord, the King of Israel.'"

Elamadad added, "They were putting their coats on the ground for him to ride over and others put down palm branches to carpet his way."

Annas spoke, "What could be worse?"

Rabsaris spoke on, "We learned that Jesus set out from Bethany this morning. There were crowds of people already waiting for him there and they only got bigger. The man is no fool with how he gathered his followers in this morning. The people were lured to him by the false report being spread by his disciples, that he had raised a man known as Lazarus from the dead."

Rabsaris continued to recount the morning's events, "When he came into the city, riding on the donkey, I sternly ordered that man to silence his supporters. But he was defiant." He spoke with a particular anxiety in his voice, "The crowds couldn't have been larger! He held the people spellbound!"

Caiaphas who had been remarkably restrained during these reports now showed his temper, as he interrupted, "No! He holds them with illusions and sleight of hand. He has no real power. The real power is here among us. And we will use our power to deal with him before the Romans step in and do something against us because of him."

Now that the members had a firsthand report of the morning's events they worked toward making more sense of it.

One of the scribes, Bacchus, spoke out from the middle of the room, "With this grand entrance he made, he is giving us something to react to. But what is it?"

Now a Sadducee called Zethan added, "He came into Jerusalem and the people treated him like a victorious battle commander, as if he were the savior of our city." He paused to scoff and laugh, and then concluded, "But he has fought no battles and he hasn't saved the city from anything either."

Caiaphas spoke out, "But what can we do about a man who came into the city on a donkey? I don't like what he did and I certainly don't care for the man either, but what exactly is his crime? We have got to pinpoint it!"

Bacchus added, "There is something more to this, but what is it? Is he saying that he sees us, or the Romans, as so weak a force that he can ride on a donkey in the hopes of conquering us?"

The conclusions the Sanhedrin began to formulate were tentative and uncertain.

And so Elamadad countered, "But he wore no victor's Loral wreath."

And Abihuel added to that, "He carried neither an olive branch for peace nor a weapon for war."

Bacchus then spoke again, "Is he taunting us into a fight, or toying with us before the people?"

To which Abihuel countered again, "Riding a donkey is not a threat to anyone. It is a humble act."

And as they wrangled back and forth, Bacchus opposed him saying, "Entering Jerusalem like he did is a sign of something, but what are we to make of it?"

Annas stood up and strongly pointed out, "So what, that it was a donkey? That doesn't matter! What matters is that he rode in to the praises of the people. They called him the 'Son of David' and said 'blessed is the coming Kingdom of David!' His entrance is clear proof that he is someone who supposes he can be a King over us! Want further proof of his ambitions? He went straight to the Temple as if he was presenting himself to be anointed and crowned our King."

But an Elder, Dathan the Counselor, who was as exacting in speech as he was in producing triple redundantly proofed scrolls, spoke to correct the retired high priest, "Come now, the Temple is where priests are anointed. Herod's old palace that the Romans confiscated for their Praetorium is the place where kings are crowned. Thankfully, he didn't go there. Let's be more realistic in our evaluation of his actions here."

There was a forward looking chief priest Jonas who spoke now, "We should all be weary of what he will do next."

"Yes, he is right!" Neriah, a Phariseedic scribe shouted, as he added, "There is a prophecy in Zechariah. It may be that this man knows it and is acting it out to gain supporters."

Annas' attention now focused on this man as many in the room were speaking out of turn and making complaints against the Rabbi.

Someone asked, "What prophesy? What does it say?"

The room grew silent and everyone listened to hear what the prophecy said.

A venerable old scribe, Kelal, who was leaning on his staff, spoke in a weakened voice, "You may be right about his Kingly ambitions, but not about the donkey not mattering. His choice of the donkey is deliberate."

A scribe who aided Kelal, named Zethan, had been holding a scroll that he now opened, with the help of another scribe, so that the old Kelal could read aloud, "The scroll of Prophet Zechariah; 'Rejoice greatly, O daughter of Zion! Shout aloud, O daughter of Jerusalem! Behold, your king is coming to you; righteous and having salvation is he, humble and mounted on a donkey, on a colt, the foal of a donkey.'"[10] He paused for just a moment and then spoke again, "You see, he is supposing he can be a king over us. Let there no longer be any lingering doubt about that."

Then countered Sadducean chief priest Hebrek, "He may have entered the city like a king to be crowned but we all know that will never happen. We won't be endorsing him, and the Romans will not let him rule over us either."

"Agreed," said Elamadad as he spoke again, "But we don't need to be alarmed. Our people may not have recognized what his actions portray. They may not know about that prophecy, so what does it matter?"

But in opposition to his more neutral view, Elamadad strongly countered, "I will tell you what matters! We know it and he knows that we do. He is deliberately trying to intimidate us by this mockery of a victor's procession. It is a veiled threat to us. That is why he came into the city."

In support of this chief priest Jonas added, "His entrance was a threat and it was not veiled. Everyone in the city saw him descending down the Mount of Olives. This man is no dunce with how he acts and stages himself. He clearly knows how to orchestrate a situation and manipulate our people. He is using this grand entrance to kindle the nostalgic memories our people have. The timing of it is uncanny. Don't we all know that today's events have a striking similarity to when Jehu was anointed king, and to Simon Maccabeus as well? The people laid coats out for Jehu to walk on and they shouted that he was their 'king.' And again when Maccabeus entered the city they shouted his praises and spread palm branches on the streets for him to walk on, just as they did again today for this Rabbi. This stunt the Galilean has just pulled off has too close of a resemblance to those events to go ignored. This false prophet from the north wants them to feel like they can

---

[10] Zechariah 9:9

overthrow these Romans and win their freedom from them." Chief priest Jonas said it aloud clarifying for everyone the notion that they had been talking around.

Another Sadducee spoke out, "Do you mean that the Nazarene believes he is the Messiah and will become our Savior by delivering us from the Romans?"

But that was uncomfortable for chief priest Jonas to hear and he did not care to have anyone put words in his mouth. He respoke and made it clear what he had just said a moment ago, "No, that is not what I am saying. That is what you said, not me. What I am saying is that he has stirred up the people who would love to have a king of their own to rule over them again. They may hope that as David defeated our enemies, this Jesus will overthrow our oppressors and their yoke of bondage that is upon us."

Jonas took a moment to think before he said anything more and then he looked at that Sadducee and with a smile said, "Yes, I agree, fully. Now he looked to everyone in the room with a great winsome smile and nodded 'yes' as he said, "I agree as should we all. There is an urgent and growing danger here, even though he has committed no crimes that we have been able to identify as of yet. But if he continues on as he has, I am sure he will become a Law breaker. His use of these scriptures and our history is not lost on the crowd either. Whether they know of these events or not, or of this scripture passage or not, is somewhat secondary. The people, they know how he made them feel today. And they love feeling this way. With the Passover Festival just days away this will only grow worse when our people connect today's events with the remembrance of our ancestors' deliverance from murderous Pharaoh and the bondage he held our people in while they lived in Egypt." Now his voice grew very contemptuous, sputtering out spit as he spoke, "This Jesus of Nazareth could not have picked a more critical time of the year to pull off this kind of stunt to launch his campaign. He may already have enough followers behind him to begin a revolt. But neither he nor anyone else could raise up enough warriors from our people to overcome the empire and defeat them."

There was a deep roar of voices that now rose in the room. The chief priest Rabsaris spoke out forcefully, "And don't think that the Romans didn't take notice of this from their high citadel. They know what this Rabbi did, and they know us and our history. And if they are unsure about any of it, the Herodians will no doubt fill them in on the details."

Fear radiated in waves across the room and was felt by all as Hebrek shouted, "Already the Romans have brought in large numbers of their troops for the festival. If there is an uprising, they are ready for it."

The room erupted into an uproar of small conversations between all those who were gathered. Caiaphas felt the burden in full which was now felt by the members of the Sanhedrin. As he sat there he felt as if his head was starting to spin. As he looked around the room, its walls seemed to be wavering as if they would collapse. He worried that he would become sick and thought about leaving the room because he was overcome by all the worries the Rabbi caused him.

Annas was no longer able to just sit there any longer. He stood to address everyone in the room again. As he held his hands up the room went quiet. He spoke with an anxiety filled voice, "What else can we conclude from all this but that he is leading the people astray and into danger! His parade this morning was a threat to our leadership and everything we have." The roar in the room rose again in agreement with him.

Caiaphas worried what the old man might say or ask the Sanhedrin to do, so rather than leave that to chance he gathered his strength and rose to speak. "Thank you Annas for your words. Now I will speak." He really didn't have anything on his mind to say, so he paused and walked a few paces back and forth, thinking and pointing to his head with a finger, picking at his scalp, as if physically probing for something to say. "I think we have covered enough ground today, so we can be dismissed. I will keep you informed as I learn more. Thank you for coming. Good day to you all."

Chapter Twenty-One
Jesus Cleanses the Temple

On Monday in the week of the Passover it was necessary for everyone to search their homes thoroughly and cleanse it of all leaven. And so as Jesus and his disciples set out for Jerusalem that morning, Martha and her sister Mary were preparing to search and cleanse their entire home of leaven.

As Jesus and the twelve neared the city it seemed that everyone along the way knew who he was. They not only yielded the road to him as he walked by, but gladly stepped off the road and bowed to give him honor. They enjoyed giving him the full width of the road to walk on because they considered him to be a prophet and in so doing they showed him their adoration. Jesus passed through the city gate and made his way to the Temple as had been his practice whenever he visited Jerusalem. Many of the residents of the Holy City were celebrating his presence in their hearts. There had been a five hundred year absence of prophets in their land, other than John the Baptist. Now the people had a renewed sense of national identity, in spite of the Romans, and that gave them the joyous feeling that God was truly with them, close with them again.

The Holy City's population had grown immensely as worshipers arrived from the Judean countryside, with Galileans who journeyed from the north, with Jews returning for the Passover from the dispersion who were living in Gentile lands and with proselytes who were Gentiles that had converted to the faith of the Jews. There were even those from abroad who were neither converts nor monotheistic in faith, but they recognized the God of Israel as a true god within their belief in many gods. And as it had been in the countryside, where Jesus was recognized and honored, so also in the swelling of the city's population everyone stepped to the side to allow the newly recognized Prophet and his disciples pass freely. Their hearts and minds rejoiced gladly and they were thrilled to overflowing, whether it was the first time they saw him or if they were seeing him again.

As Jesus approached the Temple complex he could see that it was already overly crowded and filled with activity. He entered the outer court through the Huldah Gate, and though so many were thrilled to see him he remained calm and silent. He soon blended in with the great crowd that was there and his notoriety among the people was temporarily lost. Rabbi Jesus tried to walk through the Court of the Gentiles on his way to the Royal Porch, but he was redirected by a well-dressed Pharisee who spoke in no uncertain terms to him and his disciples saying that the Court of the Gentiles was closed while they were setting up their exchange. He could see that they already had set up rows and rows of animal stalls that were filled to capacity with sheep, and that more were being built by workers in preparation for the Passover.

Another man who was bringing in a great herd of sheep shouted and told Jesus to "look out" and then put his hands on the Rabbi and stared at him as if to say, 'move or be moved'.

But Jesus didn't step aside for him so the man coarsely pushed Jesus aside. Jesus remained silent and stood there in disbelief as the herd of sheep passed by him. The animals were followed by a company of men who told the Rabbi that he wasn't supposed to be in the court, that it was closed to everyone so they could set up their tables for the money exchange. These men had carts with boxes of

Temple coins in them, and they were followed by another horde of what looked like assistants carrying in table after table. Unlike his experience all morning of being recognized and honored by those he passed, now those Temple workers walking past him only gave him insult. He looked at the entrance to the court and saw that the large crowds of Gentiles who had come to pray and worship there were shut out of the very chamber provided for them to gather in.

Jesus could not stand to see this go on any longer. It was time for the Feast of Unleavened Bread and just as everyone was taking time this day to cleanse their homes of leaven, so also he could see ever so clearly that his Father's house must be cleansed of this unrighteous leaven. Though he spoke softly to himself, but Peter, James and John were still able to hear what he said, "This is the Gentile's Court where they come to worship in my Father's House." Then Jesus took in a deep breath, it was different than usual though, and then he took in a series of short breaths that started and stopped in quick succession, the kind a soldier would take before entering into battle. Then he raised his voice as never before. It was loud and forceful as he commanded, "This is the Gentile's Court, for all the nations to gather in! Tell me where will they worship, now that you have taken over their place in the Temple?"

The money changers in front of him stopped what they were doing. Everyone did. Jesus had their attention. He had everyone's attention. Although his voice rang out so powerfully, the money changers only paused in their work temporarily, and one of them responded to the Rabbi, "Who cares? Don't you know that this is Passover week? This is our busiest time of the year." The force of the Rabbi's words did not carry well enough to get them to stop their evil or to get them to recognize the grievous error of their ways.

For Jesus, this was not just the week of the Passover. It would become the fulfillment of the Passover; when he would give his life for the sins of the world. This Passover the Lamb of God would be sacrificed, once for all, for all the sins, for all of time. The Master could no longer bear to see this continue. He could not restrain the righteous anger that had welled up inside him and was now overflowing from him. He was appalled, and with still more power than before he raised his voice and with a commanding shout, "What are you doing to my Father's House? How in the world are the Gentiles going to be able to enter their own court to worship? How could anyone pray in this place? It is too noisy and you have filled it with animals! This must stop immediately."

Now he commanded the attention of the money changers and the animal handlers. Not that they were in agreement with him, because they weren't. But these Temple workers feared he would somehow interrupt their business with his incessant shouting. They looked projecting the shaming expression of a parent's disappointment over a misbehaving child, thinking that Jesus would feel shame for what he had said and was planning to do. But that would not work on him. How could it? Jesus marched past the animal pens and took a handful of leather lead cords, wrapping the ends of them around his hand. He tugged at them to ensure they would not come loose from his strong grip as he surveyed the room with all seriousness. His eyes grew large and his breathing was hard. He lifted this arm above his head and swung the cords round about. Then, with a sure grip of his hand he snapped them forward, then suddenly backward with the hard recoil of his arm. The terrible crack of its whiplash was heard by everyone.

That sudden movement of his hand changed the flow of things going on in the great hall. Jesus addressed everyone, including those being barred outside of its entrances, "Listen to me! Every one of you! This is the Court for all the Nations to gather in! It was built so that the Gentiles could come here for prayer and to worship the Living God!" He walked in a circle looking at everyone in it, appealing to them. "But there is no room left for them to gather inside. There is no room because you have shut them out of their own place. There is no room because you are using it as a den of thieves, so you can rob every one of their money by stealing away everyone's obligation to bring their own lambs, that they have raised themselves."

Those who were trying to do their wholly unrighteous business there were aghast at what Jesus was saying. But his words did not and could not persuade them to the side of the truth. Jesus looked at them with indignation. Having a passion in his voice that sounded like a battle cry, "I am making room so that the Gentiles can gather and worship in here!" Even still the animal handlers and the moneychangers did not move to leave; they stood their ground, standing in front of their tables and stables as they widened their stances in a show of defiance. Jesus now knew that it was only by a matter of force that they would move, so push came to shove. Jesus marched over to the animal handlers as he shouted at them, "Go on, get out of here and run with these animals." He walked from animal pen to animal pen and opened their gates as he cracked his whip driving the animals out by fright, into a mad stampede. The sheep bleated and tore out of there in such a wild chase that anyone standing in their way had to rush clear. Some even had to dive to get out of their way, escaping any which way they could.

Without hesitation he continued until all the pens were emptied. Then he came to the moneychangers tables. So hardened were the hearts of these men that they did not foresee that Jesus would also carry out the wrath of his judgment on them with equal vindication. Again he lifted his arm high and swirled the leather cords roundabout like a whip and cracked them high in the air. But that warning did nothing to move those men from greed to flight. So, confronting them directly, he lifted up one of their chairs and asked them, "Why ever did you bring chairs?" Then he smashed it to pieces on the floor as he shouted to them, "You're not staying!"

He went directly to the first table sweeping his whip forward. Then with a quick tug backward, it gave off a reverberating sound like thunder. With broad sweeps of his arms he reached across the table top wiping it clean of the ledger sheets and boxes of money placed there. There were several rows of money tables set up in the room and he meant to end all this in short order. As the Master moved to the next table, the money handler who worked there moved to stand at the end of his table as if to block Jesus from sweeping it clean. He tried to look intimidating and he was a large man, but that was because he loved to fill his belly by overeating. His actions only served to escalate his own impending problems because Jesus picked up the table at the long end and lifted it above his shoulders high into the air. Everything that was on it rolled down and onto the belly of that man, knocking him over and pinning him down to the floor where he screamed out. Then Jesus threw the table with great force into the table next to it, knocking it over and sending its contents on to the floor. The strong boxes, filled with Temple coins, were made of sturdy wood construction. Jesus picked them up and tossed them into the air, sending them flying about until they smashed onto the floor, breaking open and spilling their contents everywhere. Jesus continued on in his rampage, taking more strong boxes he tossed them as if it was no effort at all, into the great stone walls of the room. There they broke open, their coins flying out like the spray of an ocean wave breaking across a rocky beach.

All of the animal keepers had left with the stampede of their sheep and were elsewhere trying to regather them. But the moneychangers were a more tenacious sort. Fear had driven out the animals, but these men were not so easily moved. No. In their greed they tried to salvage their losses, picking up their coins and putting them into broken strongboxes, into bags and into anything they could find. Some tried to stuff their robes and coats with the loose coins, but then they were so weighed down that they could not stand back up again. Jesus roared as he spoke to them, "What are you still doing here? Do you value your money over your life?! You should have left in the stampede with the other animals!"

From one of the few tables still standing, the Rabbi lifted a stack of several strongboxes up high and then slammed them back down hard onto the table. The table's legs collapsed bringing everything down onto the floor with an overwhelming sound, as if the building had collapsed in on itself. Though he was hard at work in his Father's House, he never came to exhaustion or even slowed his pace. Rather, he continued relentlessly as he overturned the last of the tables, tossing some of them into the air with a great heave-ho, and sending them tumbling on their long axis, end over end. The last one he flung across the great room and it spun about like a flat rolling ball.

But in all of this, the moneychangers simply would not leave! They had dogged the flying debris and cowered under the remnants of their broken tables for shelter. And though their faces were struck with horror, it was clear that their only worry was over losing their money. One of them called to Jesus, "What do you think you are doing here? What authority do you think you possess that you can act this way towards us in our Temple?" Jesus stopped what he was doing and listened to him, having a glimmer of hope that some of them might see the sin of their ways and turn to God in repentance. But that would not be this man. Jesus spoke to them all, "Rightly did Ezekiel prophesize against you saying you make gain of your neighbors by extortion; and you have forgotten me, says the Lord." [11] Jesus was not sure if he had their attention or if their money was still at the center of their thoughts. He clapped his hand together loudly and said to them all, "'I strike my hands together at the dishonest gain you have made and I will purge your filthiness out of you. Because your officials are like wolves tearing apart their prey and destroying lives to get dishonest gain.'" [12]

But by the stiffness of their necks, coupled with their love of money that made hard their hearts, it was easy to see that they would not be moved. One called out with scorn, "How dare you speak such a word against us! We are here by the commission of high priests who have entrusted us with this work."

At such a statement Jesus found it easy to now turn from his serious attitude and begin to mockingly laugh at

---

[11] Ezekiel 22:12
[12] Ezekiel 22:13

them, "The high priests? That must be why the people call this place the Bazaar of the sons of Annas! What did Moses write to the priests concerning honest exchanges? You ought to know, right? 'You shall not cheat in measuring, you shall have honest balances and weights, for I am the LORD your God, who brought you out of the land of Egypt.' Everyone knows that your exchange of money is unjust. You pride yourselves in knowing what Moses wrote, but it is Moses' words that judge and condemn you."[13]

The moneychangers continued their efforts to recover their money, scurrying about looking under everything for every last coin as they looked nervously over their shoulders to see if Jesus was coming their way. One now stood up to speak and he almost seemed to have tears in his eyes, "We…" he paused to take in a deep breath as he was choked up, "… we have been providing…" again he paused to take in a breath, "… an essential service here…" still suffering from being choked up he had to pause again, "… a money exchange of foreign coins for Temple coins."

Jesus looked directly at him as he listened to his every word. Then with all the force his voice could carry, he spoke as if his words were the sharp blade of a battle sword, "Everyone knows, even you know that you have been overcharging and stealing money in here! Their foreign coins purchase more food in the market place than your Temple coins. More than ten times as much. Everyone knows what thieves you are, but because you have put yourselves into the seat of Moses there is nothing they can do about it."

Then Jesus turned his piercing eyes to some of the animal keepers who had returned to repair their stalls, "And you there, you are no better than these thieves." One of

---

[13] Leviticus 19:35-36

them spoke back, "We provide approved animals for the worshipers to sacrifice."

But Jesus would not accept what he said, "Animals? The people are supposed to go through the difficulty of raising their own lambs and then experience the heartache of seeing them sacrificed. How else can they know how terrible the price of redemption from sin really is? You say you 'are providing what they needed?' Not so! You took away from them what they needed to provide for themselves and endure through for the forgiveness of their sins. What you have been offering is evil, disguising itself as holy. Do I need to explain to you what you should already know? You twice rob the worshipers. First of their money, because you overcharge them for the lambs, sometimes charging over ten times what a lamb is worth. And again when you take away their experience of raising their own lambs for sacrifice."

Jesus shook his head in disbelief that the Temple workers were still challenging him. He looked at the one closest to him as he was gathering up coins from the floor, "That money is ill gotten gain, and since it doesn't rightly belong to you in the first place, don't take it anywhere!" The man's face was filled with greed as he gathered up the coins, but it quickly changed to horror as he heard the voice of the Rabbi speaking directly to him. Yet, as he looked back to his money the look of greed once again returned. Jesus was shocked by the resilience of the greed that had enslaved this man. Jesus walked over to him and bent down to look him directly in the face and with fortitude he shouted, "Now go on, get out of here!"

The man cried out unintelligibly in fear as he crawled away, before he rose to his feet dropping the coins in his hands to the floor, and ran out of the room.

Jesus stepped back and looked the room over again and saw its desolation. He walked to the doorway to exit the room. As he turned to look back, he breathed in deeply, seeing that his work was all but done there. He called out for all to hear, "This house must be cleansed of all its unrighteous leaven. It is written that my Father's House 'shall be a house of prayer for all the nations.' It should never have been used like this; as a market and a bank for thieves and robbers. Hear me, everyone. All of the leaven that was in this place, that I have found and that which cannot be seen, though it be as dust on the floor, is now removed and this place has been cleansed."

Jesus' disciples gathered at his sides and the Rabbi prepared to leave but suddenly some of the chief priests and elders came rushing in. Their faces were in shock and disbelief as they surveyed the room. One of the chief priests named Rabsaris spoke out with such furor that it was deafening, "Jesus of Nazareth, what is going on here! Just look at the clutter you have created and the animal filth you have spread everywhere."

Though the priest was so enraged, Jesus was not moved by his attempts to be intimidating. The Lord simply and enjoyably replied to him as unawares, "Clutter? Filth? What clutter, what filth? Don't you know that in preparation for the Passover Feast you must search your home over on this day and find all the leaven in it to clean it out? I have cleansed the Temple and gotten rid of the unrighteous leaven that you were harboring." Jesus walked right past him and his companion. He and his disciples with him in single file because they needed to show that they were not intimidated. All but Judas, who lingered but a moment as he looked to the money strewn about and shaking his head in disgust, albeit a disgust that was of a different opinion about the money than Jesus'.

Chapter Twenty-Two
The Bloody Plan

When the High priest Caiaphas heard the report of what Jesus did to cleanse the Temple his, blood came near to a boil. He held that any sin committed on or near to the occasion of a holy day made it twice the offense, for that reason alone. Not that what Jesus did was a sin, it was not. It was a very righteous thing that he did in cleansing the Temple. But Caiaphas, a blind leader of the blind, did not see it that way; to him it had to be a terrible violation of the Law in one way or another, it simply had to be. In his twisted thoughts he was sightless to perceive that what Rabbi Jesus did was to correct the sin that was ongoing under his administration as the high priest. So he sent out a hasty call for an emergency meeting of the Sanhedrin at his palace.

At the meeting there was, of course, Caiaphas and the former High Priest Annas, many chief priests, several scribes, included among them was the venerable Kelal and his attendant Zethan, as well as some of the elders.

Chief priest Rabsaris looked directly to the eyes of Caiaphas and Annas before speaking, "You have heard what he has done in our Temple and what he said in there! This man is outrageous! Do you know that he has accused all of us before the people? Our public trust has been severely damaged, and it could be ruined if this goes on any further. You must unite all of us together against him; it is the only way we can prevail over him."

Caiaphas did not care at all for what Jesus had done, but he also did not personally like this chief priest. So he took a moment to enjoy rendering a sarcastic answer to him as he snickered and said, "Apparently he has no fear of what you can do to him."

Rabsaris looked at the high priest with the look of a pleading man, hoping that the matter at hand could be dealt with forthrightly.

Caiaphas continued, "If there is a way to unite together all the bodies of the Ancients, the Priests, Scribes, Pharisees, Sadducees and even the Herodians it is this; by using our common hatred of this Nazarene Rabbi."

Old venerable Kelal feeling no support or passion from Caiaphas for their cause against the troublesome Rabbi, in somewhat of a desperate effort said, "High priest, I'm ready to call for the Temple guards and have him arrested." Caiaphas had already grown weary of the complaints that came to him daily now, of how Jesus was making regular appearances in Jerusalem, and teaching subversive messages. So he looked at Rabsaris with a look of exacerbation as if to say 'Help me deal with this fellow.'

The chief priest looked at the old scribe and deepened his voice, "Don't over step your bounds. The guards do not take orders from scribes."

But Kelal did not back down, even though he knew the chief priest was right. He focused his eyes firmly on Rabsaris and spoke with great assertion, "Then you do it! You have the authority to arrest him! And do it soon!"

The chief priest made a fist with his right hand and put his knuckles into the palm of his other hand and slapped them together a few times. His mind took him somewhere else for half a minute as he was imagining something. Then, his thoughts returning to the meeting, said, "I wish we could. But just look at how all the people strain to hear him. They stand and listen to him for hours unending, captivated by his every word. If I have him arrested it will push his followers into rioting and the people will overwhelm the Temple guards in order to save him from being arrested. Then our own people will turn on us, unleashing their wrath. It would become a worse disaster than when he drove the sheep out of their pens and disrupted the money exchange."

Old Kelal didn't care for his hopeless outlook. He took his own turn with a sarcastic remark, "It is hopeless then, isn't it? I mean for you. It looks hopeless for you doesn't it?"

Rabsaris looked at him with a nasty smirk on his face shaking his head slowly from side to side.

"Here is what needs to happen," the chief priest spoke pragmatically; "The lawyers have told me that with all of our efforts to catch him so far, he has said nothing incriminating yet. So they advise that any plan to deal with this one must begin by catching him in his own words. We need to catch him saying some blasphemy against Moses or against the Holy One so we can use it to arrest him and throw him into prison. If he is found guilty of a crime like this, our people will turn away from him. Or, better yet, we need to be able to accuse him as a traitor and for treason against the empire. If we could accuse him of being an insurrectionist who wants to incite war against Roman rule, that would be best. Personally, I prefer to let him be caught in a crime against the empire, so that we can hand him over to them and let them deal with him in their own way. Then the people will not turn on us. Instead their anger will burn against our oppressors. You have seen how the people hang on his every word? Follow this plan and you will see what will happen to him."

Rabsaris explained how his plan to catch him in a crime would be carried out, "This is what must be done. I will have our lawyers instruct your spies to lure him in with deceitful questions and trick him with his words. And we need to be certain that no less than two of our informants are there, hidden among the crowds at all times, so that they can later serve as witnesses against him so that the Law may be kept. The witnesses must listen carefully to everything that is said, and committing it all to memory; everything that is said, especially what the Rabbi says. Once our spies have tricked him into incriminating himself, and we have our witnesses, then we can bring him before the entire Sanhedrin. But all of our members must be present at his trial for us to condemn him as a false prophet."

Caiaphas and Annas looked at each other; Annas shrugged his shoulders and wondered if it would work.

Caiaphas was not so sure it would work. He was not so subtle about his doubts, as he mockingly laughed out loud. "You think it is going to be that easy, do you? We will see. If he incriminates himself, if it goes to trial, if the witnesses agree, if we see it happen. Then maybe our problems will be resolved. Maybe."

Caiaphas stood to his feet and paced back and forth as he thought to himself. Then his grim face grew bright again as a sudden thought occurred to him. He spoke clearly to all in the room, "Don't you know anything at all, any of you!? The solution is so simple. It would be far better to have this one man die for the sake of the people than to have our entire nation brought down to destruction because of this same man. We will have to put him to death. And if we work the Romans right, they will put him to death for us. This way we can stop an uprising before he can get it underway. And for us, it is best if we continue to live as we have under their yoke. Thank you everyone from coming. That is all we can discuss for today."

Chapter Twenty-Three
Jesus' Passover Lamb

The day in Jerusalem was draining, more so than any other. Jesus had been fully overcome with holy zeal when he cleansed the Temple and his physical exertion was extraordinarily exhausting. Not that he was not used to it, or up to it, he was. His years of work as a carpenter had given him great strength and greater endurance. But in addition to having tossed tables and heavy coin boxes around, he had experienced extreme emotions: outrage and righteous anger. And he had also gone face to face with those wicked money changers with their obstinate resistance to abandoning the evil they were perpetuating. All these combined factors came close to emptying the stores of his final reserves of energy. The Rabbi was glad to have left the Temple a better place because of his work in cleansing it, and he was glad to leave the Holy City and return to the village of Bethany for the peace and quiet if offered.

It was late in the afternoon, and as he and his disciples approached the village, there was at the same time three shepherds coming in from the fields with their flock of sheep. They led the sheep into the corral on the edge of Bethany. Jesus sent all but his inner circle of three: Peter, James and John along with Judas, ahead to the home of Mary and Martha. They would all spend the night there but first this small group went directly to the corral.

The oldest of the three shepherds, Aaron, greeted them, "Welcome, Rabbi Jesus, welcome!" Jesus bowed his head slightly, placed his hand on his heart and returned the greeting, "Good afternoon Aaron, Jacob and young Jonathan! You remember my disciples, Peter, James, John and Judas." They all exchanged greetings and then Jacob spoke, "Rabbi, this is our herd; they are all well cared for. You can make your selection from any of these." Jesus was grateful for their service to him in providing a lamb for the Passover and told them, "I would have raised him myself, but with my travels that was not possible."

Jesus, with his disciples, entered the corral and looked at the sheep, but all of them shied away, as sheep usually do. Jesus bent down to his knees and extended his hand out to call one of them to himself. All but one continued to shy away. This one came over to him and sniffed his hand. Then the lamb came close to his side and nuzzled his head into Jesus' side as a sign of affection. The Lord reached out his hand to pet his head and then looked into his eyes, "Here, let's take a good look at you."

Peter, James and John joined Jesus as they closely examined the lamb to see if it would fulfill the obligations required by the Law. They kindly held the lamb in place and ran their hands over the legs to ensure that they were sound and had no signs of having been broken. They pulled aside its wool to inspect the skin and assure that it had no infestations or blemishes. Its overall contour was viewed and considered to assure that it had proper proportions from head to toe.

As the examination came to a fruitful conclusion, Aaron asked, "What do you think Rabbi? Will this lamb be the one?"

Jesus grinned widely and looked at the lamb with pride, "Yes, I think so. He is fit and perfect in every way. A lamb without spot, wrinkle or blemish as Moses requires. Thank you for your work in raising him.

Jacob had something on his mind. He almost began to say something, but hesitated.

Jesus looked at him and asked, "Is there something else that you wanted to say?"

Jacob humbly spoke, "You do know that those priests at the Temple may not accept the lamb that you have chosen for Passover. They reject most. Some days they reject everything that the people bring no matter how perfect they are."

Jacob did not know about the work that Rabbi Jesus preformed earlier in the day to cleanse the Temple and rebuke those who sold animals and exchanged money.

Jesus did not make mention of it though. It had been a long day for him, but he did look at Jacob and said, "I know. I don't think that will be a problem after today. It is a terrible disservice they do to our people. From the beginning, it was God's plan for us, that we would endure the difficulty of raising our own lamb, one that is perfect enough for sacrifice at the Temple. Our heavenly Father wants us to bond with the animal, so that we can go through the experience of seeing it die for our sins, even though it is innocent. When the priests reject the lambs that the people have raised, they rob the people of that experience. And when we can't raise our own lamb, we are supposed to select it on this day, so that we can live and bond with it for no less than four days; from the day it is selected until the day it is sacrificed for Passover. The way they have handled it at the Temple the people can only bond with the lamb that they take possession of for only a matter of minutes, which is not bonding at all."

As they talked, the youngest shepherd, Jonathan brought over a lead cord and placed it around the lamb's neck and handed it to Jesus.

Judas then stepped forward and opened the purse holding Jesus' ministry funds and took out the price of a lamb, "Here, I will pay you."

He handed the coin to Aaron, who in reply said, "Thank you."

And with that completed, Jesus and the lamb, along with his disciples, turned and made their way to the home of Mary and Martha.

Chapter Twenty-Four
By What Authority

Jesus left Bethany early that Tuesday morning and walked with his face set toward the Holy City. He arrived at the Temple as things were just beginning to get crowded. He went directly to the Woman's Court, took a seat and began to teach. Soon after he began speaking, some of the chief priests, scribes and elders entered the great hall at a hurried pace because they knew that Jesus was there. They looked determined with their stern eyes as they gazed the crowd over. When they spotted Jesus, they walked directly over to him. Standing firm with their arms crossed over their chests, they contemptuously listened to him for the moment. Though there was a sizeable crowd already gathered to hear his lessons, it now grew exceedingly large as people took notice that the Temple authorities were there with something on their minds.

Jesus was teaching about life values saying, "Therefore, do not worry so about your life, because it is our Father's pleasure to give you the Kingdom."

The Rabbi paused to look the Chief Priest Zerubash in the eyes just as he was interrupted by him, "Jesus of Nazareth!" He was shouting, "Tell me by what authority are you doing these things in our Temple? By whose authority are you teaching, and by what authority did you disrupt the money changers and animal keepers yesterday? Who do you think you are, and who is it that you think gave you this authority?"

The great crowd that had gathered watched and listened with interest, their heads went back and forth as they listened to the two speaking with each other. Jesus responded to the chief priest asking him, "You want to know by what authority I do these things? I will also ask you a question, and if you can tell me its answer, I will give you my answer to your question."

Jesus paused but they did not object, so he continued, "So, John the Baptist; he was the son of the Priest Zechariah, who was of the Priestly Order of Abijah. His father served God here in the Temple, but John served God as a prophet and baptized in the Jordan River, rather than as a priest here among you. Now here is my question, John's baptism: was it of his own design, or did he receive it from God?"

The chief priest looked directly at Jesus and then squinted his eyes and gave a hateful look to the Rabbi. He stated the question back to Jesus sarcastically, "From God in heaven, or was it his own idea?" The chief priest looked like he was very irritated with what he considered a bothersome question. He acted as if this was a great nuisance to him. It took him a half a minute, but then he said, "We will need to discuss this among ourselves." The high priest hesitated because he really didn't want to do this, but then he turned to the others with him. They all moved in close together and discussed it in hushed voices. Their hands moved about with some gestures that suggested to everyone that they were all upset by the question Jesus had put to them. And it appeared by the shaking of their heads that they did not have an answer for him. But whatever it was that went on in that discussion it was certain that it was an intensely heated one.

Now if you were close enough to hear them, and some were, you would have overhead one of the scribes say, "If we say, 'From God,' he will say, 'Then why didn't you believe him and repent of your sins?'" To which a very nervous elder responded, 'Ba... ba... but people believed that John was a true prophet from God. If we say that it was his own idea, they will become enraged and stone every one of us here before we can escape! Just look at how worked up they are right now!" In a minute Zerubash would have to speak for himself and for those with him, he very anxiously asked the others, "So whatever should I say to him? All the people are waiting to hear our answer."

An elder advised him, "I have found that it is best to say that 'I don't know' when I have been in situations like this one. Yes, that is what is best to say." The others took a second to think about that and then heartily agreed.

Finally, they all turned in unison toward Jesus and Zerubash turned three shades of red as he searched for the courage to give an answer to the question the Rabbi posed upon him, "Jesus. Ha... Rabbi, we, ah..." He looked around as if he was hoping something would occur out of the blue to distract everyone away and he wouldn't have to give an answer for himself. "Well, no one has ever asked us that before. We can't give you an answer right now..." He found that his mouth was parched, so he paused to swallow and wipe the sweat from his brow, "... because we don't know where John's baptism came from."

Jesus was looking down and nodding his head as he heard their answer and it was no surprise to him what they said. He had a sour look on his face that told the authorities who had gathered to challenge him, and everyone else there, that he knew they were lying and that he didn't care for their lack of honesty with him. He looked each of the authorities in the eyes one by one. But they were cowards every one of them, and would not return a direct look at the Rabbi. Instead they turned their blushing faces aside. Jesus spoke with all frankness, "Isn't that interesting! Moses gave you the standard by which to measure a prophet and yet you have no idea how to use it? Well then, you can continue in your ignorance, because I'm not going to tell you by what authority I am healing the sick, making the lame to walk and revealing the mysteries of the Kingdom of God."

The authorities looked more than a little humiliated and were jittery, as if they were anxious to leave. Perhaps they were frightened of what the people might still do to them. The chief priest who led them gave another dirty look to Jesus, squinting his eyes and shaking his head. Then he turned quickly and stormed out of the court along with those who had come with him in tow.

Chapter Twenty-Five
Vineyard Justice

Jesus regained his calm and was relaxed as ever, even after that confrontational encounter with the Temple authorities. Now he not only resumed teaching, but he shared a specific parable just for this very occasion, because it was a direct reflection of the times. "Hear this, all of you. A landowner worked hard to plant a vineyard. He built a stone fence around it and dug out a wine press in it, and he also built a watchtower. Then he leased it to tenants and went away to another country to live. When the harvest season came, he sent a servant to collect his share of the produce of the vineyard. But the tenants took hold of him and beat him so badly that he was left with severe injuries."

The crowd who listened all expressed their distain over the violence done to the landowner's servant.

Jesus continued the story of the parable, "So the owner sent another servant, but they stoned him with rocks and left him for dead."

Again those listening to the Rabbi showed that they were offended with the way the servant was abused.

Jesus continued, "The owner sent a third servant who they wounded badly and threw out. Then the owner asked himself, 'What can I do about these tenants? They are criminals! I will send my beloved son; they will respect his authority and then they will give me my share of the produce.'"

Again those listening commented among themselves, agreeing that the tenants would respect the son.

Jesus continued the parable, "But when the tenants saw him, they decided to kill him…" Some of those listening now gasped to hear this. "… and claim that vineyard for their own. So they mocked him and took hold of him by force. They threw him off the property and then ruthlessly took his life. Now, after all this, what do you imagine that the vineyard owner will do? He will come himself and put to death all of those murdering tenants."

The crowd wholeheartedly agreed out loud.

"Then he will lease the vineyard to others who will give him his portion of the produce at harvest time. Therefore, know this: everyone must produce fruit in keeping with repentance and every branch that does not bear good fruit will be cut from the vine and thrown into the fire. So do not doubt in your hearts that the Kingdom of God will be taken away from those who are unfaithful to him, and he will give it to those who will faithfully provide the fruits of the Kingdom of God."

Those who had listened to the message reacted strongly as they called out, "Heaven forbid that such things are possible!"

It was clear by this that they felt very uncomfortable about the message they had been given. But it was unclear if any of them made the connection between the parable and its meaning which was about their Holy City, their Temple, and their faithfulness to the God of Abraham and Sarah, and the religious faith that was entrusted to them.

Jesus spoke to them again, this time it was with a more direct message, "Haven't you ever heard this scripture passage from the Psalms and wondered what it means? 'The stone that the builders rejected has become the chief cornerstone. Everyone who falls on that stone will be broken to pieces; and it will crush anyone on whom it falls.'"

Chapter Twenty-Six
To Catch a Prophet

Immediately following the Parable on Vineyard Justice, Jesus noticed that he was being watched by not just the people. He was also being scrutinized from a distance by members from the Priesthood, Herodians, Pharisees, Sadducees, scribes and elders. He was not yet aware that there was a mix of spies that had been sent to blend in with the crowds and that they had instructions on how to trick the Rabbi into saying something incriminating. These men approached Jesus at random throughout the day, and with increasing frequency as the day rolled on.

A spy from among the Herodians named Malluch approached Jesus with his question of deceit asking, "Teacher, I have heard you teaching and have come to know that you are sincere when you teach the truth about God, and your words are true for all people, regardless of their standing in life. I would like to hear from you the truth about this, and have you settle this question that I struggle greatly with. I want to continue to be completely faithful to the LORD and our nation, but the Romans who are pagans place their demands on us too. I do not know what to do. Can you tell me if it is lawful for me to pay the tax to the Emperor that is demanded, or not?"

Once Jesus understood where the man was going and what his question would be, he laughed loudly. "Are you asking me this as a pretense? It sounds to me like these are not your own words that flow from your heart, but that they are actually the words of someone else that you are repeating." Just then another man standing nearly next to him turned a bright shade of red. It was clear that Jesus had correctly spoken. The Rabbi went on, "What is the real reason you are putting me to the test? Is it so you can have a reason for reporting me to the Roman authorities?" Jesus paused to see if the man would react to his question, but he didn't, so he continued, "You know that many of our people quietly say that this tax should not be paid, don't you? Are you hoping I am going to publicly say that too? But so that you may have my answer on it, hold out one of the coins that are used to pay the Emperor his tax and let me examine it."

Malluch was not happy with the course this conversation was taking and he begrudgingly reached into his sash, took out his coin purse and dug around until he found the right coin. He was not at all happy to show everyone there that he was so wealthy, and still worse for him, he did not want everyone to know that he had one of the emperor's coins in his possession. This immediately destroyed his facade of innocence over the use of the Roman coin. Still again, worse for him, was that he brought it into the Holy Temple, which made him feel very embarrassed. And it showed on his beet read face. He looked disgusted with himself; as if he could not believe he was falling into his own trap. Neither could he believe that he was actually doing it, holding up the disreputable coin himself as he offered it to Jesus.

But the Master would not take hold of it as he said, "No that is quite alright, "Simply hold the coin up for me to see, would you?"

The Rabbi looked closely at it without touching it and having seen the one side he asked, "And what does the other side look like?"

Malluch appeared to be in pain as he turned it to the other side, and impatiently held it up for Jesus to examine it. It was clear he did not like becoming a servant to Jesus over a question he had posed in the hopes of disgracing the Rabbi.

Jesus asked him as unaware, though he already he knew the answer, "What does the inscription say?"

The spy resented every bit of how he was being handled by Jesus. He knew that the Rabbi was giving him the treatment that he had meant for the Rabbi to suffer under. That was the position he had coveted for himself in this effort to find him guilty of a crime. Now he reluctantly answered the question "The inscription is in Latin and it translates 'Caesar Augustus Tiberius, son of the Divine Augustus.'"

This was a great offense to all those who had gathered in close to hear what would be said; that the emperor should call his own father a god on the coins that were used in the Holy Land.

Jesus then asked him, "Whose image is this on the coin?"

The spy answered again, "It is the image..." It was clear to all that it was emotionally painful for him to admit to what he had in his hand, "... it is the image of the emperor."

Jesus nodded 'yes' and said, "Ah ha, his image, his name, his father a pagan god, is that right? So this must be his coin then?"

The conversation had only grown increasingly painful to the spy who would have rather just walked away than continue it in. But he was being watched at a distance by the groups who had united together to catch Jesus in his words. Nearby him were their witnesses who were there to hear every word spoken and commit them to memory so they could testify against the Rabbi. The Herodian reluctantly answered Jesus, "Yes, it is."

Jesus was enjoying every bit of this man's discomfort, but then he didn't go looking for him. The man had come to Jesus. The Rabbi looked around at every one who was watching to see what would happen before he spoke again, "Look, here is an amazing dilemma and no one in our land has found the solution to it yet. The emperor wants to charge the people of our nation with taxes because he rules over us. He wants his tax to be paid with his coins that are used here among us." Now the Lord looked directly at the spy and innocently asked, "Have you ever paid this tax in the past?"

Now the spy actually gave serious thought to throwing the coin as far away as he could from himself, and just running away, as he looked at Jesus and then looked away to the entryway of the Women's Court. His face grimaced and he voiced a painful grunt as if he were ready to let out a cry for help or to scream in agony. He looked to the people knowing that he was caught in the sins of Jacob who had deceived his own father. He looked down, not wanting to be seen by anyone anymore. He shrugged his shoulders up and then down but said nothing.

Jesus looked to him with all sincerity, and then raised his eyebrows, as he turned his head slightly to the side, revealing his curiosity.

Finally the Herodian looked down and shook his head 'yes.'

But just before that very moment Jesus looked away and said to him, "Never mind that."

The Herodian now was beyond his wits because he had mustered up all the courage he had left just to shake his head and admit to his great shame something no one ever cared to admit to. Jesus prolonged the man's agony, "But you still say you are still not sure if you should pay his tax."

The man's legs shook as if he was about to collapse from fright or exhaustion. He answered Jesus' question though, "No Rabbi."

Jesus wanted to work this question to its final conclusion so that everyone would know the wisdom he possessed. "Where was this coin made?" he queried.

The Herodian responded as if he no longer had control of his will, "It was struck in the emperor's imperial mint. It is from his treasury."

At that Jesus was now prepared to give his full answer to the question that made so many in their nation uneasy, "I think that if the coin has his image on it, his name, and his title on it too…"

Everyone listened intensely, but the spy could have cared less to hear the answer at this point. He just wanted to leave.

Jesus continued, "…and because it was struck in his mint and it is from his treasury…"

Everyone held their breath for fear that Jesus would say something incriminating and even the informants there stepped in closer to hear him.

"… then it is certain that the coin belongs to the emperor." said the Rabbi.

The answer was at the same time both anticlimactic and profound. It made sense and it was so simple to understand.

Jesus now concluded as he spoke to Malluch, "So, because it is the emperor's coin you should then give Ceasar what belongs to Ceasar. Satisfied? Oh, one more thing and it is the weightiest matter before you today. Malluch, start giving to God the things that are God's."

The spy heard what Rabbi Jesus told him and he wondered why he had to endure so much agony to get the answer. He was calloused to the fact that Jesus treated him just as he had conspired to treat Jesus. The answer he walked away with was not the incriminating answer he wanted and suffered so to get. This answer should have meant something good to him, because he should have felt a sense of relief that he hadn't sinned by having paid the tax in the past. He went in armed to bring Jesus down and came out disarmed and beside himself, because of the ordeal that he brought ended up coming down upon himself.

This next Phariseedic spy was named Jesse, and though he had seen the prior spy turned away in exhaustion and shame, he was not going to be deterred in his mission. He walked right over to Jesus before anything else could transpire, because he did not want to miss his opportunity. He spoke clearly, rendering a complement to the Rabbi, "I am impressed with your command of the Scriptures and how well you answered the Herodian. I listened and learned something from you today, Rabbi. Now, I too have a question for you. 'Which commandment in the Law is the greatest and which is first of all?'"

Jesus, without hesitation, answered, "Moses wrote what he received from God saying, 'Hear, O Israel: the LORD our God, the LORD is One.' And that we, as his people, 'shall love the LORD our God with all our heart, and with all our soul, and with all our mind, and with all our strength.' This is the greatest and first commandment. After this is the commandment like it, 'You shall love your neighbor as yourself.' There are no greater commandments than these two and by these two all of the Law and Prophets are understood and fulfilled."

Jesse stood tall and listened to the words Jesus spoke. He was breathing deeply and freely as if they were life to him. He had a pastoral calm about him as he replied, "You are right, Rabbi Jesus, and you have spoken well. Loving the Lord our God and our neighbor as ourselves are the greatest commandments. These two are even more important than all of our burnt offerings and sacrifices."

The Pharisee had not brought a very challenging question to the Rabbi and Jesus was pleased with this man's faith. He spoke to him kindly, "Lawyer, if you believe this and live your life by them, then you are not far from the Kingdom of God."

Jesse listened and nodded happily and with a smile he said, "Thank you Rabbi Jesus." Then bowed low, turned and casually strolled away.

Next up was a Sadducean spy named Ezod who felt in his pride that he would fare better against the Rabbi than all the others. Not that he had a better deceptive trick but for the reason that in his self-conceit he believed in himself. "Rabbi Jesus, Moses wrote that when a man's brother dies and leaves behind a wife, but no children were born into their marriage, that his brother must marry her and raise up children for his dead brother so that they may care for their mother's needs in her old age. So then, there was a couple whose marriage had brought seven sons into the world. The oldest brother married but he had an unfortunate and early death and he left behind a widow with no children from their marriage. So the next brother married her but he died without having a single child by her. So did all of the brothers likewise, and then, finally the woman died. Now here is my question for you Rabbi, if there is a resurrection, which brother will she be the wife of in heaven?"

Jesus knew the question; it was one that was commonly used by the Sadducees to defend their denial that there is a resurrection and eternal life in heaven with God. Jesus nevertheless listened dutifully, as if it was a new one for him to ponder. He gave it thought for about two seconds and then asked, "You want me to answer you and say which brother she will be wife to in heaven?" Ezod nodded 'yes' and looked as if he was excited that Jesus would soon stumble as he tried to give an answer to him.

Jesus looked at him squarely and spoke sharply, "Ezod the Sadducee, you are in error. Many of them, actually."

Upon hearing that his heart sank hard and his face fell.

Jesus continued, "And it is all because you don't understand the Scriptures or the power of the LORD our God."

Now the Sadducee felt very vulnerable. He had taken great pride in knowing all the holy writings, especially the Books of Moses, which the Sadducees viewed as the only true Holy Scriptures. He had at first shown his pride outwardly, because he believed that he would be able to put Jesus to the test and prevail. Now he had his doubts and his face showed that he had become fearful. Perhaps he worried that his fate would soon be the same as the Herodian's. Jesus spoke clearly and slowly, as if the Sadducee was not so bright a fellow. He fashioned his answer as though he was explaining it to a young child, one whose ears were too young to come into knowledge of what all a marriage includes, "When two people are joined in a marriage covenant they become one couple together by God's blessing. When one of them dies, the marriage covenant has ended and the one remaining is freed from the covenant. Now, when they are raised from the dead by God and given everlasting life they are no longer married, because death released them from the covenant, remember? Instead they are like angels in heaven and angels do not get married."

The Sadducee could have just melted right there as he felt streams of sweat roll down his face and over every surface of his body. Everything he was to say was carefully orchestrated. He had been coached and rehearsed thoroughly on what to say, but now it all was turned against him. He had one more question, though, and he held out hope that this one would clench the noose he had put before the Rabbi. He summoned up his courage and blindly spoke, "But I don't find anything in the Scriptures that tell me that there is a resurrection of the dead, or everlasting life in heaven for mortals.

Jesus, in all fairness, listened to his question. It, too, was one he had heard before. But now he would share with this Sadducee an answer that he had never heard before but sorely needed to hear. "You don't find anything about the resurrection in the Holy Scriptures? Haven't you read what was written in the Books of Moses? How God said over and over again, 'I am the God of Abraham, the God of Isaac, and the God of Jacob?' You do know that these words he spoke were said long after the death of these patriarchs, don't you?"

The Sadducean spy looked intensely at the Rabbi and nodded, 'yes'.

Jesus watched his response and then spoke on, "Understand by these words that the LORD does not make himself known by those who are no more, but by those who are now living eternally in heaven with him. Therefore, he is not the God of the dead, but is God of the living."

As the man heard the answer, the words overtook him like a sudden storm, because Jesus had just demolished the falsehood that was so central a belief in his sect. There was nothing more he could say, and so he hastily bowed his head as if he was showing a sign of respect to the Rabbi, and then he just walked quickly away.

The chief priest, Rabsaris, who was overseeing the effort to incriminate Rabbi Jesus looked on with his companions. He spoke angrily, "Do you hear him? He sees right though us. He is destroying us by his craftiness." He shook his head as if to say he believed their plan was hopeless. You must recall your spies; don't let anyone else test him."

But to his dismay a Pharisee had already approached the Rabbi and one of his companions told him, "Too late."

Another member of the sect of the Pharisees, Gilnash, approached the Rabbi, "Teacher, I have another question that I have been unable to find the answer to, even though I have searched the Scriptures over very thoroughly and asked many learned and wise men. Help me to understand how it is that …."

Jesus grew weary of the continual efforts that were being made to incriminate him. He spoke forcefully to interrupt the lawyer, "Before you bring another question to test me with, I have one for you. What do you think about the Messiah? The scribes say that the Messiah is the son of David. What do you think of that?"

The Pharisee took a moment to clear his head of the question he was going to ask and focused on listening to Jesus' words and then he said in agreement, "Yes. That's right, the scriptures say that the Messiah must be a descendant of King David, making him David's son."

Jesus made it clear they were in agreement also, "Right. But how then is it that David spoke by the inspiration of the Holy Spirit when he prophesied, 'The LORD our God said to my Lord, "'Sit at my right hand, until I put your enemies under your feet'"? So David also rightly calls the Messiah his Lord.'"

The Pharisee was still listening carefully and after a moment of thought gave his opinion again, "Yes, he did call him his Lord in the Scriptures."

Now Jesus took the conversation to a higher level of pondering, "Of course he called him Lord. But now answer me this. How can the great King call the Messiah both his son and his Lord?"

The mild Pharisee whose calm was until now unshaken, offered what he expected to be an intelligent answer to the situation, "Ah..." was all he could say as his voice fell short of rendering an answer. He was used to being able to just rattle the answers off one by one as he heard the questions of others. But this was new territory for him; not just the question, but also of not having the right answer just roll off his tongue. He had long prized himself as being such a studious person that he could give an answer to any question thrown at him. But now he was failing himself and his eyes revealed his concern that he might have met his match. He paused, his thoughts working hard at producing an answer, but none was forthcoming, leaving him with nothing to say. Dumbfounded as he was, he did manage to make a sound, "Hum..." He looked down and then nervously looked over to the chief Priest Rabsaris who sent him in to deceive the Master. Gilnash gave Rabbi Jesus an honest answer though, "I never saw it that way before. How is it possible that he..." he paused as he asked himself the question "...how is it possible that he calls his son his Lord?" There was a longer pause than before as he gave thought to it; it was quite a hard riddle for him to come up against. "It will take me some time to look into this. I will need to bring it up with some others for their consideration, too."

Jesus answered him smartly, "Yes, look into it why don't you." The man began to leave but Jesus needed to remind him of why he had come in the first place before letting him go, "What about that question you wanted to ask me?"

The Pharisee turned and faced Jesus but then walked away backwards because he wanted to get away before anything else happened to him. He simply answered, "It will have to wait. It wasn't that important anyway." Then he turned and walked, almost running, to get away.

The group of Temple authorities who sent in spies to do their dirty work felt only a small portion of the grief and exhaustion that their spies were overcome with in the aftermath of it all. The group all showed their disgust to the Rabbi as they pridefully paraded past Jesus on their way out. Then the final one, a scribe, who was very elaborately dressed, as if it was for the occasion, walked slowly by with a slight strut in his walk. This had been part of their plan for that day, but they had conceived of it as a victory march after they had trapped the Rabbi by getting him to incriminate himself. Now, in their abysmal failure, it became a show of pride before the people, who were not taken in by their deceptions. To them the authorities looked more like a rag tag band of fools, whose cause was a lost one.

The show and trial of dishonest questions was over and the Woman's Court began to return to its usual activities. That included the giving of offerings to support the ministry of the Temple. Jesus looked around and saw the line of people waiting to make contributions. Mixed in with the common folk were several wealthy ones who were making large donations. The many receptacles for the offerings had a large wooden box as its base. There were mounted on the top of these metallic billows that the coins were put into and then they rolled, very noisily, down into the lower wooden collection box below. Everyone listening knew something about how much was being given by the noise their donation produced. The larger the gift, the louder the sound the metallic coins made as they struck the metallic billows.

Jesus was distracted by the goings on there. Not that he was against the offering though; it was the noise they made that was an irritation to him. It was very bothersome to see and hear those who made it a practice to stand nearby and watch who was giving the most. These ones would call out loudly and offer praise to the ones who gave the most. But then something caught the Rabbi's eyes that took his thoughts elsewhere. He saw his disciple Judas taking too great an interest in the offerings being made. Jesus expected his disciples to be attentive to his lesson. They needed to learn all of them well. And also to be attentive to those he taught and to serve as repeaters when the crowd grew larger. Judas, however, had become fixated on something else that day.

Jesus took on a look of disgust because of Judas' attention to such a distraction as the giving. Then he went on and began teaching his next lesson to the people, "Look out for the authorities like the ones who paraded before you only a moment ago. They love to walk around in their lo-o-o-ng robes and put on a show, hoping everyone will take notice of them. These are the ones who love to be given formal greetings of honor and to be publicly shown extraordinary respect. In places of worship and at banquets they like to be ceremoniously seated, as others watch them receive their special attention, as though it is due to them. They have been entrusted with the responsibility of overseeing the care and maintenance of widow's estates. But no one is overseeing them as they secretly sell off what the widow's husband left for her to live on. They steal her property and money for their own lavish lifestyle, depriving the widow of her living until she is destitute. You see, no one, not even those who seek to live a religiously devote life can serve two masters. No one can love and serve God, and love and serve money at the same time. Anyone who appears to live a religious life but loves money is compromised in their devotion. They become the ones that you hear making long and loud prayers in public so everyone knows what their petitions are. They appear to do well for themselves on earth, but that is not their end. In the end they will receive greater judgment for their sins."

Chapter Twenty-Seven
Ting, Ting Goes the Widow's Mite

On this day in particular, Jesus had been sparring with an endless barrage of spies disguising themselves as common people, acting as though they were coming to learn from him. They all had a similar trait. They each asked questions designed to ensnare the Rabbi as a lawbreaker against Moses, the Romans, or worse to blaspheme against God. This was nothing new to him, but the large number of them lining up in a row to speak to him one after the other was new. He wondered if they were trying to wear him down so that in his weariness he would say something they could charge him with. Their ongoing questions were irritating to him and while it did wear down his patience a little, his wisdom remained boundless in the face of their trickery.

Finally, Jesus had enough of their foolishness. They were keeping him from teaching the people and nurturing them in the faith. He turned the tide to his favor and got them to stop badgering him by asking one of them a question he could not answer. So his opponents gave up and left. Finally Rabbi Jesus would be able to teach without interruption, or so he thought. But there were so many who crowded into the great hall that day who had just arrived for the Festival. They were not all there to be taught. Most were there to give their annual tax to the Temple. Others, who were pilgrims, came to give their contributions to the Temple Treasury for its support. And there were those who came to sing their praises over the ones who made large offerings to the Temple Treasury.

All this took place in the Women's Court, or so it was referred to as such. It was actually the Court of the

Treasury, but it was instead commonly called the Women's Court because this was the farthest a woman could enter into the Temple complex. Beyond a richly ornate gate in this court there was a stairway that led up to the Court of Israel were only Jewish men could enter. It was in the Women's Court that the offerings were received and those who brought their gifts stood in line to place their coins into large wooden chests.

As Jesus continued teaching, his listeners, including his disciples, gave him their undivided attention. All but one anyway. It was Judas, who held the purse of money for Jesus' ministry, who was preoccupied with the Temple offerings. Jesus had taken notice of that, because it held Judas' attention all too well and diverted him away from his Rabbi's teaching.

From the Court of Israel there stood at the top of the stairs one of the chief priests, Akiv. He was glaring at Jesus, and with him a few other priests were also glaring down at the Rabbi, and looking the room over. As Akiv looked about he noticed the connection between Jesus and his distant disciple, and wondered why this one was off by himself. Then he made the connection between Judas and his preoccupation with the Temple offering, and understood why he was off by himself. Akiv knew that the life of a disciple of a traveling Rabbi was a Spartan one. They went without personal luxuries, going from one patron's house to the next, or frequently camping outdoors. They had no home, nor money of their own to speak of. They had only what they could carry and what was given to them.

Akiv looked at the other priests, and pointed his finger at Judas and commented, "This disciple stands apart from the rest. Do you see what he is most interested in? The offering? And he admires our most generous contributors."

One of the priests pointed out that, "His eyebrows rise and fall by the sound of the coins rolling in." He laughed a giddy melody and said, "And he rises on his feet as though he is dancing to its noise."

They all lightly laughed together.

Then Akiv beckoned his spies, who though mixed in with the people, were attentive to his call and came to his side. He longed to have an informer in the Rabbi's inner circle and now he discussed with the three of them how they might conspire to use this disciple to their own ends.

At the collection boxes, as the contributors made their offerings, the money made its noisy clatter. Most people gave no more than a handful of coins that they had saved up over the year and now, on their annual pilgrimage to the Temple for worship, they gave a year's offering. Several large donations came, the coins making a clashing sound that rang out louder than any other gifts that hour. And as the offering was made, the donor looked around at the people watching him, giving them a knowing nod and a smile. More than a few people cooed and awed as others called out for all to hear, "This man richly provides for the needs of our Temple! Listen to his generosity given to support the work of our priests." The donor took pride upon hearing that and then waved to the man who had spoken saying, "Thank you, thank you everyone."

Judas stood apart from the crowd, as if he was overseeing the people and their offerings. His arms were crossed over his chest and he proudly held high his head. He bounced up on his feet as though it was energizing to him, and he nodded his head in approval to the donor as if he was a person of importance.

Most donors who passed through the lines had little or nothing said about them, and no loud praise was given because their gifts were not substantial enough. But then came an especially large and noisy offering. The man who poured it in had to empty a heavy bag of coins, shaking it a time or two so all the money would come out. His coins slowly tumbled in making several large clashes. Once done, he looked up to see the people's responses and he nodded knowingly as though he was admired by them all.

Judas took great interest in this man, more so than any before him. He bounced at the knees and let his head merrily bob about at random as his eyes blinked in rhythm with the sound of the coins rattling their way down the trumpet.

One of Akiv's spies casually strolled over by Judas and made what appeared to be a simple remark of chance in passing, "Where do people get these large sums of money?" This was actually a leading question to get him thinking in a certain direction, as was cleverly devised by the chief priest.

The offerings continued nonstop as so many were visiting the Temple that week from near and far. It did not take long for another contributor to come by with a monumental offering. It clanged long and loud into the trumpet, and by its size it drew nearly everyone's attention. A man yelled out, "This man provides for the needs of our Temple, enough for an entire week!" The voices of the crowd that lingered there rose in praise over his generosity. Another man called out, "Give thanks to this righteous man! He supports the needs of our Temple generously!" As the final coins rolled down the offering trumpet, the benefactor looked up and raised both of his hands waving to the people, "Oh, thank you everyone. You don't need to say anything, but thank you!"

Now a second spy of Akiv's strolled by Judas and slowed down as he whispered aloud a remark that was meant to sound like it was only for himself to hear, "I wonder what it would take to acquire that kind of money?" And as simply as he had walked that way, he moved on and disappeared back into the crowd.

Finally, a third spy came by Judas. This one was well dressed and finely groomed, a robust man who looked like he lacked for nothing. He displayed a sense of refined confidence about himself that was complemented with a jovial manner. He stopped near to Judas and then turned to face the offerings being given. After a brief silence he leaned into Judas' ear and spoke clearly, "Imagine what you could do with that kind of wealth, hum?" Then he chuckled warmly and looked at Judas as if to encourage him to join in the laughter.

Judas had no misgivings about the man, no notion that the chief priest's spies were working in ways other than by directly challenging Jesus in public. He took to their bait and shared his private thoughts with the stranger as if he was opening up to a close friend, "I like the sound of that jingling rumble as the money goes down the trumpet the best." Then he took hold of the ministry's purse that he carried. As he looked down at it he showed lament on his face that told of his dismay, that it was not very full. Then he shook it as he turned his ear to hear the jingle of the coins in it.

The spy showed a congruent sadness on his face and agreed with Judas for the moment. But then he became cheery again, "Yes, the sound of the coins is a delight to one's ears and to my heart also."

They both took notice of a widow coming up to offer her gifts. Her clothes were old, faded and worn thin. Judas expected that her gift was not going to amount to anything to get excited about and his eyes wandered. The stranger also looked away for the moment, away from the widow and away from Judas. This too was part of the covert plan; he was hoping Judas would notice his affluent appearance. And so, too, Judas took advantage of the moment as he took notice of the man, looking him up and down from head to toe, and began to covet the fine garments he wore. And worse, he coveted the man's larger, fuller coin purse that was hanging from his sash.

Judas' Rabbi also took notice pausing in his lesson to look around at that moment. He took note and showed an interest in the widow who was waiting in line for her turn to offer her gift. He also noted that Judas was apart from his other disciples, apart and taking an undue interest in the collections being taken for the support of the Temple's operating needs. He noticed the man next to Judas, he knew this was a spy, and he took displeasure in the coveting he saw in the eyes of his disciple. Then Jesus continued on with his lesson while keeping an eye upon the widow.

The spy was pleased that Judas took an interest in his purse and fine clothing, and responded in kind. He took hold of his large and full purse and showed it to Judas and he jingled it about like a musical charm. He spoke as if he was confiding in Judas a deep secret of his own, "Do you know what is really one of the greatest things that you can experience for yourself in this world?" He was laughing now and his fat belly bounced in rhythm to the sound of his chuckling voice. He projected an almost euphoric atmosphere. "To go to the market and purchase some fine garments like these and not have to worry about what they cost!" He now bellowed with joyous laughter. He turned directly to Judas and looked into his eyes, "I just look and point. The man waits on me and shows me his finest embroidered linen robes. They are lightweight, cool, even in the heat of the day, and so soft to the touch. Here, see for yourself what they feel like." The spy put out his arm for Judas to reach out and touch.

Judas looked at it and moved his head about to see it from several different angles. Then he reached out his hand and took hold of the sleeve of the spy's garment. He pinched the fabric up and rolled it between his thumb and fingers.

At that very instant everything ceased to move forward, Time was suspended, and the gates of hell opened with all subtlety, as the form of a snake came out from the rich man's sleeve at the cuff, and its head appeared. Its mouth opened and its two pronged tongue slithered in and out to test the air. Its head moved about quickly and then, with a spiraling crawl, it entered into Judas' cuff. Its terrible form was seen moving quickly, racing up under his sleeve and across his chest until it disappeared over his heart.

Then time returned, and Judas continued the conversation, "It must be terribly expensive?"

The man shrugged his shoulders and opened his hands and arms outward as if he was unaware, "I don't even consider the price until I have what I want." He turned outward to the crowd as if to imagine a merchant and his shop were there in front of them. He gestured with his hands as if he were offering the merchant payment and said, "Then I just reach out and say 'Here, I will pay you' to the man" all the while chuckling and giggling in a joyous show.

Judas was so lured into the spy's act that he felt as if he were there in the market with him, and a part of it all. Again the rich man turned, now with the greatest of speed, and faced Judas directly. Time ceased to move again. The face of the stranger faded and what appeared was so frightful that it was nearly impossible to look upon. His face was a ghoulish pale white, decayed like a leper's skin. Judas' face also became just like his, pale and sickened with disease.

The man reached out and took hold of Judas' wrists tightly and held him bound as he leaned into his ear and spoke with a whisper, "By stealth and craft work my will in what you do and great shall be your reward, I will see to that." And as speedily as he had turned to face Judas he returned to his former place at Judas' side and time moved on again.

The rich stranger nodded his head as he spoke again, "Oh, it is expensive all right, that you can be sure of, but I truly enjoy the experience so very much." The man grew euphoric again, lifting his hands up as though he was holding the world in his control, "And there is nothing else like it in this world" he laughed.

Judas shook his head and wondered out loud to the man, "How do you come by so much money?"

The stranger was still overcome with his laugher. But he stopped his happy snickering and then spoke as if he was explaining how to play a joke on someone. Though he laughed occasionally as he spoke it was a fiendish and cruel laughter, "I have others do the work for me. I use them to do the labor and I make the money. I pay them a token for their work and keep the rest for myself. Then I sell their work for as much as I can get for it. I love what I do and I love putting them to work for me so that I can get whatever I want."

Judas thought about it for a time and then an idea came into the eyes of his imagination. He saw himself getting money from the high priest; a bag full of money. It made him feel like he was a part of things at the Temple, as though he was in their service, and a man of some importance among them. And then he felt as if his loyalty to the Rabbi and duties of caring for his ministry funds were now being transferred to the work done with the finances of the Temple. He imagined how he might gain a position there as one of the trustees of the Treasury. But then he could not imagine how he would tell Jesus that he was leaving him. His heart felt as if to do something like that was a betrayal of trust. But then he found comfort in the thought that there really was not a large difference in the two jobs, and that it was all in the service of God after all, wasn't it?

Now finally, it was the old widow's time to place her gift into the Offering. As she prepared to do this Jesus called out loudly for everyone in the Women's Court to listen, "Wait everyone, wait! Quiet, everyone and listen!"

The rooms drone fell silent and those who carefully listened heard the faint sound of two small tings, amplified by the trumpet's billows, followed by the sound of her two coins rolling their way down as the widow passed by, unaware that anyone was paying her notice.

Those who had sung out the praises of the great contributors were silent; they shook their heads as though they were rejecting the sound they had just listened to. Many in the crowd wondered what it was that they were supposed to have listened for, and asked each other what did they miss? Everyone was disappointed over what they considered a very anticlimactic letdown. Rabbi Jesus stood up tall to speak again and all eyes turned to him as he softly resounded the echo of her contribution. "'Ting ... ting.' Ah, how wonderful is the sound of it!" The people looked at him curiously because they did not find any meaning in what he spoke. Jesus looked the people over with a nodding head and a knowing look in his eyes. He turned and made a point of looking at those who were there to sing the praises of large contributors, to ensure he had their attention, then he spoke again, "This poor widow has just put in more than all the rest of these noisy others combined and multiplied one hundredfold!" He held up his right hand and pinched his index finger and thumb together for all to see. "Those others, they gave only the smallest pinch." He let go the pinch of his fingers to demonstrate, "The smallest pinch of their great wealth." Again, he looked around the room and his eyes came to rest on Judas for a moment. He recognized, as only a prophet could, the evil that had worked its woe in his disciple's life. Then he continued his gazing the people over until again his eyes met with those who had given their praises to men for the large gifts they had offered and regained their attention, "If you, over there, praising the contributors want to honor a generous giver, let this women be honored far above all the rest. She is an honorable daughter of Sarah and Abraham. By God's righteous measure she gave the most of all, because out of her poverty, she gave everything that she had to live on." The room remained silent, but for only a moment and then it returned back to its usual roar of noise and unchanging practices.

But changed was Judas. Having been captivated by his encounter with the spy, he now gave thought to finding a way to get a large sum of money just for himself to have, so that he could spend it on whatever his heart desired. But he would not get it by pilfering the ministry's funds this time. Yes, he had taken a coin here and a few coins there from it himself in the past, but he knew that if he took too much for himself to make a purchase of fine clothing, that would not go unnoticed.

In a final word the spy spoke to him again, "As a man with your refined tastes in life you should, of course, consider treating yourself to such an experience as mine sometime soon."

Judas agreed, "I just might do that. If I can find a way to get the money," he nodded affirmatively, "I will do that."

The spy now rose on the balls of his feet and turned toward Judas one last time. He placed his hand over his heart saying, "Peace be upon you."

To which Judas said, "And upon you as well."

Chapter Twenty-Eight
Judas Conspires

Judas took delight in the notion that had been implanted in his heart; that to purchase a fine set of clothes would give him the same laughter and sense of fulfillment that the well to do man possessed. And with that for his goal, he set foot in the direction of a chief priest called Jonas. He saw him in the Temple often and knew his name, so now he went to seek him out and meet him. Jonas had been standing together with a Sadducee named Kallahadad atop the stairs that led into the Court of Israel, but they had just turned and gone inside.

Judas hurried himself up the stairs and approached him with a degree of humility for show on the outside, and a heart filled with conspiracy and greed deep within it. "Sir, I would like to see the high priest. I have information for him."

Jonas held back his laughter, but not very well, and as he chuckled he tried to disguise it as a cough. But if there was any doubt about his sense of humor in this, his widely grinning face gave him away. For him it was hilarious that a man with no title, and unbeknown to him, had just made such an outlandish request to see the high priest.

Kallahadad, though somewhat skeptical about the request, spoke with interest, "What kind of information?"

Judas could see he wasn't making the best of first impressions. So he spoke now with an eager voice, as if he was doing them a favor, having something of great value to offer them, something they truly needed and desired. He turned his head quickly about to the left and then to the right to see if anyone was watching or listening in. He urged them with a motion of his hand to come in closer for what he was about to say, "I know that the high priest would like to take Jesus under arrest, and I know where the Nazarene can be found most any time of day or night."

Jonas shook his head in disbelief because if what Judas was saying was true, he must be one of the Rabbi's followers. He wondered, "Why, then, would he be saying this?" Then he posed the question, "How is it that you are so sure you can lead us to him and tell us you know where to find him so readily?" And then he huffed as he said, "Are you one of his followers?"

Judas had hoped it would not be as difficult as this, "Don't you recognize me? I am one of his disciples actually. Haven't you seen me with him in the Temple before?"

Jonas looked at Kallahadad and the two shrugged shoulders as Jonas said, "Maybe, maybe not. I have not personally paid attention to who his disciples are. They do not interest me."

Kallahadad, being more direct than Jonas, questioned Judas, "You are one of his followers and you know where he goes?

Judas nodded.

Kallahadad told him, "Wait here for my return."

Jonas and Judas stood there in an awkward silence that seemed to go on endlessly. Neither cared much to talk to the other. Neither wanted to be the first at attempting to chitchat. As they waited, time slowly rolled on. Neither of them cared to break the chill of silence between them that was meant to interest the other somehow.

It could not have come sooner when finally, Kallahadad came back, much to their relief. He spoke to Judas, "Come with me, I will take you to the high priest, he is in the Hall of Hewn Stones right now."

Judas was lead into a private hallway and to a large doorway with two doors side by side. Two Temple guards stood to attention. Kallahadad motioned to the one and the guard opened the door. Judas followed the priest inside then he was told, "Wait here and don't say a word."

The Sadducee left him and approached the high priest Caiaphas, stopping about ten feet from him. Caiaphas was in a whispered discussion with several others. The high priest took his time, and then looked at Kallahadad and gave him a nod, as he turned his head in the direction of the doorway where Judas waited. The Sadducee bowed to the high priest, returned to the doorway for Judas and walked with him over to the high priest. Both stood in silence until Caiaphas stopped his conversation with the others, and turned his attention to them. Both Kallahadad and Judas bowed low.

Then the high priest spoke, "I have seen you with Rabbi Jesus before haven't I? You're one of his disciples aren't you?" But the truth be told, Caiaphas had never noticed Judas before. He simply said this as a ploy to warm Judas up for the conversation they would have. Then the high priest said to those around him, "Will you all excuse me while I talk to this man?" His companions all stepped away, but not so far away that they would be unable to hear everything that would be said. The high priest motioned for Judas to come in close for their conversation.

Judas felt well regarded, now that the high priest stated that he recognized him. But as Judas looked at his face he could not remember himself ever having actually seen the high priest before. He wondered why such an important man would take notice of him, out of so many people that crowded into the Temple every day. After a short pause for his pondering, Judas spoke for himself, "Yes. I am Judas Iscariot."

Caiaphas asked him, "So, you asked to meet with me. Why?"

Judas had trouble finding his voice as his mouth opened but he fell short of knowing what to say. Then, as he thought about his plans for the money he hoped to get, he found the words coming out of his mouth, "I know that you want to arrest Jesus. I have seen your Temple guards and how they react to him. They take a personal interest in the Rabbi's teachings. One day this week they looked like they wanted to arrest him, but they were hesitant about approaching him because they were fearful of what the people would do. I can help you with that."

Caiaphas gave nothing to Judas for credit, "Help me? How?" he demanded.

Judas offered his help to the high priest, presenting it as if he was really doing him a service, "You want to avoid the crowds don't you? I know that. That way they won't see Jesus being arrested and start rioting. I know where the Rabbi can be found when there are no crowds around him, and I can lead you to him."

Caiaphas was interested in peeling back the layers of the conversation so that he could find out if he could actually trust Judas to do this to his Rabbi, "You would do that for me? Why?" Caiaphas was expecting some intrigue or higher motive to be disclosed to him.

It was to his disappointment what motivated Judas who now slyly said, "What will you pay me if I do this for you?"

Caiaphas nearly laughed aloud as he heard those words, but unwilling to offend his new informant he concealed his contempt for the man. He moved in closer to Judas as if it were a gesture of friendship and kindly reached out and held him by the arm. Then, from up inside Judas' sleeve out came the snake, as before. It twisted about as it held its head high, its two pronged tongue sliding out and slithering about to test the air. Then it worked its way quickly up the sleeve of the high priest until it came to rest over his heart. The two men were oblivious to its presence and movements, which was only possible because they both suffered from spiritual blindness. But because Caiaphas had taken Judas by the arm, Judas was led to believe that was a sign that their relationship was quickly becoming a warm one. While they worked to come to an agreement on the surface, as though they were suddenly close friends, underneath lay a fragile sense of suspicion for the other and a greater sense of mistrust between the two.

The high priest now spoke directly to Judas' interest in doing this, asking, "Why would you do this against your Rabbi?"

Judas did not want to admit that it was for greed and coveting, That would be too cold. So he waited to give his answer thinking that it would appear as if he had not already had something in mind. "What would it be worth to you? How much would you be willing to pay me for him?"

The high priest stared into his eyes as he spoke and then nodded knowingly, "Would you mind waiting over there while I talk with the others to see what they have to say?"

Judas nodded in agreement, bowed and stepped back far enough for them to talk in private.

Those who stood in waiting all stepped together and whispered among themselves.

Caiaphas spoke to the others first, "With this man's help we can arrest Jesus. He has assured me that he can lead us to him when he is not mixed in with a large crowd of people."

Chief priest Jonas asserted, "Absolutely. It must not be done in public, that would lead to a disastrous uprising."

Kallahadad added, "Not like the last attempt. We must better prepare the guards that are sent to take him so they don't cower again." Another chief priest spoke, "This must be carefully planned out. We must have a squad of guards standing by ready to do this at a moment's notice."

Caiaphas agreed, "Yes, that will be done. But for right now all we need to consider is his offer. He wants to know what we are willing to pay him for delivering Rabbi Jesus into our hands."

Kallahadad spoke out with a quiet laugh and then asked, "Really? That is all he wants, money? How does one hundred pieces of gold sound?"

The high priest said, "I would pay any price to have him arrested. But let's start out with a lower price."

Chief priest Jonas said, "Offer him thirty pieces of silver, it has a nice sound to it."

Kallahadad offered his advice, "If he objects ask him what he would accept. Then we will wear him down."

Caiaphas looked to the group to see if anyone else would comment and hearing nothing more he said, "Then we are in agreement. I will speak to the man. Someone go get the money."

As the others stepped away, and he called Judas back to his side. He spoke as if he was very pleased to make this offer, as though it was a generous sum. He smiled with glee as he spoke, "Judas, we have decided to make you an offer for your help. How does thirty pieces of silver sound, hum?" He laughed now hoping that he could secure Judas agreement.

Judas was not accustomed to meeting with such ranking authorities and felt uncomfortable in his surroundings. He was anxious to conclude his business with them and didn't give it much thought before he answered because he had already reasoned that whatever they offered him, it would be enough. He smiled and chuckled with Caiaphas as he said, "That will do so long as I am paid now."

Caiaphas nodded and said, "Agreed. And of course I will pay you now my friend." He motioned to the man who had returned with the money to pass it to him. Then the high priest put the bag of silver over his heart and said, "Peace be upon you."

At that moment the snake moved under Caiaphas's garment and slithered from his heart and down his sleeve. As he reached out his hand to pass the money over to Judas the creature's ugly head reappeared out of his cuff.

Judas reached out to accept the silver and the snake moved back up his sleeve and returned to his blackened heart. Judas happily returned the greeting, "And peace be upon you as well." The two chuckled together.

Now Caiaphas began to walk Judas out towards the door and then Kallahadad stepped over to walk with him as Caiaphas returned to meeting with the others. The two men walked back to the hallway leading to the Court of Israel before Kallahadad bid Judas goodbye.

Chapter Twenty-Nine
Prepare the Passover Meal

Thursday morning in Holy Week came quickly, but then the week had been a very busy one for Rabbi Jesus and his disciples. On Monday the Rabbi had made the selection of his Passover lamb. Peter and John had been there for that. Now they came to Jesus to ask him where they would celebrate the Passover.

Peter spoke for the two of them, "Master, where will you have us prepare for the Passover?"

Jesus had been anticipating that they would come and ask him this. He stopped what he was doing and said, "Peter, you and John take the lamb that I have selected and go to Jerusalem. Enter though the Fountain Gate and there you will see a familiar man who is the servant of one of our benefactors. He will have a jar of water with him that he filled from the fountain. Go with him to his Master's home and say to him, 'Where is the guestroom that you have offered to our Rabbi so that we may prepare the Passover for him?' Then he will show you the room where we will observe the Passover. Prepare it there for us."

"Yes Rabbi" they both said in unison.

Peter and John took the lamb that Jesus had picked out and made the short journey to Jerusalem. It was only about two miles away but with the lamb the short journey took them a little longer. They entered the Holy City through the Fountain Gate as Jesus had said, and then looked about for the servant with his jar of water.

John spotted him first, "Look Peter, there is the man."

They walked over to him and Peter greeted him, "Our Master, Rabbi Jesus from Galilee, told us to look for you at the Fountain Gate. I am Peter and this is…"

John felt he needed to speak for himself so he interjected quickly to say, "John, I am John."

The servant was curiously surprised, "You were looking for me? Why? How did you find me in this crowd?"

Peter explained, "Rabbi Jesus said look for a man you have seen before. He will have a jar of water with him. Now I don't wish to offend you, but how often do you see a man doing the work of a woman, carrying a water jar?"

He laughed a little as he spoke, "I suppose you are right. I had not thought about it that way, until you said something. I am Mikhail. Come with me I will take you to my master's home."

The walk to the benefactor's home was a short one. From the outside it was very unassuming; it had a simple entrance that did not suggest it was the door to a large and well-furnished residence. On the outside of the building was a stairway that led up to another entrance to the home. Mikhail pointed to it and said, "That leads to the upper room that you will use. But come inside, this way, and meet my master." As they entered the home they were met by other servants who rushed to their sides, and washed their feet, and offered them cool water for their thirst. Mikhail led Peter and John into a room for receiving and entertaining guests. Then entered their benefactor. Mikhail turned to face him, bowed his head and spoke, "Sir, this is Peter and John. They are disciples of Rabbi Jesus from Galilee."

Peter and John bowed their heads in respect as their names were spoken.

"Thank you, Mikhail" he said, as he turned to face the disciples before speaking, "I am Zechariah. Welcome to my home."

Peter raised his hand to his heart as he addressed him, "Our peace be upon you and your household. Our Lord requests the use of your guest room so that he may observe the Passover meal there with all of his disciples."

Zechariah answered, "Of course. Mikhail and my other servants will see to anything that you need." With that said, Peter and John bowed their heads to him and Zechariah did the same before he turned and walked away.

Mikhail spoke softly, "Here, follow me."

Peter and John were led upstairs and into the upper room from within the residence. They looked about and took notice of its fine furnishings; a large U-shaped table for the dinner, more than a dozen reclining couches, and more tables and cabinets along the walls. Peter's eyes swept the room over but stopped at a place on the wall where two fine swords were hung. John, too, in looking the room over came across the swords, and there, too, his eyes stayed. The two of them admired the fine weapons for a while before they realized that they had been spellbound by them.

Without taking his eyes off of them, Peter stepped forward and took the swords off the wall and placed one in his sash and the other one on a table next to the wall. He strutted about the length of the room, looking like a rooster overseeing a gaggle of his own hens. Then, as suddenly as anyone could, he sprang into action and drew the sword out, pointing it forward at an unseen enemy. Its sound was of iron slicing across iron as he withdrew it from the sheath. The sword was highly polished and it was easy to see that its blade was razor sharp. Peter stared forward as if he was taking stock of his newly imagined foe. Then, as suddenly as he had drawn the blade, he moved it about in a series of forward offensive strikes intermixed with high and low defensive blocking moves.

John couldn't help but see all that Peter did. His eyes had grown large as he first watched in amazement over the fisherman's swordsmanship skills. But then he grew fearful of Peter's display and worried that he might come too close to him as he acted out his fight. John slowly made his way over to the table by the wall and cautiously picked up the other sword. Then went to stand near a back corner of the room. John spoke with concern in his voice, "How is it that you know how to use a sword so well Peter?"

Peter boldly spoke out swinging his sword about to colorfully illustrate what he said, "*There - are - thieves - in - the - land.* I caught fish and then sold them. That was my business. I handled the money too. Our boats and equipment are very valuable. I had to be ready for them, the bandits, you know. I had to fight them off on a number of occasions and I haven't lost a fight to any of them yet. There are a few of these *acquaintances* of mine out there who have been marked by my blade. They don't go about so openly anymore, with the improvements I had to make to their faces after they attacked me." John wondered if what he was hearing was true or if it was just Peter being Peter and embellishing his story.

Peter continued his imaginary sword fight against his invisible adversary. He made defensive moves as if to block an attack as he shouted, "Your blade shall not strike me by day or by night! My sword is more protection to me than any shield could be." Then switching to the offense and lunging forward he shouted, "This blade will pierce you through in a dozen points and I will wear down the fight in you, or it will cost you your life if you do not yield the victory to me." Now having won in this display of

239

single combat he smartly sheathed the sword, then held it in his hand and put the tip over his shoulder as he confidently swaggered about.

He spoke to John with poise, "Do you know what just occurred to me?"

John found relief that Peter had won his little battle and that the sword play was over. He answered him, "What?"

Peter continued strutting about and added to that the waggling of his head in a jocular motion, and then he answered John, "Well, with Jesus coming to Jerusalem, it seems that the Kingdom of God is soon to be restored in power and might again, doesn't it? Very soon it could be that the dust my battle horse kicks up will choke and blind the eyes of the Romans. It could be that God will soon deliver us from the emperor's grip and send them limping home, if I let them live."

John took a serious interest in this new direction in the conversation, "Tell me Peter, has Jesus spoken to you about...?" John paused in the hopes that Peter would pick up on what he was saying and would finish the sentence for him.

But Peter didn't catch on, "About what...?" he asked.

But John was glad to say it himself, "Has Jesus spoke to you about who his commander will be? You know Moses had Joshua to lead the army and King David had Joab to lead his army."

Peter caught on now, "No he hasn't told me in so many words that I will be the commander of his army. But when he does ask me, I have already decided that I will accept that great honor. After all, I am naturally bold and courageous, and with what I know about swordsmanship, just imagine the great victories I will win for him." As he walked about he looked even more than ever like a strutting rooster as he bounced about on his legs. He went to the window and gazed out, imagining himself leading in a victorious battle against the Roman army.

John wondered if Peter was just embellishing the truth, or if this could really happen. He murmured quietly to himself, "You mean to say that you are immaturely brazen and impulsive."

Peter heard a comment but not what was said, "What'd you say?"

John grew tired of Peter and his uppity ways, "Nothing, I was just talking to myself." John found himself growing still more tired of Peter and now felt the need to react. He raised his sheathed sword and then waved it about rather comically to mimic what Peter had just done with his. He remembered how Peter had started his comment, 'No he hasn't told me in so many words...' and from that he became very concerned that Peter had spoken with too much certainty and too little truth.

John played on Peter to draw out from him more about what fantasies he had lingering in his heart and asked him, "So, how do you think things will happen? I mean, will we each get a legion of angels to lead into battle? Or, will we lead the men of our nation into battle? Or still, will we lead both men and angels? How will it take place?"

Peter spelled out his version of how he wanted it to take place, "I think that ah, I will be the general of all the armies of our nation. But you, young John, you will first need to become a man before you can lead men. I think that if you are fortunate enough you will be my squire. Or, maybe I will have you serve in my stables and care for my many fine horses. Then, when you have finished there, you can shine my armor and put a fine edge on my swords."

John was not at all surprised by what Peter said and he could have even accurately guessed what Peter would say in advance. What he did not expect was the belittling he got. But young John had been a disciple for nearly three years now, and by Jesus' instruction he had grown mature and bold enough to face down this much from Peter as he spoke out against him. John shook his sheathed sword a little and boldly said, "You are not a general yet, and I don't take orders from you Peter!" John could hear in his own voice the confidence he wanted to display and he was satisfied by it. He didn't care what Peter thought of him now and not wanting to get into a verbal match with him either, he said in a huff, "I'm going outside. Alone!"

Peter understood he had gotten to John with his pointed tongue and so he relented, "Alright then! I'll let you be my sergeant." As John made his way to the door Peter suddenly sprang in front of it and blocked the way out. He stared at John as if he was a man ready for a fight, and raised his sheathed sword directly at John's heart. Peter expected a fearful John to withdraw and cower from such a threat, but to his amazement and John's as well, better instincts than that took over.

John shouted with a deep and reverberating grunt that could have crumbled a mountain into sand. "Ahhh!!!" and with his sword still in the sheath he reacted with a defensive strike which moved swiftly, like a flash of lightning sweeping across the sky, knocking Peter's sword so hard that it flew out of his hand. Then John moved quickly, putting his sword to the side of Peter's neck and sawed gently with its sheath to show that he could slit his throat with ease. John was shocked to see himself act so valiantly; he didn't know it was in him until that very moment. It all happened so fast and with such precision that John was most pleased with himself.

Peter reacted with eyes that opened so wide his eyeballs looked as if they were in danger of falling out. He was frozen in place, and in fear he dared not move for the horror that his throat would be slit open. Then he remembered that John's sword was still sheathed and he was in no real danger. He privately recognized that young John was not to be toyed with anymore and neither was he to be thought of as a youth any longer. Peter realized that he was leaning backward almost to the point of falling down, as he had tried to escape the point of John's sword and his own death. "Easy John, easy" he calmly said. "I was just fooling around, that's all. I had no idea that you had such fight in you." Peter looked at John as if he was asking for his permission, then reached up with one hand to cautiously move the sword away from his neck.

John spoke as a man of great self-confidence, "You should *not* have jumped in my way like that. I wasn't expecting it. So I took due course, as you would have, and I stood up for myself in battle. It is a good thing for you my sword was still sheathed."

Peter spoke apologetically, "Yes, you're right, I should have known better." Peter realized that he was still blocking the door, so he stood to the side to allow John to pass. Then he offered this complement as a means of endorsing John's manhood, "I could use a man like you. Maybe I *will* ask you to lead a legion of men and angels."

John jutted his chin out because he didn't want to leave that point up in the air, "Maybe? If it comes to war just try and stop me." John went outside and after the excitement wore off he returned to a quiet Peter who was sitting on the edge of one of the couches.

He looked at John and said, "Well, let's return these

swords to the wall and start our search for leaven."

Then John said, "Peter, they were supposed to have searched and cleansed the house on Monday, four days before Passover."

Peter answered, "Yes, and I am sure they did, but we must ensure it is done, even today. If we find leaven it must be removed from the room and we will wash the area where it was."

John nodded in agreement and said, "Yes Peter."

They lit all seven candles on two of the Menorah candelabras that were on the table. Then they carefully went over every surface of the room by candle light, searching for leaven and cleaning with dusting cloths all the furniture and sweeping the floor thoroughly.

They found only a little dust and dirt on the floor and so they brought it outside and recited in unison these words, "All of the leaven that was in this place, that we have found and that which cannot be seen, though it be as dust on the floor, is now removed and this place has been cleansed. Amen"

Chapter Thirty
Passover

The upper room was prepared. Peter and John, along with the help of Mikhail and some of the other servants, had worked very hard all day. Then in the morning the two disciples had gone to the market district and purchased all that was needed for their Passover meal, which included the bitter herbs of parsley and celery. There were the many ingredients for the Charoset, whose name means *clay,* of all things, and though its name doesn't sound very appetizing, it is in real life very tasteful. The reason for it being called by this name is that it is meant to represent the mortar mix that their ancestors, as slaves, used in their labors as they constructed buildings for Pharaoh in Egypt. The recipe was simple; roasted almonds finely crushed, dried apricots, tart apples, dates, honey, raisins, with a little cinnamon and salt that is made into a creamy dip for the bread. They also purchased many, many loaves of unleavened bread. Their host, Zechariah, provided the wine for the meal.

First thing in the afternoon, Peter and John had gone to the Temple with the lamb and had it sacrificed for them by a priest. Once they arrived at home they began to roast it in an open flame in the inner courtyard of their host's home.

Later in the afternoon Jesus made the journey from Bethany, over the Mount of Olives, past the cemetery on the western slope and into the Holy City. When Jesus, along with his other disciples, arrived he was greeted by Zechariah and welcomed into his home.

As the sun first began its final descent into the horizon, Jesus made his way into the upper room where his disciples awaited him. The room was dimly lit by lamps on the tables and cabinets next to the walls. On their dining table were three separate candelabras, each holding seven candles. These would be lit just before the meal would begin. Their Master assigned their places around the low U-shaped dining table. Jesus, of course, was on the couch at the head of the table. To his right was Judas, Thomas, James the Greater, Philip, Thaddeus and then Simon the Zealot. On the Rabbi Jesus' left was John, followed by Simon Peter, then Andrew, Matthew, James the Lessor, and finally Bartholomew.

As the disciples all went to their couches and sat on the sides of them, they anticipated that the servants would come and wash their feet. Jesus stood at the head of the table next to his couch and waited for the servants as well, but not with the same expectations as his disciples. The servants entered into the room with all that they needed to wash everyone's feet. Jesus took particular interest in this; he had been waiting and watching for this time to come. First, they came to the Rabbi. He is their Master and his feet would be washed first of all. But Jesus did not sit on his couch when they came to him. Instead, he took off his outer robe and set it aside on his couch. He looked to the servants and asked them to assist him. They looked at each other wondering, whatever did he mean by saying this?

Then Rabbi Jesus took a large towel and wrapped it around his waist. He knelt on the floor before John and motioned to a servant to give him a basin. He lifted John's feet into the basin and then reached for a water pitcher from another servant. He slowly poured the water over John's feet and used the towel around his waist to very thoroughly wash them. Though it made all the servants uncomfortable, none of them questioned it or tried to stop him. They knew that was not their place. Then he motioned to the servants for a towel and he dried John's feet. When he was done he handed the basin of dirty water to a servant who took it away for disposal and another gave him a clean empty basin to begin with again. Their Master went around the room, going from disciple to disciple, washing their feet clean from the dust they had gathered from the road. Though the servants were becoming more comfortable with what he was doing, his disciples themselves were very uneasy with what was being done for them by their Master. But none spoke out against it, that was not their place, either. The room remained very silent, uncomfortably so, throughout it.

Lastly, Jesus came to Peter and knelt. As history has shown of him, Peter was not as shy as the others, nor was he one to remain silent, even though his Master had not initiated a conversation or told them why he was doing this. Peter looked downward, and though this was hard for him, it was not right in his mind that his Master's head should be beneath his own like this. He spoke quickly and with great urgency, "My Lord, what is this that you are you doing here, kneeling before each of us like a lowly servant and washing our dirty feet? How can you possibly bring yourself, as our Master and Rabbi, to do this thing? Why are you coming to me and kneeling as if you are going to wash my feet? You are over me and I am beneath you, and so is washing anyone's feet."

Jesus did not get up from his kneeling and he did not immediately answer this distressed Peter either. He wanted his disciple to wait for his answer, hoping that the waiting would calm him and open his mind to a new lesson.

Jesus looked up at Peter and looked into his eyes with understanding, "I am doing this for you Peter, for you. It doesn't matter if you understand it or not for now. The time will come when you will know why I have done this for you." Jesus' hopes that Peter would be more open and receptive did not materialize, not yet anyway.

Peter remained insistent about having his way, "I cannot allow this, Rabbi Jesus! I cannot let you wash my feet! I know and you know that what you want to do is far beneath you."

Again, Jesus was silent as he hoped to reach Peter and open his mind to a new understanding, "Your feet are dirty. I must be the one to wash them." Jesus looked up at his disciple but Peter would not look at him. It was too much for him to see for now. Jesus spoke to him again with a firmer tone, "Peter...," he waited for his disciple to stop shaking his head and he made eye contact with him again. Peter had heard his name and was expecting Jesus to continue speaking, but Jesus' silence followed again, so he looked down at his Master who then spoke with a firm but quiet voice, "...Peter, if you don't let me wash your feet clean...". Jesus paused to consider an uncertain thought he was having. He determined he must say this as he nodded 'yes' in certainty and then finished his sentence, "...then there is nothing we can share in together, ever again."

Peter's heart fell to his feet and his countenance dropped as he feared that he would be dismissed as a disciple. Quickly he accepted that Jesus would wash his feet saying, "Then yes Lord!" And in his typical enthusiasm he went a bit too far, as he added, "Yes and not only my feet, but wash my hands and my head also."

Jesus chuckled a little in the gladness that he had won Peter over to not only having his feet washed, but also because of his additional offer to let his Lord wash his hands and head. Jesus shook his head 'no' as he smiled and chuckled again to himself, "You bathed in preparation for this meal; you do not need to bathe again. Only the dust from the street on your feet must be washed, and you will be clean again." So Jesus knelt before Peter and washed his feet. Now at the end of this work, Jesus unwrapped the towel he had fastened around his waist and gave it to the servants, who poured water over his hands so that he could wash them before he put his coat back on.

Jesus stood tall at the head of the table next to his couch as the disciples looked at him. "Now all of you are clean, all but one. Every one of you knows that it is the place of the youngest or the lowliest servant to wash the dirt off our feet. But you must understand why I took the place of the youngest and the lowliest servant and washed your feet clean. I am called Rabbi, Master and Lord by you, and rightly so, because this is who I am. But on this holy night I have also become as the youngest among you and as the lowliest servant here. By this, from now on, each of you must follow in living out devoutly the example of my life in your own lives and become as the youngest and lowliest servant to everyone. And not just to each other but for all the people as you serve them in my name. As my servants you are not greater than me but lower. I send you out in my name as messengers who will bring the Gospel of my Kingdom to the world. Remember that you are not greater than the one who sent you to preach and to serve in humility. That is why I have used this holy occasion to first show you that my heart is a servant's heart, and then I explained it to you. This way you will never forget what I have done for you. By my example you must always live in servitude for others, without hesitation. Only then will your service to others be blessed by my Father."

The sun had set and now was the time for the very ritualized Passover meal to begin. The servants waited at the door for Jesus to let them know when to begin bringing out the meal. And so as the Lord nodded to them, they returned carrying small hand towels for everyone, six water pitchers and bowls of water for everyone's ceremonial hand washing. Along with that, they also brought wine chalices and pitchers of wine, bowls with saltwater in them for dipping bitter herbs into, serving plates with parsley and celery, napkins and a plate for each with a stack of three pieces of unleavened bread.

When the table was set Jesus rose to speak, "Light is the symbol of God's very presence among us, and so I kindle the festival lights on this night reminding us that God is always with us." He took an oil lamp and lit all of the candelabras on the table. Then he returned to his place at the head of the table and spoke the first prayer,

"Ba-ruk A-tah Ado-nai Elo-hey-nue Me-lekh
ha-'o-lam a-sher kid-sha-nu B'mi-tzvo-tav
"Blessed are you, O Lord our God, King of the
Universe, who makes us holy by your commandments
v'-tzi va-nu I'-had-lik ner shel shabbot yom tov."
and commands us to light the Festival Lights."

In this meal it is customary to not fill your own wine chalice, but to fill the chalice of the person next to you and to have them do the same for you. And so, the disciples took turns as they shared in filling each other's chalices. With that complete, Jesus spoke to them, "On this night we celebrate the Passover Feast. This is the beginning of a tragic story and the beginning of a wonderful story. On this night Moses spoke the words of the LORD to our ancestors saying, 'I am the LORD, and *I will bring you out* from under the yoke of the Egyptians.' Let us bless the LORD as we drink the cup of our sanctification." Then they all joined in the prayer,

"Blessed are you, O LORD our God, king of the universe,
who has created the fruit of the vine. By your mercy you
have provided us with all things that are necessary for life.
Amen"

And everyone drank their chalices empty.

Jesus said, "Let us wash our hands clean as God has commanded us. As we wash we call upon the LORD to cleanse our hands and hearts."

And all the disciples responded by offering a blessing to the Holy One of Israel,

"Blessed are you, O LORD our God,
King of the Universe,
who makes us holy as we wash our hands."

Again, as it was with filling each other's chalices, now they took turns pouring water over the hands of the person seated next to them. They took care to ensure that the water ran between their fingers and into the bowl below. And then they all dried their own hands with the towels that the servants had provided them.

Jesus spoke again to his disciples, but with words unfamiliar to them from Passover meals of years past, "I have solemnly dedicated myself to eating this Passover with you before I suffer. And I tell you that I will not eat this meal again until all that it holds is fulfilled in me by the unfolding of God's Kingdom on earth."

Some of the disciples spoke to each other in a low chatter, questioning what it was that their Rabbi meant, but oddly enough none of them thought to ask him.

Jesus held up a bowl of saltwater in one hand and a plate of celery in the other saying, "Tonight we eat bitter herbs dipped not once, but twice in saltwater. With the first dipping we remember the tears that were shed and the painful suffering of our people as they endured being tortured as slaves while they were held in bondage in the land of Egypt. With the second dipping we remember that the LORD delivered us from bondage and gave us freedom in the Promised Land."

All the disciples nodded knowingly and looked to each other in affirmation as they recited the blessing;

"Blessed are you, O LORD our God,
Ruler of the Universe,
who creates the fruit of the earth."

Jesus, as the presider at the head of the table, was the first to dip his celery into the saltwater, once, then twice before eating it.

The disciples followed in doing the same. And the attentive servants came into the center of their U-shaped table and removed the plates of bitter herbs and saltwater bowls from the table.

Then began the part of the meal when everyone would share in recalling the history of their people's lives when they lived as slaves.

Jesus began, "In Egypt our people had to leave in haste so they took their dough before it was leavened and put it in their kneading bowls and wrapped it up in their coats. In remembrance of that, there are three pieces of unleavened bread on our plates. This bread is the bread of affliction and pain. So then I ask you, why do we hide the middle piece of bread in our napkins?"

In homes with younger children, they would be the ones that were prompted to answer this question, but there were none present and so the disciples took turns answering the questions that now followed.

John who was at Jesus' side answered first, "When our people were in slavery they never knew when or where their next meal would come from. So they hid some of it in case they needed it."

Now the Lord took from the three pieces of bread the middle piece of unleavened bread and lifted it up for all to see saying, "Now we will hide the middle piece of unleavened bread in our napkin for our dessert." He continued with the story of their people, "Our people groaned because of the harshness of their slavery and they cried out as they suffered. Their cries rose up to God and he heard them, and he recalled his covenant with Abraham, Isaac, and Jacob."

The Passover dinner now called for everyone's wine chalice to be filled. So Jesus and the disciples took turns filling each other's chalices.

Jesus asked the next question saying, "On this night the children of Israel ask, 'What are we celebrating and why must we do it in only this way?'"

Judas' turn was next and so he stated, "We will tell them that this is the Passover sacrifice to the LORD. On this night our ancestors were held in bondage and in bitter lives of slavery to Pharaoh. It was then that the LORD passed over the houses of the Israelites but struck down the first born of the Egyptians. He spared our houses because the blood of the Passover lamb that was sacrificed was put on our doorposts to cover our sins. So our people bowed down and worshiped the LORD. And Moses told the people what the LORD instructed him to say, which was,

'Hear, O Israel: The LORD is our God, the Lord alone. You shall love the LORD your God with all your heart, and with all your soul, and with all your might. Keep these words that I am commanding you today in your heart. Recite them to your children and talk about them when you are at home and when you are away, when you lie down and when you rise. Bind them as a sign on your hand, fix them as an emblem on your forehead, and write them on the doorposts of your house and on your gates.'"

Jesus again asked a question, the third one, "Why is this night different from all the other nights? Why is it that on all other nights during the year we may eat leavened or unleavened bread but on this night we must eat only unleavened bread?"

Now Peter shared the answer, "On all other nights we may eat leavened or unleavened bread, but on this night we can eat only unleavened bread because our ancestors could not wait for their bread to rise when they were fleeing slavery in Egypt. So the unleavened bread was flat and hard when it came out of the oven."

The story continued to be told in spontaneity by all the disciples who each took their turn.

Thomas was next, "Tonight we break our bread to remember the brokenness of our ancestors who lived in slavery; it is the unleavened bread of our affliction and the bread of haste."

Andrew continued, "We break bread to remember when the LORD parted the waters of the Red Sea and delivered our people from Pharaoh's army. This is the bread of our freedom from the bondage that they held us in."

He was followed by James the Greater, "We eat unleavened bread to show that we were a broken people but we are now healing."

Jesus asked the fourth question, "Why is it that on all other nights we eat all kinds of vegetables, but on this night we eat only bitter herbs?"

Mathew was the next to share, "Tonight we will only eat bitter herbs. This is to remind us of the bitterness of slavery and harsh demands that our ancestors endured under their taskmasters in Egypt. We eat them because Pharaoh made life intolerable with harsh labor and the killing of our infants."

Jesus continued with the questions, "Why is it that on all other nights we do not dip our food, but on this night we must dip our food in saltwater, not once but twice?"

To which Phillip replied, "We dip them once in salt water to remember the tears shed by our ancestors as they were held as slaves. We dip them a second time to remember how God delivered them and replaced their bitterness in life by taking away the burdens of slavery and sweetened their lives."

Again Jesus asked, "Why is it that on all the other nights of the year we dine sitting upright or reclining, but on this night we must recline?"

Now it was James the Lessor's turn to answer the question, "We recline because tonight we live as if we are kings at this holy meal. In ancient times only a free person could recline to eat but the slaves had to stand."

Rabbi Jesus continued on asking, "On all the other nights of the year we can eat meat that is roasted, stewed or boiled. But on this night why must we only eat roasted meat?"

Thaddeus answered, "We eat only roasted meat on this night because when our ancestors were delivered from slavery and bondage to Pharaoh, Moses instructed them that the LORD wanted them to quickly prepare their lambs that were sacrificed for their meals. Then he ordered them to take the blood of the lamb and place it on the door posts of their homes. That was a sign to the LORD so he would pass over their homes."

Now Jesus said a blessing;

"Blessed is LORD our God who fulfills his promises,
who is ever faithful to his servants
who put their trust in him."

The Rabbi continued on, "This night is different from all other nights of the year because on this night we remember what God has done for his people, the Israelites." The questions were completed and so they all shared in telling the story of their people beginning with the time of Abraham.

Bartholomew began, "The days of our people began when the God of our Patriarch Abraham appeared to him and said, 'You must leave your homeland and your family, and journey to a land that I will show to you.' So, he left all behind and settled in Haran. After his father's death God told him to move to this country in which we now live. At that time God did not give him any of the land to possess, but he promised to give it to him as his own and to his descendants. Then Abraham's children suffered from a terrible famine that came upon them in the land where Jacob and Rebecca lived. So Jacob and his family journeyed to Egypt where there was food for them to eat. Their family grew very large in numbers and they became a nation in the land of Goshen in Egypt. But Pharaoh, who ruled over Egypt, became fearful of the Israelites and forced them into slavery. He ordered them to work hard.

But our nation continued to flourish in spite of four hundred years of slavery."

As he came near to the end of his portion of their history he looked at Simon the Zealot to indicate he would now continue telling the story, "So Pharaoh ordered that all newborn baby boys of our people be thrown into the Nile River to die. But a Levite mother defied Pharaoh and put her son into a basket and hid him in the reeds of the river. Pharaoh's daughter found him when she went there to bathe. She made him her son and called his name Moses. Moses grew up in the palace as a prince. Later he discovered that he was an Israelite. Then when he saw an Egyptian slave driver beating an Israelite he became very angry and punished the Egyptian by putting him to death. But then he had to flee from Pharaoh's anger over the incident. In the fullness of time God appeared to Moses out of a burning bush in the desert and said to him, 'I am the God of your ancestors, the God of Abraham, the God of Isaac, and the God of Jacob; meaning that as he was faithful with them so also he would be faithful with Moses. The LORD said to him, 'I have seen the suffering that my people are enduring, and their voices have been heard. Now I will visit them and bring them out of bondage and slavery. I will rescue them and bring them into the land long ago promised to my servant Abraham, into a land flowing with milk and honey.' So Moses went to Pharaoh and asked for freedom for our people. But Pharaoh hardened his heart against God. Each time Pharaoh was asked, he refused to grant them freedom, so God brought many terrible plagues against him. On that final night God said that he would pass through all the land of Egypt and strike down every first born, of men and of animals, and bring his judgment against them. The LORD told Moses that each household must sacrifice a lamb and put its blood on their doorposts as a sign, so that when he saw it, he would pass over our people and the plague of death would not touch them."

Jesus now began an especially reverent part of their remembrances as he spoke, "Tonight we do not rejoice over the destruction of our enemies, but instead we join with them as we too, mourn the losses they suffered when they refused to obey the LORD. Now we will dip a finger into our wine and allow a drop to fall on our plates for each of the ten plagues as I name them."

And in the centuries old custom, everyone repeatedly dipped their right index finger into their chalice and then allowed a drop of wine to fall onto their plates for each of the plagues as Jesus spoke;

"The plague of the water of the Nile turning into blood.
The plague of swarming frogs upon all the land.
The plague of gnats upon all the land.
The plague of swarming flies upon all the land.
The plague of disease on all of their livestock.
The plague of festering boils upon all the people.
The plague of hail and thunder upon the land.
The plague of devouring locusts.
The plague of darkness upon all their land.
The plague of the death of their firstborns."

Jesus concluded this part of the observances with the words, "God showed great signs and powerful deeds through his servant Moses and freed his people. He brought them out of bondage and slavery in Egypt through the parting of the waters of the Red Sea and gave them this land that we now possess as our homeland."

Now the servants who were waiting to hear those words came in with several large serving platters of roasted lamb that they had carved and placed them on the table.

Jesus looked to his disciples and spoke the words, "Beginning with the day of the fall, God promised to provide redemption for the sins of the world. In those days, God warned Adam and Eve that on the day they eat of the forbidden fruit of the tree of the knowledge of good and evil that they would die. And when that day came God offered up an innocent lamb to die in their place for their sins so that their lives could be spared. When our people were slaves in Egypt, when the days of Pharaoh's judgment had come upon him, God returned Pharaoh's sins back upon him and required the life of the first born from all of his people. Our ancestors were spared from that judgment because the LORD had instructed them to sacrifice a lamb for their protection and the forgiveness of their sins. The blood of this lamb was placed upon the door posts of their homes as a covering for their sins, and the LORD passed over them because their sins were covered over."

Next there was a traditional hymn from the Psalms that was sung responsively. Jesus began and led while the disciples, in harmony, responded their reply.

"Praise the LORD! Praise, O servants of the LORD;
praise the name of the LORD."

"Hallelujah."

"Blessed be the name of the LORD
from this time on and forevermore."

"Hallelujah."

*"From the rising of the sun to its setting
the name of the LORD is to be praised."*

"Hallelujah."

*"The LORD is high above all nations,
and his glory above the heavens."*

"Hallelujah."

*"Who is like the LORD our God,
who is seated on high,
who looks far down on the heavens and the earth?"*

"Hallelujah."

*"He raises the poor from the dust, and lifts the
needy from the ash heap, to make them sit with princes,
with the princes of his people."*

"Hallelujah."

*"He gives the barren woman a home,
making her the joyous mother of children.
Praise the LORD!"*

"Hallelujah."

*"When Israel went out from Egypt,
the house of Jacob from a people of strange language,"*

"Hallelujah."

"Judah became God's sanctuary, Israel his dominion."

"Hallelujah."

"The sea looked and fled; Jordan turned back."

"Hallelujah."

"The mountains skipped like rams, the hills like lambs."

"Hallelujah."

"Why is it, O sea, that you flee?
O Jordan, that you turn back?"

"Hallelujah."

"O mountains, that you skip like rams?
O hills, like lambs?"

"Hallelujah."

"Tremble, O earth, at the presence of the LORD,
at the presence of the God of Jacob,
who turns the rock into a pool of water,
the flint into a spring of water."

"Hallelujah."

And now as their hymn was ended they all blended their voices singing in harmony,

"Ah, ah, amen"[14]

Their meal continued with Jesus reciting the scripture, "On this night Moses spoke the words of the LORD to our ancestors saying, 'I am the LORD, and I will *deliver you from slavery.*' Let us bless the LORD as we drink the cup of our deliverance." And together they all offered the blessing to the LORD;

"Blessed are you, O Lord our God, king of the universe,
who has created the fruit of the vine.
By your mercy you have provided us with
all things that are necessary for life. Amen"

In unison everyone lifted their chalices and drank them empty. And again Jesus offered a blessing to the LORD for the unleavened bread;

"Blessed are you, O LORD our God, King of the universe,
who brings forth bread from the earth.
Blessed are you, O LORD our God,
King of the universe,
who has sanctified us with your commandments,
and commanded us to eat unleavened bread."

With that part of the meal completed, the servants in waiting now carried in the rest of the food, the roasted lamb, the bitter herbs and the charoset, in and placed the platters on the table.

Jesus looked to his disciples as he lifted the charoset mixture for all to see and spoke these words about it, "Tonight we eat the mix of fruit, nuts and honey with our

---

[14] Taken from Psalms 113-116

unleavened bread to remind us that our ancestors were ruthlessly forced to perform harsh labor by mixing mortar and making bricks for the construction of Pharaoh's buildings." Then he lifted the bowl of charoset higher before setting it down. He broke off a piece of his unleavened bread and used a knife to spread the charoset on it and then added another piece over it to make a sandwich of it before eating it. The disciples now also did the same. And with that completed the meal progressed to its next stage.

Chapter Thirty-One
One Will Betray

The Passover meal now progressed into a time for dining without any more formalities until the close of the meal. This was the time for the disciples and their Rabbi to simply relax and enjoy each other's company, conversation and the generous hospitality of their benefactor.

Most of their conversations spoke about times past and times to come. They recalled with great joy the surprised, and even pleasantly shocked, faces of people who Jesus had instantly healed and worked miracles for, cleansing lepers, given sight to, restored their hearing and making the lame to walk. With it being the Passover they, of course, made connections between the days of their ancestors' desert wanderings in Sinai and the ministry of Jesus. There was the miraculous provision by God of food in those days, the manna which was bread from heaven and the quail that they ate. Though Jesus did not provide them with any birds to eat, he did provide food by multiplying loaves of bread and a few fish for many thousands to eat. They recalled the parting of the Red Sea as Pharaoh's army pursued them, and though Jesus had not parted any waters, he did save them all from death by calming the raging storm and walking upon the water.

This was the third Passover the disciples had celebrated with the Rabbi and while these feasts were amongst the most memorable of their lives, everyone would agree that this one was the greatest of them all. At this one they all had the highest hopes that their Rabbi, their Messiah, would soon restore those golden years when King David ruled their land and their people. They dreamed about having the Roman's leave, taking their pagan ways with them. They all truly longed to be free of their taxes, laws and of their very presence.

Now Jesus gestured to his disciples that he wanted their attention so he could speak to them again. The disciples' voices fell silent while they motioned to each other to turn and attend their Rabbi. Jesus looked across the table to view each one. Seeing that they were ready to listen to him he appeared to be summoning his courage to speak. As they looked to their Rabbi he opened his mouth to speak but, for the first time ever, they saw him struggling to say something. They were listening. Jesus was supposed to be saying something, but there was nothing but silence. The disciples grew concerned at this very unusual occurrence. What they saw was equally unknown to their Rabbi, that he would be unable to speak to them. Jesus struggled to disengage from his effort to speak and then he became most sorrowful and troubled. It was then clear to everyone that whatever he was going to say was so terrible that he could not face it for the moment. Their Master trembled with his hands, his arms and shoulders, and it looked as if he might collapse into weeping as he had at Lazarus' tomb. Throughout this minute of uncertainty and struggle the disciples looked to each other and wondered if they should say or do something, but of what would that be their minds were void.

Jesus regained his composure and then spoke with great certainty, "I must tell everyone with all truthfulness that tonight one of you will betray me into the hands of the chief priests."

The quiet and rapturous delight that had only a few minutes ago filled the room was suddenly lost as if the death of someone had just been announced. It was such a shock that the disciples felt like they were doubly frozen in that moment of time. If it was hard enough to imagine that anyone would betray the Lord; then it was all but impossible to imagine that one of their own should be the one who would do this. As they slowly regained their poise and were able to come to terms with this terrible prophecy, they felt like they were being weighted down, as though they were wearing heavy water soaked robes in the sea. Some reacted strongly with deeply felt emotions, some made threats to kill the man who would sink so low to do this. Others then wondered if it could somehow be them, or who among them it might be.

Judas swiftly grabbed his wine chalice, gulped hurriedly and swallowed hard as if he had just had an awful bout of heartburn that suddenly came up to scorch his throat. Then he reached behind his sash to grab the ministry's coin purse and his own newly acquired coin purse, and held them tightly, as if he were fearful they had been misplaced. He continued to hold them tightly in the hopes that somehow the money would bring him comfort after the distressing words Jesus had just said. But neither the coin purses nor the wine could sooth his troubles. Still, worse, a frightful thing came upon him, one that he had never known of before or experienced. It was a sudden, mind gripping flashback. He saw himself at a distance when he was in the Temple talking with the well-dressed man who had boasted so much about his money and his affluent life. He saw himself and the way he had clenched the ministry purse then, as he lamented that it was not completely full. The flashback made his heart nearly stop when he saw the rich man put his arm out for him to take hold of. He saw for the first time what he was blinded to then. He saw the movement of the snake, its mouth open, and its two-pronged tongue testing the air. So terrible was the flashback that it was all he could do to keep himself from screaming in uncontrollable horror, as he watched its twisting form quickly racing up his sleeve and then disappear over his own heart. Judas looked about the room fearful that he might give himself away somehow and then be put to an unbearable end at the hands of another disciple, like Peter or Simon the Zealot. His hands began to shake and he began to suffer from a massive headache as he feared that suspicion would fall on him.

The rest of the disciples were also having very strong reactions to the announcement that one of them would betray their Lord. They looked each other over with sharp distrusting eyes as they tried to care for their own flood of heartbreaking emotions that were surging through their veins. They each looked at the others to see if the betrayer would admit to his guilt and they asked each other, "Is it you?"

Even though Jesus had not called for anything to be done about this offense against him, Peter readied himself for action. He determined to take this matter into his own hands, if only he could discover who it was. The tall disciple pounded his fist hard on the table top, but in the trauma of the moment no one noticed it. He stood to attention and then turned to the swords on the wall. He was fully ready to pull one down and put it to use. He spoke out loudly, "I remember you said something about this during our travels, that you would be betrayed and put to death. But I didn't understand it then, and even now I can't believe it is possible, not by anyone counted among us here." He looked down at each disciple one by one and with slow, careful consideration. But no one looked at him as if they were the one that he sought, and no one admitted to being behind this terrible plot.

Then all of the disciples looked to Jesus to see if he would say something more or give some sign of who it was. But nothing more was said, not by Jesus and certainly not by the one who would betray him.

Judas was able to conceal his guilt well enough for the time being, and because of his contorted heart he was even able to live in moments of complete denial to himself of his guilt. In his twisted thoughts, even though he knew he was the one, he also had thoughts of wondering who among them could this possibly be. In the contradiction of his deceit he even wondered if someone else also had their own clandestine plan to betray Jesus. He was not worried about trying to put up an innocent appearance. His biggest problem was struggling with the horrid flashback that he had just seen of himself.

And now he was made captive to another flashback. He saw himself from a short distance away, when he was with the high priest, and he asked him, "What will you pay me if I do this for you?" Judas' stomach suddenly tightened, and a fearfulness gripped him in a way he had never imagined possible. He bent forward and reached for his stomach, as if touching it would bring him some relief. He looked down and saw that his belly was bloated and it extended out significantly. But for him there was no relief possible, not for this, not for anything anymore.

The other disciples were so preoccupied with themselves that they did not notice how Judas' reaction was very unlike any of their own. Some had broken down into tears, some queried the others methodically, and a few sat speechless, mindlessly staring into space. Peter continued to look everyone over again and again, slowly, meticulously and with great misgivings. There Judas sat, and though his distress was uniquely his own, no one was able to discern by it that he was the guilty one among them.

Bartholomew raised his hand to gain everyone's attention and spoke loudly, "Whoever could this be? I demand you confess yourself to me now!" But no one did.

Thomas, the elderly gentleman, in disbelief questioned everyone, "How could this be one of us, with all that we have been through together?"

And Matthew stood up and insisted in his disbelief, "No! I cannot imagine that any one of us would do such a thing."

Phillip stood to attention, agreed with him and questioned the possibility of it insisting, "Why would anyone do such a thing?"

Simon the Zealot, who had taken pride in the idea that he was in all things vigilantly watching out for Jesus' safety, was ready to manhandle the traitor, "Who is going to do this? Declare yourself to me right now! I demand it of you!"

And Peter joined him in his militant stance, "Why must this happen? I am going to put an end to this right now. Who among you is it?"

Judas was nearly compelled by their demands to offer himself up, so intense was the effect of those demanding to know who among them it was. But the urge to give himself up was undone as he was struck again by a gripping flashback.

Suddenly, as before, he was taken to the moment when Caiaphas spoke to him face to face saying, "Judas, we have decided to make you an offer for your help. Thirty pieces of silver."

Judas shook his head saying, "No, no, no!" in the hopes of shaking the flashback from his mind. But it would not leave him. It went on and on, flooding him with terrifying emotions. He saw himself up close, he looked into his own eyes and smiled as he said, "That will be enough, so long as I am paid now." Then he felt the hand of Caiaphas again on his shoulder. But this time it was not a kind or gentle touch as it had first been. It was a weight beyond what he could bear, a weight that crippled him down and would not let him go, even though he longed for it. He saw up close, too close, Caiaphas' face when he had said his final words to Judas; words that now echoed over and over again in his ears like the terrible screech that vultures make when fighting over a rancid carcass. It was enough to make him nearly collapse to the floor as he saw the high priest putting his hand over his heart, holding the money bag of thirty pieces of silver and saying, "Peace be upon you." He wanted to scream over the horror of it all as he saw the moment when the snake moved from under Caiaphas's garment, and as he reached out his hand to pass the money onto Judas the creature's ugly head reappeared out of his cuff. Judas saw himself reaching out to accept the silver, and the snake moved back up his sleeve and returned to his blackened heart. This was too real for him. He batted away at his arm as he tried to fight off the snake that appeared in his flashback. But it was to no avail. It was too late for that. It was only a flashback of what he had already condemned himself to do.

The room began to return to some order and already Jesus, John and several other disciples had returned to reclining on their coaches. Peter breathed a sigh hoping to bring relief to himself, but it did nothing to help him. He reasoned, *'Since Jesus has not said who it is and the traitor has not revealed himself despite the demands placed on him to do so, then perhaps John would be able to persuade Jesus to tell him privately'*. He turned slowly and spoke quietly into John's ear, "I cannot stand this intolerable mystery of not knowing. Something must be done. Our Master must not be betrayed. John, privately ask him who he is talking about and then confide with me in secret."

John gave it a moment's thought and then nodded a barely detectable yes. He turned back toward his Master and leaned in very close to his side and casually rested his head on Jesus' chest. He spoke with calm, "Lord, show me whoever could this be that you spoke of?"

With John still leaning on his chest Jesus whispered privately into his ear, "Watch for this sign. It will be the one that I give this morsel of bread to when I have dipped it. Do nothing against him and say nothing to the others."

Jesus looked about the room to see that everyone had surprisingly moved on from the distressful news of a betrayer among them to casual conversation. No one seemed to be looking at him, other than John, and so Jesus dipped a piece of bread into the charoset and kindly gave it to Judas by placing it into his mouth. No one else noticed. Why would they? This was commonly done between friends at a meal.

Judas received it with a broken smile, a smile that was not fully able to conceal his distress or his guilt. He had hopes that Jesus' gesture might bring him a feeling of relief, but then he was overtaken by a gripping cramp in his swollen belly, and a final flashback of himself and Caiaphas chuckling together as they parted company. However Judas knew no peace though he longed for it as never before. Such a thing for him was no longer possible. He was accursed, and his demise was of his own doing.

Jesus turned and spoke again to John, "David prophesied rightly by the Holy Spirit, 'He who ate my bread has lifted his heel against me.'"

Judas overhead the Master's words and looking directly into his eyes spoke to him, "Is it me that you are speaking of now?"

It might be said that Judas was courageous for stepping out and asking that question. But the fluctuation of his voice did not sound courageous. It sounded fake, as though he was lying and doing a poor job of it at that. Jesus looked at him and said nothing.

Judas spoke again, "Rabbi, it can't be me can it?"

Jesus looked directly into his eyes but remained silent. The Master would not lie to Judas, but he was not going to accuse him either. He was going to let Judas do that for himself.

Judas attempted a lighthearted laugh but it came out forced and phony, "Ha, ha, why would you say that about me? You trust me."

Jesus did not respond, and so Judas asked him, "Is it me Lord?" His face grew contorted and disturbed as he spoke those words and it was clear to John that he had given himself away.

Jesus now spoke truthfully to Judas, "Yes Judas, it is you."

Now Judas worried for his life; about what Simon Peter or Simon the Zealot might do to him if they learned of it. Judas knew about the swords hanging on the wall, but what really worried him more was what they would do with their bare hands against him. He worried about a slow death or of having his neck broken and an agonizing death at their hands.

Jesus spoke on but it was not at all what Judas expected to hear, "So what you have made plans to do, go now and do it quickly because the night is upon us."

Judas understood the words, but they were strange to

him. He fully expected that Jesus would reveal him to the rest. He did not ask, though he wondered to himself, 'why didn't Jesus reveal to the others that it was me after announcing that it was one among them? Why didn't he ask me to back out of my plans, and why did he send me on my way?' Judas did not seek to understand Jesus on those matters, and he did not seek to defend his own actions. He heard Jesus' words to "Go now and do it" and that was all that he needed to hear. This gave him a twisted sense that he wasn't doing anything wrong, and a doubly twisted feeling that it was somehow acceptable that he was betraying the Lord. He was glad to get out into the night air where he hoped he might find some relief for himself. Glad to get away from the room where he had just suffered the greatest distress of his life. He rose like a clumsy old man and his hands shook with palsy. As he came to the door he was forced, as before, to endure another dementing flashback of when he was walked to the door by the high priest after he had been paid the thirty pieces of silver. Then he pushed open the door and stepped out, vanishing into the darkness of the night.

Chapter Thirty-Two
The Body and Blood

The Passover meal was now nearly completed. But it was only Jesus who knew that he was more than the presider of the meal. He was the fulfillment of the meal. Once he had finished, his life was going to be sacrificed, just as the lamb they had eaten had been sacrificed. And in bringing the meal to its fulfillment, so also, he now shared a small part of the mystery that it held within.

At the beginning of the meal a piece of the unleavened bread, the middle piece of three, was hidden away in his napkin for this very purpose. Jesus removed it and presented it for all to see, and then blessed the bread saying,

"This is the unleavened bread of
our ancestors' pain and affliction."

Now his eyes turned heavenward,

"Blessed are you, O LORD our God,
King of the universe,
who brings forth bread from the earth.
Blessed are you, O LORD our God,
King of the universe,
who has sanctified us with your commandments,
and commanded us to eat unleavened bread."

With that said he lifted the bread up in both hands with his arms fully extended heavenward. The blessing continued,

"Worthy are you alone the LORD our God
of all creation. By your power you sustain us
and all living things with the grain of the sown field.
Amen"

These words were familiar to all of his disciples; they had been hearing them yearly on this occasion for all of their lives.

What was new to them now unfolded. Jesus again showed the bread to his disciples and said these words that would be memorialized. He spoke now with words never before heard at a Passover meal, "Take this bread and divide it among yourselves." The Master broke the bread, took a piece for himself and then passed one half to his right and the other half to his left for all of his disciples to share. Once the bread was passed Jesus lifted his piece up for all to see as he spoke again,

"This is my body which is given for you;
eat of it, all of you.
Do this for the remembrance of me."

The disciples gladly received and ate the bread from their Rabbi, which they saw as an unexpected blessing upon them.

Again Jesus led them in the Passover Feast observance saying,

"Moses spoke the words of the LORD
to our ancestors saying,
'I am the LORD, I will redeem you with
an outstretched arm and with great judgments.'

Let us bless the Lord as we drink the cup of our redemption."

The disciples offered the response in unison,

"Blessed are you, O LORD our God,
king of the universe,
who has created the fruit of the vine.
By your mercy you have provided
us with all things that are necessary for life.
Amen"

Jesus now lifted a large serving pitcher of wine heavenward, holding it as high as his arms could reach. Again he spoke words that had never before been heard,

"This cup that is poured out for
you is the new covenant in my blood,
which will be shed for you and for
all people who will believe in me
for the forgiveness of their sin."

Then, according to the custom, Jesus filled the chalice of the disciple who was next to him, which was John's, and the wine was passed until everyone's chalice was filled, as each disciple poured for the one next to him.

Jesus, with all solemnity and sincerity, raised his cup for all to see and spoke,

"This cup is the new covenant of my blood which is shed
for the remission of your sins. Drink of it, all of you.
For I tell you, I will not drink again of this fruit of the vine
until that day when I drink it anew with you

in the coming of my Father's Kingdom.
Do this for the remembrance of me."

Now he drank his chalice empty and the disciples followed as they drank their chalices empty. The final part of the meal now unfolded. This was a hymn that they sang responsively. Jesus began and led while the disciples, in harmony, responded;

"Let us give thanks to the LORD, for he is good; for his steadfast love endures forever! Let Israel say,"

"His steadfast love endures forever."

"Let the house of Aaron say,"

"His steadfast love endures forever."

"Let those who fear the LORD say,"

"His steadfast love endures forever."

"Out of my distress I called on the LORD; "

"The LORD answered me and set me free."

"The LORD is on my side; I will not fear."

"What can man do to me?"

"The LORD is on my side as my helper;"

"I shall look in triumph on those who hate me."

*"It is better to take refuge in the
LORD than to trust in man."*

*"It is better to take refuge in the
LORD than to trust in princes."*

*"All nations surrounded me;
in the name of the LORD I cut them off!"*

*"They surrounded me, surrounded me on every
side; in the name of the LORD I cut them off!"*

*"I was pushed hard, so that I was falling,
but the LORD helped me."*

*"The LORD is my strength and my song;
he has become my salvation."*

"Glad songs of salvation are in the tents of the righteous:"

*"The right hand of the LORD does valiantly,
The right hand of the LORD exalts,
the right hand of the LORD does valiantly!"*

*"I shall not die, but I shall live,
and recount the deeds of the LORD."*

*"Open to me the gates of righteousness,
that I may enter through them
and give thanks to the LORD."*

"This is the gate of the LORD;

the righteous shall enter through it."

"I thank you that you have answered
me and have become my salvation."

"The stone that the builders rejected
has become the cornerstone."

"This is the LORD's doing;
it is marvelous in our eyes."

"This is the day that the LORD has made;
let us rejoice and be glad in it."

"Save us, we pray, O LORD!
O LORD, we pray, give us success!"

"Blessed is he who comes in the name of the LORD!
We bless you from the house of the LORD."

"The LORD is God, and he has
made his light to shine upon us."

"Bind the Festal Sacrifice with cords,
up to the horns of the altar!"

"You are my God, and I will give thanks to you;
you are my God; I will extol you."

"Oh give thanks to the LORD, for he is good;
for his steadfast love endures forever!"

Then they all sang together,

"The name of the LORD be blessed
from now until the end of the age of all the ages.
Let us bless him of whose gifts we have partaken:
Blessed be the LORD our God of whose gifts we have
partaken, and by whose goodness we exist. Amen"[15]

All the disciples took delight in the wonderful feelings that had been kindled in them over the remembrance of God's great deliverance received by their ancestors': the freedom from centuries of the harshest treatment a people could endure. They reveled in the memory of the signs and wonders God wrought and the gift of their inheritance, which was the promised land, flowing with milk and honey. For all of them, life was at its greatest summit at this feast. They found courage in their history. It gave them thoughts of what they longed to experience in their own time. The hand of God upon their mighty prophet, they hoped that in their day they would see the full restoration of their ancient Kingdom, as it was in those golden years of David and Solomon. Their stomachs were full, their hearts were strong and their hopes for their people were filled with courage.

---

[15] Taken from Psalms 113-116

Chapter Thirty-Three
Bring These Swords

The Passover meal was complete, and the disciples moved about freely in the upper room and even ventured out into the courtyard of their Master's generous benefactor. They all enjoyed the rich and warm feelings that had been generated that night. In the quiet of the night they relaxed with full bellies and full hearts.

Peter spoke with the Rabbi, "Jesus, you came into the Golden Gate as a victor on Sunday. Then on Monday you cleansed the Temple of those corrupt practices. That was glorious. All the people supported you and shouted your praises. The time is now right. Many of the people believe that you are the Messiah. So, I have been wanting to know, will you restore the rule of our Kingdom to Israel again now?"

Jesus answered him, "This morning, when I sent you and John to prepare for the Passover, what did you do first?"

Peter gladly answered him, "Even though they had already cleansed it on Monday according to the Law, John and I cleansed the upper room of leaven again."

"Yes, you cleansed it of leaven to prepare it for the Passover. And on Monday I cleansed God's house, the Temple, of its unrighteous leaven when I drove out those who exchanged money and sold animals so that it, too, was prepared for the Passover. Now, tonight we remembered how God delivered his people from bondage and slavery to Pharaoh. But you need to realize that there is a far greater oppressor in everyone's life than the Egyptians ever were over our people."

Peter enthusiastically spoke out, "The emperor!"

But as quickly as Peter said, 'the emperor' Jesus spoke without a fraction of a second passing, "No. Not the Roman emperor."

Peter stepped back in surprise and was, for one of those rare times in his life, speechless.

Jesus explained himself, "There is a worse oppressor whose relentless grip goes far beyond the frontiers of the Roman Empire's reach. In this world not all the nations are subject to an emperor. But the sons and daughters of all men are slaves and in bondage to sin, every last one. I have come into the world to bring freedom to every person from the worst of all tyrants. I have come to bring deliverance and freedom from sin and death, from the grave and from Satan's tyranny."

Peter listened to his every word without moving even an inch other than to mildly move his head as unknowing. He concentrated on all that he was being told. He focused hard, but it seemed as if Jesus was speaking in a language unbeknown to him.

Jesus understood the difficulty that Peter could not overcome. But the evening was passing and there was no time for him to go over it again or explain it to him in another way. Jesus took the conversation a different direction because the hour was growing late.

He looked at Peter and spoke to him as a close friend, "Simon Peter, … Peter, you must listen to my words and be forewarned. Satan himself has appeared before God's throne in heaven and made demands before the Council of God just as he once did so he could attempt to destroy the life of God's servant, Job."

Peter heard his words, but they were very difficult for him to comprehend, so he said, "What is this you are telling me, Rabbi Jesus?"

His Master continued, "My friend, seizing the life of the son of perdition who will betray me this night is not enough for Satan's unquenchable appetite. This time he has demanded the lives of all my disciples for himself. He wants to brutally thrash all of you with a winnowing fork, like wheat that is beaten and thrown into the wind to remove its chaff, so that he can rip you from your faith in me and the salvation that I will bring to all the people of the earth."

Peter was surprised to feel the beginnings of tears welling up in his eyes, and his mind wandered to images of what he would have to endure. "I have always followed you faithfully, my Lord. Why would such a fate befall me now? Why does it have to come to any of your disciples? Won't I be spared this by simply following you? Isn't that enough?"

Jesus could not spare him or any of his disciples from this distress, but he could give Peter a hope and the means to his future, "Just as you have believed in me, believe in me still, and believe in me always, Simon Peter. For as certain as the night has fallen, so also this evil will rise up against you, you and all of your brothers here. But know that I have prayed for all of you so that your faith will not fail you."

Peter protested his interests, "I have given my life to you! I have followed you more than all these! I will go with you to all places, to prison or even to death for you, my Lord!"

Jesus spoke to him with a gentle but firm resolve as he shook his head 'no', "Where I am going you cannot follow me. But afterward, remember this, that when I rise you will follow me again."

Peter was again near the point of shedding tears, bitter tears over the thought of being separated from his Master. "Lord, where are you going?" he pleaded. "Jesus, just tell me now, why I can't follow you? You know that I left my boats to follow you and that I will follow you still." Peter's tears began to fall slowly down his face and to the floor below, "I will lay down my life for you."

Jesus spoke to him as his Lord, "Know that while it is still night you will hear the rooster crowing, but not until you have three times denied knowing me."

Peter tried to man himself up and retain his composure. He wiped away his tears and stood at his tallest, took in a deep breath and filled out his chest, and with solemn pride spoke in his own defense, "I will never turn away from following you; I will never deny you my Lord. How then can I be so humbled by a boasting rooster who does not know that the morning is not yet come?" His head became cocky as he asserted his devotion, "I will never in my life turn away from following you, and I know this with all my heart." He bowed as he pledged, "I will never, no never deny you, my Lord and Master!" Peter lifted his chin high and his head darted about sharply as looked around the upper room at all the disciples. Then he rose up onto his toes and back down again, as he made it clear that he would not be moved from the assertions he had made about his fidelity.

Jesus was disappointed that Peter did not take the difficult news as he intended, so he spoke to him with a different tone. "This will not happen as an end to your faith, but that by it you will know from whence comes your faith and strength. When I return the time will come for you to turn to me again, and when it does, know that I will not send you away or reject you. I chose you and I will restore you to faithfulness. Remember this."

Jesus now turned and gestured to the other disciples and said to Peter, "When you have turned again you must help your brothers so that they will also turn and believe in me again."

Jesus took Peter by the hands and, standing directly in front of him, looked him in the eyes and commanded him, "Remember this Simon."

Jesus looked across the room at his disciples and, knowing that they would leave for Gethsemane soon, he spoke to them all, "In the past I sent you out, without money, without a bag for your needs, not even sandals for your feet. Even so poorly equipped, did you have need of anything as you traveled?"

Thomas answered, "We lacked nothing my Lord."

Matthew added, "All that we needed was provided for us by people we ministered to."

And then James the Lessor shared, "They were more than glad to open their homes to us and give us whatever we needed."

Jesus smiled widely and knowingly said, "And it was right for them to provide for you, because you are worthy of your wages." Now the Lord's demeanor took on a most serious sound, "But from now on each of you must take both a purse with money and a bag for all that you will need."

The disciples nodded in agreement.

Again, Jesus asserted himself, "From now on you are going to find that your ministry in my name is not going to be as well received as it once was, because this scripture will soon be fulfilled in my life, 'And he was numbered with the transgressors.' And many will think of me as an outlaw and dishonorable. Now when you go out you must arm yourselves by carrying a sword for your protection. So, if you don't already have one, then you must sell what you do have and buy one."

Peter and John's ears picked up quickly what Jesus said about owning a sword. Peter spoke quickly, "Master, there are two swords here." He walked straight to the wall where they were hanging and took them down as he looked at Jesus.

The Lord looked at him and replied, "Two are enough for now, bring them both."

Peter moved with confidence as he placed one into the side of his sash so that it was hidden from view under his coat. With the other one in hand he spoke, as he looked around the room at the rest, "I found that this one has a fine blade when I handled it this morning." His eyes stopped as they came to the youngest disciple, "And John, I know that you are familiar with how to use one of these, take it for yourself." Peter looked him straight in the eyes and nodded with confidence as if the two were now soldiers dressed for battle, should one break out.

Jesus spoke to his disciples again saying, "Remember, all of you, that I did not come to be waited on by servants or by my disciples. I came to be a servant by giving my life as a ransom for many. It is time for all of us to get up on our feet and make our way to Gethsemane."

The disciples looked about the room to find where they had stored their traveling bags and staffs for walking. Several took oil lanterns to light the way. Then they all gathered at the door with Jesus in their midst, and one by one they went out into the night.

Chapter Thirty-Four
In the Garden

There was a full moon. That was a given because it was Passover, which was set by the lunar calendar. But even with the brightness of the night the disciples still carried lanterns as they followed their Rabbi down the city streets, out of the Golden Gate east of the Holy City, down across the Kidron valley and up the slope past the cemetery and into the Garden of Gethsemane, which was on the Mount of Olives.

This was not an unfamiliar end to the day for the disciples. They had spent many nights camped out in the garden over their years of discipleship. It was a well-known and convenient location to spend the night, and as such, on this night it was very full of pilgrims who had come for the Passover.

Along the way Jesus continued to instruct his disciples, giving them his final instructions before he would be betrayed and arrested. As they neared to the place where they always stayed, they saw many other campsites which were filled with slumbering families. Soon they reached their place and the disciples began to bed down for the night. They were all very tired after the long day and the Passover feast had made them sleepy. Now was the time for them to settle in and sleep, or so they thought.

Jesus spoke out, but not with a quiet or hushed voice as they would have expected in that hour. No, he spoke with a new tone in his voice, one they had never heard before. His voice was both demanding and curt, "Now listen to me, all of you!" He looked around to be sure he had everyone's attention but his neck was taut and his movements were jerky. "Do any of you realize that when the sun set this evening that evil arose, and its desire is to take my life? Tonight you must not sleep, not even a wink, not even for one minute." Jesus looked them over to ensure they were still listening to him. Some of his disciples struggled hard to keep their eyes open because they were so near to falling asleep. "Peter, James and John, you three come with me. The rest of you stay where you are. Stay awake and, above all things, pray for me and for yourselves. Of all nights, on this night I need you to be vigilant and pray the night through! Pray until the dawn comes. Pray earnestly that you will not have to come into my time of trial."

The disciples looked around at each other as unaware; they privately wondered why this urgent demand of them was made at this hour. Jesus looked at them, staring and looking impatient. So, they assumed their positions for prayers. Some stood, others sat, but as always, Thomas insisted on kneeling for prayer.

Jesus turned to walk away and then motioned for Peter, James and John to come with him. As he moved forward he began to moan, and then to weep, and it reminded the three disciples of the way their Rabbi was when he went to Lazarus' tomb. Their Master's legs grew suddenly weak and so he said, "Peter come here, my strength is failing and I need your help." Jesus put his arm over Peter's tall shoulders and Peter wrapped his arm around Jesus' waist to help him walk. James and John rushed to come closer and James went to his Rabbi's left side to help him walk. John walked at Peter's side and carried a lantern to light the way. Then Jesus said, "This is far enough. Here, let me walk the rest of the way on my own. Thank you for your help."

The inner three stood by in earnest, not knowing what to do. Their Master had never suffered with this kind of weakness before. The other disciples were not far from them, and as they heard the sound of Jesus' voice they turned their heads to listen. They could hear their Master weeping, and the sound of him talking to himself. But this did not seem like something he would normally do, talking to himself aloud. They looked at each other in uncertainty and wondered what was going on. They could see Jesus in the shadows of the night, and though the moon was bright, the many olive trees in the garden cast a certain darkness around them. The inner three could see that their Rabbi had tears running down his face and that his eyes had grown puffy. Peter wondered if he should say something to him, like asking if he was okay or if he needed anything. Though he opened his mouth, there were no words that he could muster as he looked on.

Jesus instructed them, "You must remain here next to this olive tree and begin your prayers because this night is like no other night. You must all keep watch in the night over me. Don't fall asleep. Not tonight. I am severely distressed with grief, more than my words can begin to say. My very soul is being crushed under the weight of what I am asked by my Father to do."

He began to shake and it was clear he was still having trouble standing. Even though they had eaten, and even though he was used to walking many miles in a day, he now appeared to be exhausted. So strong were the effects of his emotions that they radiated from him onto these three, covering them like a heavy blanket that weighs a person down as they sleep. Jesus turned away from them ever so slowly, like in a dream, and it was surreal to them. The three were momentarily paralyzed as they stood by and watched their Master walk a crooked line until he stumbled and fell to his hands and knees. For some reason they, too, felt suddenly dizzy and so they sat on the ground, but such was their state that it did not seem strange to them that they did so.

They listened to his prayer, "Oh, God! ...". His breathing was labored as though it took every bit of his strength and every bit of his concentration with each breath. His shaking now calmed, but it was replaced with what looked to them as gut-wrenching pain consuming him. Jesus prayed continually. The three could only hear bits and pieces of it. They saw Jesus taking hold of the grassy turf, and driving his fingers deeply through its roots and down to the soil beneath. He took a handful of the earth and lifted it up, but then, as his hands trembled, the turf crumbled from his grasp and fell like dust back onto the earth.

His neck was incredibly tense, making it nearly impossible for him to turn his head easily. He managed to look heavenward but he had to strain hard to look upward. His face was contracted and full of grief. He pounded the ground with fists over and over again as he prayed. "Abba! I beseech thee dear Father, let this hour pass me by. It is already too much for me to bear up under, that you have asked me to let them spill my blood unto death. How will I endure through it when this is already a crushing weight that consumes me? With each breath it is as though my spirit is already near to departing from my flesh. Why must I have to agonize here before my betrayer comes? Isn't it enough that you have asked me to surrender my life into the hands of sinners? So then why must this piece of agony be added?"

Jesus glanced over to the olive tree where he had left his three disciples only to see that they had already fallen asleep. This weighed deeply on him, so he found the strength to rise again to his feet. Walking past Peter, James and John he went to stand between them and the other eight as he called out to them all, "Peter, James, John!" His voice grew still louder as he called out again, "Thomas, Matthew, Simon, all of you!" His voice conveyed a message that was stronger than his words, and the disciples heard that they must waken and give their Rabbi their attention. "How can you be sleeping at this hour? Couldn't you stay awake to pray for me...?" There was a tearful pause and they knew that Jesus was feeling abandoned by them as he spoke on, "... even for one hour?" Jesus turned about to see them all as he went on, "Don't you know what this night holds for me? This is why I am asking you to stay awake and pray for me." But because it seemed to him that they did not grasp the danger they all faced this night he added, "Pray earnestly that you will not have to share with me in my trial. I know that your spirits are willing, but your flesh, how weak is it?"

Jesus stood there momentarily to see that they returned to prayer and not back to sleep again. Then he returned to the place where he had been praying before. As before, his body shook as though he was terribly cold and his arms trembled as he lifted them to cover his face. Jesus fell to his knees, hard, and he turned his eyes to see heaven again before falling prostrate on the ground. He made fists with his hands and pounded the ground as he half cried, half screamed out, "Abba! Father!" Jesus' prayer was heard by some of the disciples. Not the words though, just a syllable or two here and a whisper there from each sentence. He strained as he went on, and though near to complete exhaustion, every muscle in his body was taut and his veins were distended as they had never been before. He was sweating profusely from his forehead, and his sweat fell to the earth as it docs from an athlete who was strained to the limit when he was in competition against a great opponent.

But then there was beginning a change in him that made him swallow hard and grimace. His dripping sweat became red like the deep red of the Passover wine they had drank earlier that night. He was now praying louder so that every word could be heard, as he strained to slowly speak, "The – hour - of - my - betrayal - is - nearly - here…" These words became like a turning point, but of what was not yet clear.

His prayer continued as he pleaded, "…and my soul is so deeply troubled. I beseech thee dearest Father, save me now, save me from this trial. Tell me, is there any other way?" Jesus looked up with an expression of hope, a dying hope, that an answer could be given to him. He re-spoke, "Save me from this trial and let this pass from me if there is another way." His dying hope now became a lost hope, "Already I know that my betrayer is drawing near, and he will find me here. Is there no other way that their sins may be forgiven them? Then let it come in this hour." There came no answer from heaven and there would be no answer given. His words took on a power of their own as if all of creation were to be altered by them, "If it is possible let this cup of my blood sacrifice be removed from me. Yet if this cannot pass from me unless I drink it, then your will be done." Suddenly Jesus relaxed and he wept with tears of relief, "Your Kingdom's reign must come, your will on earth shall be done. I surrender to you, not my will but yours be done."

As it was on the night of his birth when angels appeared to the shepherds in the hills, so again there appeared angels before the Lord. A mighty legion of angels before him upon the Mount of Olives. They were ten feet or more in stature each and though their form was as clear as men of flesh they were also beings of light. They were arrayed in formation on the ground, and they rose up into the sky as if on an unseen hill. They surrounded Jesus on his every side and from above, as well. They were dressed for battle, standing in armor and wearing helmets, with shields before them and swords already drawn and in the ready. Their faces showed the war-torn worry lines of seasoned warriors. They were gathered to carry out the commands of the Son of God, of whom they were charged to care for in all his ways. Their general was a magnificent winged angel, tall well beyond that of any of the other angels, and his wings were folded as they rested upon his shoulders and down his back. He stepped forward, removed his helmet, and laid it on the ground. There, too, he stayed his sword into the earth and stood his shield against it. He bowed his head low as he slowly walked, coming alongside of Jesus, where he lay on the broken ground. He dropped reverently to his knees before he spoke, "Master Jesus, Holy Son of God, I am here to care for you." The angel gently laid his right hand on Jesus' shoulder and his wings spread open and covered them both, providing shelter in this time of trouble. The angel, with head now bowed even lower, closed his eyes and then squinted even tighter as he began his prayer. With a resonating voice he prayed. His language was one never heard before on earth, it was the holy language of heaven. He was not loud, but it somehow carried far without fading. When he finished his prayer, his wings folded and returned to their resting position. He stood to his feet and returned to his place at the head of the legion. Somehow it was understood that they would remain at the Lord's side even as they now faded away out of sight.

Jesus found strength in the prayer that the angel had offered as he stood and resumed his own prayer with his arms outstretched into the night sky. "My Abba, for your will to be fulfilled, and for the redemption of all your fallen children, I die to myself this night. Amen"

He looked about and saw the dim light of torches and lanterns being carried by a company of Religious Authorities. It was a group of Temple guards and a squad of Roman soldiers coming his way. Jesus turned to alert those closest to him only to see that they had fallen asleep again. He walked over and shook Peter's shoulder as he said, "Are you sleeping?" Peter slowly woke and looked around as Jesus continued, "Couldn't even you stay awake with me for this one hour?" Jesus called out loud enough to wake all of his disciples, "Quickly, all of you rise from your sleep and see what evil the darkness of this night has brought. The time of my trial now begins."

Jesus stood bold and tall as he pointed sharply, "Look, all of you! I am betrayed into the hands of evil men." From within the company of the guards Jesus' disciple, Judas, appeared and he moved quickly ahead of them by about 25 yards. He did this because he wanted it to appear as though he wasn't part of the rest who followed in step after him. Judas looked to his rear and then pressed onward to the Lord. The disciples reacted to the guards and soldiers wide eyed and quickly gathered to surround their Lord, to the sides, and to the back. Peter stood in front and to the right of his Master and John to the front of him on the left. They effectively provided a shield for him from those who were approaching.

As Judas came nearer he acted like he was joyous to see them, and as if the Lord was going to be glad to see him again. He ran to Jesus' side to greet him and as he drew near Jesus spoke to him saying, "Judas, do what you have come here for." He moved to step around Peter, but as he tried to passed by him, Peter moved and stood in his way again, giving him his shoulder to run into. Peter turned and stepped in closely to watch him and to keep his close eye on his hands to see what he would do. He was ready to take him down if he had to, in order to protect his Lord.

Judas moved in close as if nothing amiss was going on. He held the Lord by his shoulders and kissed him on the check saying, "Hail Master!" But before Judas let go of the Rabbi's shoulders, the snake twisted out of his cuff and climbed over onto Jesus' shoulder and moved in the direction of his heart. Jesus knew without looking that the beast was there and, as quickly as a man could move, he grasped it around the neck and threw it to the ground before him. Judas looked down upon it and feared. Jesus moved ever so quickly again, raising his right foot and stomping down upon it once with a heavy blow to its head. The snake's skull was instantly crushed and now it lay there dead.

Jesus was, of course, not drawn into the little show Judas had just put on. He spoke directly to him, "Is it with a kiss that you betray me?"

Judas stood back and put his hand over his heart and acted as if he was the one who was offended. He showed his façade of disappointment, but Jesus was not taken in by his ruse.

Jesus denounced him where he stood, "You are no longer my disciple. For 30 pieces of silver you have sold me off? You have done your part in the evil plans of this lot. Now go. You no longer have any part with me."

Judas stepped back because his ruse of innocence was over. As he did he stepped onto Peter, who stood tall and stared down at him, straight into his eyes. Peter put his right hand on the handle of his sword, and drew it out an inch.

The conspirator saw the threat being made on him, looking down and away, because his eyes could no longer keep up the deception he was playing out. He realized that he must be hated by all the disciples he had shared fellowship with for the last three years of his life. He feared what might happen to him by the hand of the Lord, who he had seen work wonders without measure. Even with the Temple guards and Romans soldiers right there he became very unsure of himself and he shook with fear as he withdrew to the rear and then ran away, disappearing into the darkness of the night.

Having deposed of Judas, Jesus moved to address the Temple authorities who had come to arrest him. He looked them over as they stood trying to look intimidating and then spoke to them with great calm asking, "Who are you looking for?"

The servant of Caiaphas, the high priest spoke out. His name was Malchus. "We are looking for the man named Jesus of Nazareth."

Jesus nodded knowingly, and calmly said, "I…"

At the exact same moment as he spoke, the shoulder of the man, and of all of those behind him, retracted as if they had been struck with a severe blow. They were all shoved backward and had to regain their footing or fall to the ground. They grunted in pain from being hit and their clothing was jostled as when handled roughly. The guards' and soldiers' armor of leather and metal made a rustling noise. They all showed great surprise and some feared. After that they were not so sure of themselves and their intimidating stance was no more.

Jesus continued on, "…I am…"

And again, at the second word he spoke, they were again shoved, twice as hard as before, in their right shoulders. Once more they stumbled to regain their footing to avoid falling over backward.

Jesus' every word acted on them in like fashion, as he continued, "I am he."

They had been shoved hard in their left shoulder, harder still in their right shoulder, and now, in rapid succession, they were struck with the greatest force yet. The soldiers, the guards and the authorities with them stumbled back, step by step backward with each word, and with the final word they were shoved the hardest. Unable to step back fast enough to regain their stance, they were knocked off their feet and hit the ground hard.

Many of them shook their heads and gasped to breathe because the wind was knocked out of them. They were slow to stand to their feet. Some had become deathly afraid for their very lives after this show of force against them. Some slowly rose to their feet and offered a hand to the others in getting up. The Temple guards had the fight taken out of them and looked as if they might like to run away. But the Romans, they took it in stride and stood fast and were ready should more come their way.

Jesus looked directly at a much shaken Malchus and spoke again, "Who did you say that you're looking for?" The high priest's servant wasn't really sure he wanted to say. The last time he did, things did not go well for him. But he did speak, timidly and he said, "Jesus of Nazareth."

Now Peter, emboldened by the miraculous display he saw, prepared to unleash on their enemy his own retribution. He looked directly at John and gained his attention. He looked down at his sword handle, grasped it and mouthed the words, 'Be ready.'

John looked back at him and, with all assurance in his abilities, nodded and moved his hand to the handle of his sword as well.

Jesus, with all confidence, spoke to Malchus, "Then it is me you are looking for. As I have said, I am he."

At those words the Temple authorities, the guards, and the soldier all fearfully cowered backward, worrying that they might be hit or shoved again. But that did not happen this time. Those who came to arrest Jesus now stood before him but did nothing to move forward or take him into custody.

So Jesus again spoke to them, "So, here I am, you have found me. I surrender to your custody. But these other men here, let them be on their way."

Some of his disciples, having heard these words said about them going free, stepped back as though they might leave. They formed into several smaller groups as they continued to look on from a few steps further away. They were not sure if they should go or not, and whispering among themselves about the situation.

Still, neither the Temple authorities nor the guards moved forward to arrest Jesus. So, he very calmly extended his arms out in surrender so that they could chain and shackle him.

Malchus then looked at the sergeant of the guards and motioned with his hand for them to step forward and take Jesus into custody. A timid man moved closer and positioned himself to bind up Jesus' hands in chains. Another guard stepped in and positioned himself between Jesus and Peter.

But as Peter saw his Lord being bound he took immediate action, jumping in and commanding them, "Don't you touch him! None of you touch him!" His hand instinctively began to draw his sword out as he stepped in to prevent his Master's arrest.

The guard who stood by Peter, seeing this as a threat, moved to draw his sword against him. Peter now charged forward, and body slammed that guard, knocking him to the ground so hard that he made a loud thud when he landed. With lightning speed Peter drew his sword out of its sheath but there was no time for him to reverse his blade forward before the guard putting chains on Jesus drew his. Peter fearlessly rushed to him and drove the butt of his sword handle with the greatest force into the jaw of that guard.

As he was struck he screeched out loudly in pain and, from the severity of the blow, his head bobbled about. He crumbled over, falling to the ground as he gripped his jaw that had been driven out of joint and fractured. Then, with fearsome strength, Peter tensed every muscle in his body shouting out a great battle cry, "Disciples, arm yourselves to fight. The Kingdom of God has just begun its reign." The rest of the Temple guards stepped back and cowered as Peter rushed still closer toward them.

John closed his eyes and whispered a prayer, "Holy God, bring me your strength. Amen" And with that he drew his sword high into the night sky and pointed it forward toward the Temple guards. He swung it skillfully into the air, round and round on his right and then again on his left, and with such high confidence that his enemy could see that he, too, meant to fight them if they were to continue trying to take captive the Lord.

The next soldier in line nervously moved to draw his sword. His voice rang out with the sound of a man who was horrified beyond words. He grabbed at it once but his hand came up empty and then he reached for it a second time before he found the handle. He looked down to be sure he had it in his hand as he drew it forward for the fight. Peter took swift notice of him, and even though he hadn't yet been able to turn his blade forward, he struck down with his handle in one straight move, using it to crush the knuckles of this guard smartly down against his own sword handle. The guard retracted his hand and shook it into the air as he screamed out in excruciating pain, his sword falling uselessly to the ground. He stepped back from the fight holding his arm at the wrist with an expression on his face that clearly showed he could not believe what just happened to him.

Peter continued charging forward and took his stand between his Master and the Temple guards. John stepped quickly to his side and with great force shouted out, "Hands off my Master!" as he pointed his sword outward as if it was an extension of his tongue. The Temple guards were again filled with such fright that they were either frozen in place or cowering to the rear. Peter, continued his aggression, charging swiftly to the next person in front of him. That was Malchus. Peter knew this was the man who led the arresting party, that he was the servant of the high priest, and therefore he bore him great ill. He grabbed the man's coat to keep him from escaping and put his sword to his throat. Peter took a look at all of those with him and spoke out ruthlessly "I will slice every last one of you from head to toe!" And then in one swift move he sliced Malchus' ear all the way off. Then he threw him to the ground, stepping back to see if any others would challenge him. He stood taller than ever, as a giant among men, drawing deep his breaths. Privately, his thoughts told him that at this time it was necessary to do all he could to save his Lord, even if it meant dying in the process. He could not have been more energized for action. His emotions could not have been more charged or his thoughts sharper for what might be next.

Upon hitting the ground, Malchus cried out in a chilling voice, "I'm cut! I'm cut! It's my ear, oh! Am I cut badly? Is my neck cut too?" He looked around for his companions' help, but they did not come to aid him for fear of getting to close to Peter. As Malchus made a feeble effort to crawl away, two guards finally came to him, bent over, almost crawling, because they did not want to appear to be a threat to Peter.

All this happened in a matter of seconds as Jesus looked on in disbelief over what had just happened. He feared what Peter and John might do next with the very swords he told them to bring. So he stepped forward to stand between his disciples. He shouted out a frantic "NO!" that seemed to never end. He was desperate to stop Peter and John and to separate his disciples from the arresting party. "No, Peter, no John, stop! No one must fight." He stood in harms' way between them, looking at both warring sides and spoke loudly, "Return your swords to their sheaths. To live by the sword is to die by the sword and none of you must die this way tonight." Jesus reached out his hands to both sides and lowered his arms to indicate that they should stop fighting. "If I choose to keep my life I would only have to call upon my Father, who would immediately release more than twelve legions of battle ready angels for me to command. But if I do that, then how would the prophecies in the scriptures be fulfilled? All that is written of me must take place in this way. I will surrender and pay the price of your ransom."

Jesus turned his eyes to the servant who was disfigured and held out his arms as he walked to him. He looked directly into Malchus' eyes with such a look of compassion that it was as if he had spoken a loving and kindhearted word of concern for his wellbeing. "Forgive the man who did this to you" he said. He reached out to him as he drew near to his side, and he saw the tears of hurt and sorrow slowing coming down his face. The Lord laid his hands on him, one on his shoulder and with his other hand he cupped the ear that was cut and healed him. Looking into his eyes he held the fearful servants attention as he told him, "You are healed, see, there is no more pain. See, you are whole again."

The servant slowly nodded in agreement with Jesus because he could feel that he was out of pain and he reached up to touch his ear and feel that it was back in place. He turned to kneel low before the Lord in speechless gratitude and did not rejoin the others who had come to arrest Jesus.

Jesus called out to the Temple guards and spoke for everyone to hear, "Day by day I travelled openly about in your city. I taught publicly in the Temple for everyone to see and hear. But you would not take me into custody by the light of day or in the presence of the people. So here you are under the cover of night, armed with swords and clubs to capture me as though…" Jesus paused, thinking about what he was saying about them, and then laughed at the absurd humor he saw in the situation. Still laughing he continued, "…as though I was a, a dangerous outlaw!" Now he looked again at Malchus and leaned over to offer him his hand and help him to stand to his feet. "Don't you know by now that no one can take my life from me?" Again he paused and opened wide his arms as he spoke out to the guards. "But so that you may know that I am laying down my life, I surrender to you in peace. Neither I nor my disciples will resist you any further."

By Jesus' word, this was that turning point. Because he

said that he was surrendering in peace the tide of things flowed in a different direction. Peter, John and the rest of the disciples were no longer intimidating to the guards who had been disarmed by the earlier word the Lord spoke causing them to fall over. The guards no longer saw the disciples as a threat, so they regained their confidence as two of them stepped forward to bind the Rabbi in chains. The rest of the guards were standing ready with their hands on their swords and their clubs already in their hands. The formerly emboldened Peter and John could not believe their senses, what they heard Jesus say and what they saw as their Lord and Master do, reaching with outstretched arms and giving himself in surrender over to these men.

As the chains were wrapped around his wrists, and down to around his ankles all the disciples but Peter and John cowered backwards. Some of them even looked behind themselves to see if they would be able to escape capture, should it come to that. As these disciples moved further and further away. the Temple guards become heartened. They began to stand tall, taking on the look of brutes again. As they snapped closed the final lock on the chains, a tall and burly guard grabbed the chains and jerked forcefully down hard on them sending Jesus tumbling to the ground. Falling face first, he cried out in anguish. Then suddenly the other guards rushed the disciples crying out, "Capture his disciples, make them pay for their resistance!"

The disciples turned and ran, ran for their lives. Madly into the garden and into the darkness they flew like the wind. Peter and John had been standing the closest to their Lord and the guards were especially anxious to get ahold of these two because they had drawn their swords against them. As these last two turned and sped away, they both dropped their swords. Peter, with his long legs, outran John

303

and made it to a place where he thought he could safely hide among some thick bushes. John, however did not fare so well. He was slower to turn and run and the guards were upon him in an instant. In a fearful fright he ran, but he could feel the hands of a guard grabbing at him. As he was fleeing from them, one guard now had a strong grip on his coat and was pulling him back. John feared that he would be wrestled to the ground. But he was not going to be taken, that was certain, and without hesitation, he loosened his coat and let it slip from him as he tore out of it and fled as fast as he could into the darkness.

Peter was not far away. As John came near he called out in a hushed voice, "John! John! It's me, Peter. Come and hide in here."

Upon hearing the promise of safety, John gladly joined Peter. Once John had caught his breath he looked at Peter with a desperate question, "How could this happen to him Peter? He is the Messiah, the Son of God, you said it yourself."

Peter had no answer. He merely looked back at John with a tear in his eye and shook his head in disbelief.

From where these two were they could not see their Lord and what was happening to him, so they ventured out carefully, trying to stay behind the cover of the trees as much as possible. Soon they could see that the guards who had given them chase had rejoined the rest and were preparing to leave. They had placed Jesus in the center of their formation with their members on all four sides. Their officer gave the order and they began marching out of the garden and down from the mount toward the Holy City below. They were immediately followed by the squad of Roman soldiers.

Peter and John looked on, standing at a safe distance.

They feared going after their Lord because if they were to fall into the hands of those guards they would be brutalized, or even killed for the actions they had taken against them. They could do nothing as they listened to the sound of marching footsteps moving away. There they stood motionless, as the shadowy silhouette of their Rabbi faded away and blended into the darkness of the night.

They stayed until the last of their torches and lanterns no longer gave away its light. Their hope for a king who would rule over them in righteousness, which had grown as bright as the sun now died suddenly like a shooting star that burns out as it crosses the night sky.

www.ingramcontent.com/pod-product-compliance
Lightning Source LLC
Chambersburg PA
CBHW070918260626
47162CB00007B/2720